You've Gone Too Far, Baby

You've Gone Too Far, Baby

Mark Karnegie

mondomagik press

You've Gone Too Far, Baby

mondomagik press
an imprint of mondomagik publications

For information address:
mondomagik press
7501 Ulmerton Road #1823
Largo, FL 33771

ISBN-13: 978-0692448243

Printed in the United States of America

To Lori:
Is it any wonder?

"If there's war between the sexes,
Then there'll be no people left."
Joe Jackson (from the song "Real Men" © 1982

CHAPTER ONE

All things being equal, Jennifer Martin often felt different from the people around her. As she stepped out of the House Office Building where she worked onto Independence Avenue, she didn't follow the crowds heading toward the parking garages, commuter lots, train or bus stations at the end of the day on Capitol Hill. Instead, she began her customary short walk home.

On an uncharacteristic Washington spring day in April 2014, rain fell intermittently from an overcast sky, while the temperature ranged into unseasonably cool, though it was expected to be the last cold snap before spring finally took over and allowed the cherry blossoms to bloom.

Jennifer enjoyed her walks, whatever the weather. Although she was a Congressional Aide (more like a glorified secretary, she thought) and could afford to drive like everyone else, she preferred to walk because it gave her a chance to relax her mind and forget about the pressure of the just completed day. She lived a few blocks from the Hill anyway.

As she crossed Independence, she dodged a few deep puddles and turned onto North Carolina. She now approached the square at Lincoln Park and made a shortcut through the plaza, stopping at the small monument in the center which was dedicated to the 29th Amendment, and, as the monument itself pointed out, it was the most important amendment to the Constitution of the United States: the Equal Rights Amendment. She liked to stop there a few minutes every day because it helped her recall her idealistic days in college when she had helped to get the very amendment ratified, and her present employer, Representative Marilyn Connors (D), elected. The monument read: *'Equality of rights under the law shall not be denied or abridged by the United States or by any State or individual on account of sex.'*

From the park, Jennifer could see her fourth-floor apartment window that overlooked the park from across the street. And as the light drizzle began to pick up, she decided to move on. The ERA was finally ratified two weeks after Jennifer's graduation from Georgetown University in May 2008, when Jennifer was twenty-one and she felt she had the world at her feet. She had majored in political science and immediately began to do campaign work for a classmate's sister, candidate Marilyn Connors of Virginia. It was easier work than expected, she thought, mostly due to the circumstances. The male incumbent for the seat had to resign because of a new ERA-inspired ruling that ordered the House and Senate must always have an equal number of male and female members. The Republicans got a female replacement to run, but she didn't have enough time to catch up, and Connors won handily. At first, Jennifer didn't question the action, or many other early measures, because she thought it was the best way for the dreams of the Equality Movement to be realized more rapidly.

Now she wondered what had happened to those dreams, as she climbed the stairs to her apartment. The dark stairwell and creaking, wooden steps reminded her of her days in the Georgetown dormitories. She had a very small apartment, meant for one, in a building that had only female tenants.

As Jennifer stepped into her modest flat and closed the door behind her, she peeled off the layers of wet clothes until she was completely naked. She dried off, but she did not put on a set of fresh, dry clothes. She simply set about to prepare her dinner, as was often her custom to walk around the house nude. She was beginning to think it was the only way she could be sure she was still a woman. It was almost as if she wanted to make sure there was nothing dangling between her legs. What with the unisex clothing that everyone wore now, and her being rather small-breasted, one might not be sure of her sex, which was the ultimate goal.

At twenty-eight, she still retained her girlish figure, but perhaps too girlish, not womanish enough for her tastes, she thought lately. Jennifer was of medium height and slender, and the unisex, short-cropped hair further confused her sexual identity. She tried to tell herself that she had to remember that one can't have sexual identity and equality at the same time. Who said that, she tried to recall? Ah, yes. Big Sister, that's who.

Big Sister is what Jennifer liked to euphemistically call Barbara Thompson, the first female President of the United States. She couldn't let anyone else hear her say that, as it might reveal her dissatisfaction with the current state of affairs. But President Thompson had become her symbol of a revolution gone askew and ideals missing their aim. It wasn't just the unisex clothing that confused Jennifer; it was the direction the Movement was taking, and some of the things being done in the name of equality.

After her dinner, Jennifer took out her journal notebook from its hiding place inside a stereo speaker cabinet. She had started making notes of how she was feeling the past few months because she was uncertain of sharing her thoughts with someone in fear of being misunderstood and branded a counterrevolutionary somehow. Jennifer often felt alone in her feelings, and it comforted her to at least think she was communicating with someone else. She was beginning to entertain a few traitorous thoughts.

As she sat naked in her favorite wooden rocking chair and stared out the window, across Lincoln Park and to the small monument, she pondered what had happened to her ideals. President Thompson immediately came to mind as she wrote:

"President Thompson was elected in 2012. I still recall her Orwellian slogans during the campaign: 'Inequality is Slavery,' and 'Equality is Freedom.' And her speeches probably made people feel quite guilty when she said, "Do you people think we've achieved equality? Why, we have yet to elect a woman president." That's all it took, it seemed, just the mention of *equality* as a catchall.

"Most people, including myself, thought it was a great victory when she won the election, but after her inauguration speech, my doubts began.

"I include this partial transcript to illustrate:

"'My fellow Americans, we are truly about to embark on an historic journey for this great country of ours, and I must thank you for the mandate I have received, which will allow me the opportunity to carry on this noble cause. It has been a long time coming, but I envision a time during my administration, when a man and a woman can truly *say* they are equal. There will be no more second-class citizens, only citizens. No *he* or *she*, only *citizens*.

"'For a long time, we have called ourselves free, but we can only be free when we are *equal* and free. We have taken positive steps already. With the ratification of the Equal Rights Amendment, we can take the necessary actions to create this new, better society. A new society where one will not be disadvantaged at birth because of one's gender. A new society where equal opportunities will be available to everyone after birth. A new society that is truly free.

"'I'd like to outline some of our goals that I and my administration intend to work for in the next four years. Let me remind you that we feel these are necessary steps to create a new, glorious society.

"'To make all of this work, people need to have the right attitudes. Old-fashioned ideas that certain things can be masculine of feminine, can no longer be tolerated. Items such as clothing will not be allowed to have separate styles for men and women. Separate is not equal. We have to get it in our minds that we are *not* men and women, but just plain people. Gender has no place in language, for example, because it demeans and weakens, and we must make a concerted effort to eradicate it from ours.

"'We also find it necessary to outlaw sex and marriage, long-standing practices of dominance and slavery. I and my staff have given this a lot of thought and found that these two things are the root causes of inequality. From the beginning of time, men have been able to dominate women through sex and marriage, not allowing women achieve their full potentials.

"'Pregnancy is the great inequity. What man has ever had to endure the pain of giving birth? We have the technology right now that creates life without sex and without pregnancy, so we have the moral obligation to use it to lift the burden, to free women from the yoke of pregnancy and giving birth. Only then can women be truly equal. All that will be required of every citizen are monthly donations of one's sperm cells or egg cell. This will give us the added benefit of population control. The government can choose what population level is best for the country.

"'I may have to make myself clear on this subject. We intend to get all sexual intercourse classified as rape, which will be punishable by castration, or, in the case of women, surgically closing the vaginal opening, while still allowing for certain bodily functions.

"'With our increasing technology, surveillance can be used to enforce this measure. Because sex has been such a private matter, we feel this is the only way to stop cheaters and counterrevolutionaries. You will be watched. But the whole world is watching us to lead the way to our destiny as a human race.'

"Needless to say, the President's speech caused a stir, but I was surprised at how little the *stir* actually was. I figured that, but then, most people didn't want to oppose equality, and if outlawing sex was going to create equality, then it must be right. Even enforcing the ban on marriage wasn't too difficult. Of course, no one had the authority to perform new marriages, and with four years of the ERA already, children were generally under state care. All that was left was separation of spouses. The control of government had grown so much that it already controlled housing, and they had the force to make everyone live either by themselves, or with roommates of the same sex.

"I have my own theory about how the changes came about so quickly, and without much resistance. It really stems from a phenomenon I term the 'wimpification' of the American male in the last decade of the twentieth century. A new feminist strategy was formed shortly after the original ERA was killed in 1982. The history books might say the women's movement died that year, but it really went underground. The idea was not to be so confrontational, and women would let it be known in subtle ways that the way for men to get their attention in the bedroom was to be sensitive to women outside it. And once men figured that out, they began falling all over themselves to show women how sensitive they were.

"Companies began requiring all their male employees to attend sensitivity training seminars to show that they were committed to ending sexual harassment in the workplace, which was long overdue. But these companies had to turn to the feminist leadership to find out how to do it right, which provided a great opportunity for indoctrinating minds according to the feminist agenda.

"Whether it was a sense of guilt or fairness, men were giving women more and more positions of power and voting them into political office. Once women had sufficient numbers in the political arena, the ERA was reintroduced and, because of the lack of solid opposition from men—who feared being branded 'insensitive'—passed.

"After ratification, many women began to be confrontational again. With the feeling that the courts were on their side now, vigilante groups of women began forming out of 'Take Back the Night' campaigns to demolish age-old symbols of inequality and oppression. Pornography was one major target. Shop owners around the country could not even display it without risking their establishments being trashed by bands of marauding women, even though laws still on the books allowed the shops to operate. The police forces, which were increasingly female, often did little or nothing to help the owners, who were now forced out of business.

"These militant women began suggesting that all sex was bad, and now, of course, it has been outlawed along with marriage.

"That never really affected me too much, at first. I was single and had been celibate most of my adult life. It was more that I had never found the right man, when it was legal, than any dislike of sex, per se. All my experiences with sex, however, were never really enjoyable. My partners always were dominating me in some way and were selfish, not taking into consideration any needs I might have had. I had never reached orgasm through intercourse.

"So I found it somewhat easy to go along with the President's plan. I knew first-hand that sex made me feel unequal. Men never had to think about getting pregnant. Even when using birth control, I could not stop thinking about it as a possibility. Nothing was ever one-hundred percent effective. Men also had the option of walking away after conception, while women did not. Women must face the consequences whether they want to or not. They must choose to either abort or carry. A woman's body also changes physiologically after conception, a fact that must be dealt with. After the fertilized egg implants itself in the uterus, everything is geared to its preservation. No more eggs are released from the ovaries. The menstrual cycle ceases. Food and blood are transferred, and the new life is maintained automatically by the mother.

"But sex was not all about pregnancy. While birth control or just careful planning, people could enjoy sex for the sake of sex. It made me think about the very nature of sex. Was it really the root cause of inequality? A woman's body is invaded by the man, after all. Was it possible that this feeling of dominance was somehow subconsciously transferred throughout the ages, by both sexes? I thought about the male body. His sexual organs are on the outside of his body. Does he subconsciously feel vulnerable and thus perpetuate the idea of male dominance to cover up this vulnerability? What about the idea that men's sex drives were always greater than women's, or that men enjoyed sex more than women? There must be some women who enjoyed sex a great deal. Some women solicited money for sex, but even that seemed to be for the benefit of men, and most of those women were completely controlled by men. There must have been some women who enjoyed sex for itself. The image of the girls with the bad reputations in high school comes to mind. They were supposed to be doing it for the pure enjoyment. Or was it for their own ego, a way for them to dominate men, perhaps? And what of masturbation? It was often thought that only men practiced this, but women did also, but it was talked about less. Most people engaged in solitary sex because of a lack of satisfaction, despite the thought it was somehow wrong for them to do it. I have my own theory, though, that mutual masturbation between a man and a woman probably could be the great equalizer of sexual relations. People could get the satisfaction of orgasm, and all the problems created by intercourse—the pregnancies, the transmission of venereal diseases—could simply be avoided."

Even though Jennifer didn't agree with the strict government control of personal lives, she had to agree with the President that there was something inherently unequal about sex. But things wouldn't have been so bad, she thought, if it weren't for the Canadian thing.

The whole affair started the day after President Thompson's inauguration. A reporter asked Canadian Prime Minister Harold Samuelson, "What is your reaction to President Thompson's speech?"

"It just confirms what I thought all along," he responded, "that the American people elected a big cunt to run the country for them. She's got to be insane. How can anyone in their right mind outlaw sex? She talks about equal rights, but the American people will be lucky to have *any* rights at all after that dumb broad is through with them.”

Samuelson had a reputation for saying what he felt. He reached the top in Canadian politics because of the admiration the people had for this very trait. As a rich Edmonton oil man, he was raised on discipline, braggadocio and old-fashioned chauvinism. Being single and in his nation's spotlight, he also was a notorious ladies' man. His remarks caused an uproar in the U.S. Thompson and the American press called for an immediate apology.

“This is an absolute insult and an outrage,” Thompson had said in a statement to the press. “I, and the American people, demand an immediate apology from the prime minister. If he does not, it will be very difficult to continue normal diplomatic relations. I will now answer any questions.”

“President Thompson,” a *Washington Post* reporter queried, “you mentioned that diplomatic relations might be disturbed. What actions might you take?”

“Well, even before the prime minister's foolish remarks, relations have been somewhat strained already. We're quite disappointed that they have not followed our lead in the fight for equality. The first step would be to recall our ambassador and diplomatic corps, and I also intend to make the recommendation to Congress the trade be limited or halted.”

“Will any actions include the closing of the border?” cried out the *Detroit Free Press* reporter.

“As a matter of fact, that is already under consideration. We are very concerned and feel that an open border would be extremely detrimental to our cause. We don't wish that Canada become this nation's motel, so to speak. The problems of enforcing the proposed anti-sex bill are obvious when we share a three-thousand-mile undefended border with a country where sex is legal. And they seem intent on undermining our efforts and laws.”

“Then, do you expect a lack of cooperation from the American people on your proposed anti-sex law?” asked the *Associated Press* reporter.

“No, frankly, I do not. I think my election shows that the American people are ready for equality, and are willing to accept whatever it takes to finally achieve that goal. This would only be a precautionary measure against uncooperative outsiders. Thank you." The President stepped down off the podium and looked flustered as a barrage of last-minute questions were yelled simultaneously.

The President's press secretary stepped up to the microphones and said, "Thank you. This concludes today's press conference," and turned away to follow the President.

The next day in Ottawa, Samuelson held a press conference of his own to comment on Thompson's remarks, and to make known his plans on any reactionary measures.

"First of all, I will not apologize for my comments because I still feel the same way. I understand that she might be upset. It must be that time of the month, you know. Let me tell you what, Barb — I'll make it up to you. About these sanctions, I think we ought to discuss it first. You can come here, and we'll talk over dinner. And then, maybe we can catch a movie."

The members of the press caught the joke and burst out in laughter. "But seriously, sir, how do you feel about the threat to close the border?" a reporter from the *Vancouver Gazette* finally asked after the chuckles ceased.

"Well, I'll tell you—" Samuelson's face and voice became very grave. "I honestly think of such an action as a prelude to war. The longest undefended border between two countries in the history of the world suddenly defended by troops? I think the new lady leader doesn't want to look weak to the rest of the world. So she intends to pick a fight with the big, bad, male chauvinist pig. That's me." He cracked a smile. "I feel that the closing of the border will eventually lead to an attack by the United States. So, I intend to react to such an action by defending our borders."

A *Toronto Star* reporter raised the question: "In past history, Canada has been used by Americans as a haven from unpopular laws. Do you intend to return or prosecute any Americans seeking refuge here from the anti-sex law?"

"No. That is one thing I won't do. I won't help them, but I can't find it in myself to hinder them. I guess I'm giving the American people a choice. And that's more than I can say for their president."

After that comment was made public in the United States, about 400,000 people took the prime minister up on his 'invitation' in the following two months before the border was officially closed. More than half came in the first four days. In a nation of 300 million people, it could have been worse, but it was an embarrassment to President Thompson. Both countries were in a state of military preparedness, each expecting an attack from the other. Canada was larger in land mass, but much smaller in population. So the government decided to press into service all adult males for short periods of time, as needed by the government, but not to be part of the standing armed forces.

The United States tried guarding the 3,000-mile border with regular army troops, but soon discovered that they were strategically thin in other parts of the world. They came up with a similar solution to the problem. All citizens of ages 18-30 would be eligible for call-up to serve two months of military training and actual guard duty along the border.

Jennifer had already been notified, and her time was fast approaching. Her report date was June 1st. She wasn't too anxious to be trained to kill, but she thought of it as her duty. She never had thought of going to Canada when it was possible. The people who did go just couldn't give up sex, she thought. What selfish people. Was sex that great that it couldn't be given up? She did. She could miss it, she thought. But did she really know what she was missing? She liked the idea of what she thought sex ought to be, but because she never had achieved orgasm through intercourse, she wasn't exactly sure what it was like. Had it just been that she never found the right man, or was there no right man to find? She tended to believe the former because she had known one man whom she thought could have been the right man. That man was Paul Kennedy. Paul was Jennifer's mysterious knight in shining armor. There was more about Paul that she didn't know than she did. She didn't know what had become of him, and she only remembered half of her last date with him.

"If I had married Paul at the time," Jennifer wrote in her journal, "I might have had something to fight for. Maybe my resistance would have been stronger to what's been going on. And it makes me wonder, are there any others left in this country who think the same way I do? If there was just some sort of resistance movement out there to give me strength—or is everybody left of like minds?"

Jennifer first met Paul the summer after her freshman year at Georgetown. They were both taking the same American History class, but they didn't actually meet in class. Jennifer's roommate Sheila had dated Paul's roommate Tom for a short time. So when Sheila mentioned that she knew someone who shared an avid interest in chess, Jennifer had to tag along one time when Sheila visited Tom in his dormitory. Jennifer wanted to find someone new to play chess with; she already had beaten all the novices in her dorm so that they never wanted to play her anymore.

When she went with Sheila, she was introduced to Tom and Paul, and she struck up a conversation with Paul immediately. She asked him the usual rote college conversation openers, such as, "What's your major?"; "Where are you from?"; "What's your GPA?" But she couldn't wait to ask him about chess. She noticed the chessboard in the corner with the pieces all set up.

"So, I hear you play a little chess?"

"Yeah, I play a little, to relax from studying. Most people probably think that's kind of weird," Paul said.

"No, no, I understand. You're probably pretty good, right?"

"Not as good as I'd like to be."

"Would you like to play a game with me? I play when I get the chance, which isn't often during the regular semester."

"Well, sure. I have a board all set up and ready to go." They started to play, and paid little attention to Sheila and Tom, who paid them little attention either. They were in another part of the room horsing around, doing what young lovers do when someone else is in the same room, giving each other feels and touches, occasionally kissing, unable to completely control their burning desires. In the middle of the game, Sheila made an announcement of her plans to Jennifer.

"Tom and I are going to go down to the cafeteria for a while. We'll probably go to the library to do a little studying afterward. Paul, is it okay for you to walk Jen across campus? She shouldn't be out there alone at night." She winked at Paul.

"Sure," Paul said, unaware of the meaning of the gesture. "No problem. We still have to finish our game."

"Bye, kids. Have fun," Sheila said. "Don't do anything I wouldn't do. Or maybe I should say, don't do anything I *would* do." She giggled as Tom led her out the door. Jennifer better understood Sheila's innuendo. She also knew that she would not actually go to the library to study. It was just her prearranged signal to let Jennifer know to stay away from the dorm room for a couple of hours. Sheila never went to the library.

Jennifer and Paul ended up playing four games in five hours. Enough time, she thought. It was ten o'clock when they finished. She didn't mind, though. Jennifer thought Paul was kind of cute. They didn't talk much during their games, but she learned about his chess style. Jennifer liked to attack, sometimes brilliantly, sometimes recklessly, while Paul liked to defend a strong position and then counterattack. It could make for an interesting relationship, she pondered. They split their four games.

"Well, that does look like mate, so you win another to even things up," Paul said. "You know, I haven't played against someone as good as you in long time. It was refreshing."

"Thank you," Jennifer replied.

"I could probably play all night, but I have to study for an American History quiz on Monday."

"That's a coincidence. So do I. You wouldn't happen to have Professor Collins, would you?"

"Yes, third period," Paul confirmed.

"Hey, isn't that something? I don't know if I've ever seen you there, and maybe I just don't remember."

"Well, I usually sit in the front row."

"And I usually sit near the back, but I'll look for you on Monday." Jennifer was glad she had found something else in common with Paul, even if it was just a class. From the short time since they'd met, she liked him, and she was hoping that he would ask her out. He seemed really nice to her, but she wanted to know *how* nice, so she offered, "You know, you don't actually have to walk me back, if you don't want to. It's only a short walk."

"That's okay. I don't mind."

They began the short trip to the other side of the campus along one of the tree-lined walks. It was warm, but comfortable, quiet summer evening, the only sound being the cooling breeze off the Potomac rustling the leaves. Neither talked on the way, as their minds were unwinding after five hours of hard concentration on chess maneuvers. Paul didn't even make a move to hold her hand, so Jennifer finally decided to hold his arm, and Paul didn't protest. Her protector, she thought. She was surprised that she felt that way about someone because she had always been very independent.

When they got to her building, Paul said, "Well, I hope we can get together again sometime to play more chess. I really enjoyed tonight. Thank you."

"You're welcome." Jennifer was hoping that he would ask her for a date though, or kiss her goodnight, at least, but he did neither. They said goodbye to each other, and as Jennifer was about to turn and go, she made the decision and gave Paul a quick kiss on his startled lips. Then without another word, she quickly ran upstairs to her room.

When she got in the door, Sheila was there. Tom was not. Sheila had to ask, "Out pretty late, huh? So, how did it go with you and Paul?"

Jennifer explained that she liked him a lot, and was interested. She wasn't sure if Paul was, though. Sheila told her a little bit more about him. He was painfully shy, but probably the nicest guy she ever wanted to meet, she told her. From the few times they had met, Sheila said he was okay to talk to if there was no one else in the room, but if there were other people around, he became visibly uncomfortable, and talked very little. Sheila told her not to worry, but if she was really interested, she would have to let him know she was available for the taking, and he'd come around. Jennifer wasn't too keen on that advice, though.

Jennifer saw Paul a lot that summer, but only in class, or after class on days of nice weather. They would set up a chess board on a shady knoll that overlooked the Potomac and play a few games, whatever they had time for. But they did start talking more during their games as they got more familiar with each other, and it didn't seem like one opponent purposefully distracting the other. Neither one minded as they were just playing for fun. But Paul never did ask her out, and Jennifer began to think about Sheila's advice and whether she would have to move. She decided to wait a bit longer, if after five more games of chess he still hadn't asked her out, *she* would ask *him* out. The summer was almost over.

The day the fifth game arrived, she decided to follow the normal routine, but talk to him during the game about how he felt. It seemed the time he was the most comfortable with her.

"Well, we have our history final coming up next week," she said. "How do you think you'll do?"

"I think I should do okay, but I'm so close to an A or a B. If I get an A on the exam, I should get an A in the class. If I get a B, I should get a B in the class," Paul explained. He opened their chess game with the tried-and-true Pawn-to-King-Four.

Jennifer responded with Pawn-to-King-Three, the French Defense. Conservative, but it was a good, strong, defensive position from which to work. "I'll probably get a B, no matter what I do on the exam, unless, of course, I fail."

As the game progressed, Jennifer fianchettoed her bishop and castled. She was offensively cramped, but she was defending well. But to win, she felt that she had to attack. "So, Paul, how come you've never asked me out?"

Paul looked up from the board and gave her the quizzical eye. "What do you mean?"

"I mean, we've known each other a while now, and we play chess together all the time. I thought you liked me, but you've never asked me out. Don't you like me?"

Paul saw the attack and countered. "Yes, I like you very much, and I thought about it, but I thought you only thought of me as a guy to play chess with. I thought if you would say no, it might ruin our friendship. Do you want to go out?"

"Of course I do. You're a really sweet guy, and I think we should go out one night and have some fun. Then we'll see what happens from there."

"You know, I haven't dated much, so I'm probably not very good at it." He tried to fend off the attack, but he was two pawns down, crucial in the endgame. "What would you like to do?"

She kept the pressure on, keeping him in check. "I know this quaint place down on Dumbarton Avenue. They have a live band, and we could go for a few drinks or something."

"I don't drink much, either, but I'll go with you. I like to hear live music. How about the night after the exam? We can celebrate the end of our freshman year."

"Sounds great. And I believe that's checkmate."

Paul tried to figure a way out of his hopeless position, but, "You're right. Checkmate it is."

On the night after the final, Paul came to call on Jennifer at her dormitory. He had to call up for her to come down to meet him. They were both happy about how they did on the test and looked forward to a night of fun and relaxation. They got off campus and walked hand-in-hand down P Street, cut over on Wisconsin and down Dumbarton on their way to the Allnighter Jazz Club. They talked about the different musicians they had seen play live. Jennifer was hooked on jazz, while Paul like more mainstream and some classical.

"You know whom we're going to see tonight?" Jennifer asked. "G.G. Slimush and the G Clefs."

"I don't think I've ever heard of them."

"Well, they are just a local band, but they're good. G.G. plays a hot eighty-eight."

"A piano, right?" Paul guessed. And she confirmed her lingo. "Good, I always like to hear a good pianist, no matter what style he plays. It's a great instrument. I even play a little, you know."

"You do? That's cool. I've always wanted to play an instrument, and I guess that's why I admire people who do so much. I'd like to hear you play sometime."

"Well, I'm not that good. So maybe you wouldn't want to."

They could see the flashing neon of the club sign from down the street. They hurried across 29th Street and made their way through the crowd into the Allnighter. The place was already jumping. G.G. was knocking out the crowd with his patented dink-dink-doodley-ahs. Paul and Jennifer had to wait a few minutes to be seated, but they eventually got a table off to the side. To Paul, there seemed to be too many things going on at the same time, and he became uncomfortable because he liked to know everything that went on around him. His eyes quickly darted around the room, but he could only concentrate on one thing at a time. He looked at G.G., the piano player, then the guitar player. His attention was diverted by the waitress who walked by. She served drinks to patrons at a nearby table, and then he looked at all the people sitting at the tables around him. There was an array of sounds: the band, of course, the clink of glasses, and the people talking. They talked all at the same time, and the sound gave him a mental picture of a pen full of gobbling turkeys on a farm. Each added its own unintelligible sound to make one giant unintelligible sound. So Paul tried to focus his attention on one conversation for a few seconds, then another, then to Jennifer. Oh, Jennifer was saying something to him. "I'm sorry. What did you say, Jennifer?"

"I said, what would you like to drink? The waitress is here."

"Oh, I guess I'll just have a cola."

"Just a cola? This is supposed to be a celebration. Just relax. Have a real drink. It'll help you loosen up."

"Well, I just never liked the taste of alcohol, is all."

"Then I know the perfect drink for you. A Strawberry Daiquiri. You won't even taste the alcohol," Jennifer guaranteed. "Do you want to try one?"

"I guess it wouldn't hurt to try one."

Jennifer turned to the waitress, "That'll be one Strawberry Daiquiri, and I'll have a Whiskey Sour, please." She turned back to Paul and said, "I guess you don't do this too often, do you?"

"No, I don't. I guess I'm a little uncomfortable with everything going on around me."

"That's okay. We're just here to relax and have a little fun. Do you like the music?"

"Yes," Paul answered. "I like it a lot. It is good, like you said."

Their drinks arrived, and Paul took a sip of his daiquiri. He was surprised at how it tasted. It was very sweet, and the alcohol was hard to detect, but he could still taste it. He sipped it slowly while they continued their conversation. Actually, Jennifer continued it. Paul mostly listened. He liked to hear Jennifer speak, and he knew that he never spoke that well, and he had to exert himself to be heard over the music. Because Jennifer liked to talk, it seemed to work out well enough. Jennifer had a few more drinks in the time it took Paul to finish his first one. Then she asked him, "Would you like to dance?"

"I don't dance," Paul stated flatly.

"Come on. Anybody can dance these days. It's not as if you have to know that ballroom crap to know how to dance. You just sort of have to move your. . . . Now take that couple over there on the dance floor. Not your most polished dancers, I grant you, but they look like they're having fun, right? What you need to do is sort of take a part of your body, like your hips, and move it back and forth to the beat of the music. Then you do the same thing with your legs and arms, and you're dancing. Come on, what do you say? You don't want me to dance by myself, do you?"

"Well, I don't know. I haven't made a fool out of myself all year. I guess I can afford to tonight. But, just one dance, okay?"

"Now you're talking."

When he got out on the floor, Paul started slowly, as he was unsure of what to do first, but after a few seconds, he concentrated on the music and let it take control. He didn't know what he looked like, or if he was cool or hip, but he actually felt as if he were dancing. He looked over at Jennifer. She looked smooth. It didn't appear to be any particular step, and he figured she was following her own advice and improvising as well, but doing a better job at it than he was.

When the song ended, he began to feel self-conscious again, at how people were looking at him, and he didn't realize how tiresome dancing was. So he asked Jennifer if they could sit down again. She ordered a couple more drinks for herself as they listened to the music for a while longer, but she became even more boisterous and tried to convince Paul to dance again.

"C'mon, let's dance some more."

"But I'm no good. I can't dance," Paul stressed.

"You were good. C'mon, I need someone to dance with." She pouted at him playfully. "Do you mind if I dance with someone else then?"

"No, I guess not." He lied. Of course he cared, but he didn't know why he said that or what to do. After she found someone to dance with, Paul sat at the table alone and watched her. He thought she was probably a little drunk. Paul was starting to feel extremely uncomfortable sitting there. He thought that the music was too loud. And the cigarette smoke was giving him a headache. He wanted desperately to ask Jennifer to leave, but she seemed to be enjoying herself. However, when the music stopped briefly, he decided that he had enough, and that Jennifer had enough, whether she realized it or not. He went up to her and said, "Time to go, Jennifer, okay?"

"Go? But I haven't even finished my drink."

"Yes, you have," he told her.

"Oh. Okay." Jennifer bumped into a few tables as Paul led her out of the club. She was drunk, he thought. So he helped her by making her lean on him for support. As they got out into the fresh, night air, she said to him, "I know what you're thinking now. You're thinking that you'll be able to take advantage of me tonight, aren't you?"

He didn't say anything because he wanted her to think that he wasn't thinking any such thing. Denying it wouldn't work, but then she said, "Well, you're right. You can."

Paul stopped and looked at her. Does she know what she's saying, he wondered? As he walked her back across the campus green, he held her in his arms, and he could feel her small breasts pressed up against his side, and he thought about it. He had never been with a girl so beautiful and nice, and seemingly willing to love him. She wasn't blitzed unconscious or anything, he thought, so she might mean what she said. Or did she? He finally decided he couldn't take that chance. He couldn't do anything, and he wasn't sure how much the alcohol affected her decision-making processes. Did it simply release her inhibitions to do what she really wanted, or did it totally distort her reasoning into doing something she wouldn't normally do? Also, Paul was a virgin, and he pictured his first time under better circumstances.

When they finally got to her building, Paul asked her, "Do you think you can make it from here?" But as soon as he said it, he thought it was a bad idea. As she continued to lean on him, he said, "I guess I'll just help you up the stairs, then."

They slowly climbed the stairs, as she needed to have both feet on each step to steady herself. When they got to her room, Paul asked her, "Are you going to be all right now?"

"No. I think I'm going to be sick. I need you to come inside and help me."

He went inside her room, and Jennifer quickly closed the door behind them. As Paul's eyes were adjusting to the dark, he could see that Sheila was not there. He then realized that the bathroom was down the hall, if she was going to be sick. "Are you okay now? Are you going to be sick?" he asked.

"Yes, I'm going to be sick if you don't stay with me tonight. I need you."

"I can't do that. This dorm is all female."

"I like you a lot, Paul, and I want you to make love to me tonight." In a blink and a flourish, she removed her top. As it came over her head, she revealed to Paul that she had gone braless that night. Her small breasts still jiggled as her arms came down to her sides. She quickly went over to Paul and hugged him hard. And in between kisses, she said, "I want to have sex with you. You're so cute and sexy. I love you." And with that, she grabbed his crotch and made him a tad more uncomfortable. He gently pushed her away and looked into her pale, blue eyes.

"I don't know. I don't want you to think I'm taking advantage of you."

She stepped out of her designer blue jeans and said, "But you're not. I know what I'm doing." But the scent and taste of alcohol on her breath on her breath told Paul otherwise. She took off her bikini underwear and stood before him completely naked. She went over to him again and kissed him. "Come to bed with me," she whispered into his ear, then poked her tongue into it.

"Okay, okay." He was finding it harder and harder to resist and ignore the pleadings of a nude woman. He led her over to the bed and made her get in first under the covers. "Just wait one minute, though. Okay?"

"Okay, but hurry. My nipples are getting hard."

Paul went into the other half of the room. He had to sit down and think. Could he just let himself go and enjoy himself this one time? Probably not, he thought. He knew he would feel guilty, especially if she came to her senses tomorrow. He had to go back in there and tell that beautiful, naked creature that he couldn't go through with it. At least for tonight.

"Jennifer," he whispered. He went closer to the bed. "Jennifer." But she didn't respond. She was out like the proverbial light. He was a bit relieved, though. She was perhaps more drunk than he realized. Paul covered her bare breasts and kissed her on the cheek.

"Goodnight," he said softly, and left.

CHAPTER TWO

Athletics were definitely a problem. No one else knew what to do about it. So it ended up on her desk. Representative Marilyn Connors, (D) of Virginia, pondered this question with the intent of not only advancing her career as a junior member of the House, but also, as a way to improve the life of each American citizen by finally eradicating the last vestige of sexual discrimination in the country. It had been allowed to continue, up to now, because no one had the answer. Pressure had been building for someone to find an answer. Marilyn was given the task of drafting a bill to remedy the presumable discrimination in athletics around the country.

Before her staff had arrived that morning, Marilyn contemplated the dilemma. She wanted to get some input from her staff, but first she had to determine the concrete goals that needed to be accomplished.

Women already had been given the opportunity to compete in the major leagues of sports; that was easy, but as of the moment, no woman had made it to the majors in baseball and football. Currently, there were two women in basketball, but was that enough to reflect equality? It seemed as though the top women still couldn't compete with the top men in their respective sports. In the instances of basketball and minor league baseball, where there were women on the teams, they were in the minority and were not the stars. Women could make the same money as a man of equal ability, but the top women might never earn the same as the top men.

There was a case where a minor league baseball team benched its only female member to allow a rookie to prove himself. She charged discrimination and took it to court. The court didn't want to end up coaching a baseball team, but had ruled that it was discriminatory. The solution the court came up with was to order the coach to give the two equal playing time until an arbitrator could determine through statistics who was the better player and who deserved more playing time. That was the current ruling governing all sports, but it wasn't adequate in the minds of many. It could lengthen a few women's careers by going through the long process, but at what cost to pure sports competition? Should the government start managing sports teams? Marilyn Connors did not think so.

But what if the bill she was drafting mandated that all sports have an equal number of male and female members? Would that create equality? She tried to imagine what it would be like on football teams. Even if they had the same number of female players as male, who would score all the touchdowns? Probably the men, she reasoned. It also would have to be in the law for the male players to give the ball to the females a certain number of times. But still it would be clear who helped the team the most. Fans would know it, and therefore, would not promote the image of equal rights.

That reminded Marilyn of her days in high school. When she took a physical education class, boys and girls played a loosely supervised game of soccer on the same teams. The girls mostly stayed out of the way and usually ended up just talking to each other, while the boys ran around participating in the game. If they weren't truly equals on the field, that's how Marilyn thought it could turn out now. The girls thought they couldn't contribute, so they didn't try. The boys thought the girls couldn't contribute, so they didn't let them try. That's the way it was, Marilyn thought, but it certainly wasn't equal.

Then she pondered the thought of separate leagues. But she quickly could shoot that idea down, because her job was to close the rift between the sexes, not create one. Besides, she remembered what it was like in college. The University of Virginia's men's basketball team charged admission and huge crowds showed up. The university's women's basketball team didn't charge admission, and almost no one showed up. There was no 'separate but equal' there. Who, if given freedom of choice, she thought, would pay to see a league that couldn't hit as many home runs or couldn't slam-dunk. They could shorten the fences and lower the rim for the women, but that wouldn't be equal either.

There was still the matter of individual sports, such as track and field, tennis, golf, and so forth. For years, men and women had competed in separate divisions, but it was a foregone conclusion, it seemed, that the top men always would beat the top women. The 'world' records in track were all held by men, and then they had the 'women's' world records that were slower than the true fastest times. There was a great commotion in the early 1970s when a great female tennis player, in her prime, beat a 50-year-old former great male tennis player. The victory was supposed to be great for women's liberation, but it didn't seem to do anything. The true female reaction seemed to be one of relief, because if she had lost, it truly would have made a mockery of women's athletics. It *did* show that *any* man could not beat *any* woman, which was enlightening to many men at the time because it was a widely held belief.

Women golfers, in their own division, could earn as much as men, but they played on shorter courses. Marilyn could see she had a big problem to solve. She couldn't make the law to deny a female golfer, for instance, the chance to compete on the men's tour if she wanted to, but that should mean she would have to permit male golfers the opportunity to play on the women's tour, and that would cause chaos in the system. If she denied the male golfers, it would discriminate against them. But to keep them separate would discriminate against women.

To keep them separate would keep them unequal. It seemed like a no-win situation, and Marilyn began to realize why she was given the task of sorting it out. She was a relative newcomer, at the bottom of the ladder. And failure for her wouldn't be such a large fall, as it would be for someone at the top to risk proposing a flawed solution. So it got passed down. She figured there were probably a few lower than her on the Congressional ladder, but she truly wanted to solve the problem, difficult as it was. She just couldn't pass it on. Her staff would be in shortly to present their research.

It was a personal challenge for Marilyn. She was involved in athletics in high school, and the whole time, she felt how unequal it was. Marilyn and her best friend Jessie Fernandez were on their high school swim team. Marilyn considered herself a mediocre swimmer. She had no real talent or training, but she thought it was fun to do. Jessie had urged her to try out for the team, and she was surprised when she made it.

Jessie was a little different, however. She had talent and training. Her mother was a former college swimmer and a coach, and she brought Jessie with her to the pool at an early age. She started training her in earnest when she showed an interest, and Jessie started by entering junior competitions, and began winning. By the time she was a sophomore in high school, she was the number one swimmer on her team. And by the time she was a senior, she was dating the number one swimmer on the boys' team. Marilyn still could recall a conversation she had with Jessie back then about how they were both number one, but yet so different.

They were finishing practice one day and were heading back to the locker room to shower. The boys' and girls' teams shared the pool for practice, shared the same training and shared the same coach. Darrell Lodermeier, Jessie's boyfriend and number one male swimmer at Petersburg High School, came over to where the two were standing by the locker room door.

"Jess, you coming over later?" Darrell said as he jogged over, still dripping from the pool.

"Of course. Don't be silly. Quick, give me a kiss before coach sees us." Jessie stood on her toes to make up the height difference, and then wrapped a towel around the back of his neck to hang on to so that he could pick her up. She said she liked it when he picked her up like that because she could get close to his almost bare body. Darrell was tall, extremely lean and handsome—a real catch in the opinion of Jessie's girlfriends.

When he put her down, he said, "See you later then, baby," and he ran back to the locker room.

"Love you!" Jessie yelled after him.

"He really is something, isn't he?" Jessie queried Marilyn, as they walked through the girls' locker room door.

"Yes, he certainly is," Marilyn replied. "Most girls think you're the luckiest girl in school."

"Not really lucky. He's just a really sweet guy, and we happen to get along great." Jessie peeled off her sticky, wet bathing suit and hung it on the hook by her locker. She seemed to enjoy the freedom of walking around the locker room naked. Marilyn was a little shy, however. She would never take her suit off until she was in the shower room.

"Yeah, well, not all of us can seem to find the really sweet guys to get along great with."

"Can you grab the shampoo?" Even though they still were soaked to the bone, they headed off to the shower room to wash the chlorine smell out of their hair and off their bodies. The building steam made it harder to breathe, but the heat was a welcome relief from the cold dampness outside.

"You say Darrell is so sweet, but is he liberation-minded?" Marilyn finally peeled off her suit and hung it along with her towel in the drying area. Even though everybody else was in there also, it was the only place she felt comfortable being naked.

"I'm not even liberated. Why should he be?"

"But it is important." They walked into the shower room together with their shampoo and literally nothing else. They stepped under adjacent shower heads to continue the conversation as they lathered their hair. "It's all hunky-dory while he's number one male swimmer, and you're number one female swimmer. That's because he can still beat you, but what do you think would happen if you could beat him all the time? His masculinity would be threatened, and he wouldn't be able to handle it."

"Have you been reading *Ms.* magazine again?"

"As a matter of fact, I have. And you should read it, too, Jessie. There's a lot of good articles in there, and you might learn how to handle Darrell." They rinsed the soap from their hair and eyes, and then began to lather their bodies.

"I don't need to *handle* him."

"Then tell me this—doesn't it ever bother you that, no matter how hard you try, you probably never will be a faster swimmer than he is?"

"Well, I never really thought about it."

"But you're an athlete. You train hard and do your best. And you've seen him—he doesn't even try most of the time, and he's always faster than you. And, as athletic as you are, you're still a little flabby." Marilyn pointed to Jessie's derriere.

"Look who's talking!" Jessie grinned while looking down at Marilyn.

"Yeah, but I'm not exactly an athlete, either. You are. Darrell doesn't train as hard as you do, but he doesn't have an ounce of fat on his ass."

"Oh, you've seen my boyfriend's ass, have you?" Jessie playfully chided her, and smiled.

"You know what I mean. I see him every day in his swim trunks. But doesn't all that bother you?" They both finished rinsing and turned off the faucets as they headed back to dry off and get dressed.

"No. I can't really say it bothers me. It's just part of being a girl." She reached up for her towel and mopped off the excess water from her breasts, arms and legs. Marilyn simply wrapped her towel around herself as she walked back to her locker.

"It doesn't seem right, you know."

"But what do you want? Do you want us to be like guys?" Jessie took a quick step back, spun her towel into a whip and flicked Marilyn on her semi-exposed buttock.

"Oww!" Marilyn quickly turned around to see what had happened. "Why, you—" She set herself to retaliate by tearing off her towel, but before she was ready, she was flicked again at the tip of her right thigh. "Yipe!" she yelled as she jumped back, and then in a fluid motion, spun her towel and flicked in return. Smack! Right on target, just above Jessie's left knee. She re-loaded quickly, but just missed Jessie's left breast. The other girls started to join in on the fun. They didn't hurt each other very much, and after a few moments of their giggling, orgiastic, towel-flicking frenzy, Jessie jumped up on one of the benches—of course, leaving herself open to a few more at-tacks—to make a speech.

"Ladies, ladies, please! We're acting like animals here." She tried to sound serious, but ended up giggling again. "We must stop this now and be civilized. We're acting like—well, we're acting like—guys." The entire room erupted in laughter once again as they got in their final shots at each other before calming down and resuming dressing.

Jessie went back to her locker. She said to Marilyn, "Come to think of it, maybe it would be fun to be a boy."

"I know what you mean. We wouldn't have to worry about our peri-ods, or getting pregnant, or putting on makeup just to leave the house, or wearing bras."

"Yeah, but don't forget. Guys have one fatal weakness."

"What's that?"

"If you grab a guy by the balls, he'll have to follow you anywhere."

"Jessie!"

"What?" she said, trying to mock Marilyn's shocked expression. "It's true, you know."

"Well, seriously, about what I was talking about, you should ask Darrell yourself."

"I am not going to do that. I can't." At least that's what she told Marilyn for now. She was curious, but she had to figure out a way to be less than direct.

As they walked out the locker room door, Marilyn added, "Think about it. I'll bet he's just another chauvinist."

Jessie frequently would go to Darrell's house after school or swim practice because it was within walking distance of the school. Then Darrell would drive her home. His parents would invite her to stay for dinner so often that it was as if she were just another member of the family. She was such a fixture at his house that she was allowed to walk in the front door without knocking. But this time the door was locked. She rang the doorbell, but, after a few moments, no one answered. She hadn't noticed his parents' car in the driveway, and she thought maybe they all had stepped out, and Darrell forgot that she was coming over. But when she rang the second time, Darrell answered the door with just a towel around his waist.

"Hi, baby," he said as he picked her up again to kiss her. "Sorry, I was out back by the pool. I almost didn't hear the bell."

"That's okay. Are your parents here? I didn't see their car out front."

"No. They won't be here all evening. Business dinner or something. Is that cool or what? We can be alone for a change. Come on out back."

When they got there, she saw what was occupying his time. He had been rolling joints from his bag of marijuana. After he set up another deck chair for Jessie beside his, he sat down, picked up one of the rolled cigarettes and lit it. He took a deep drag and offered it to Jessie.

"No thanks. You keep trying to get me to smoke that stuff, but you know I don't like it. You shouldn't smoke either. It's swim season, you know. You're supposed to be in training."

"It don't mean nothing. It just gets you buzzed, is all."

"Where'd you get that stuff, anyway?"

"From the guys on the team. They all do it. Just don't bring me down, okay? If you don't want to do it, that's fine, but I like it. It relaxes me."

"Sorry. I'm just trying to take care of you." Jessie started to caress his bare arm and leg while he stretched out on his lounging chair. She quickly flipped up the towel he was wearing to see if that was all he was wearing, but he had his suit on.

"Checking to see if it's still there?" he asked with a sly grin.

"Yeah, I wanted to see if smoking weed made it fall off, like I heard."

"Where'd you hear that?"

"From the guys on the team."

"Shut up." They cuddled some more as they listened to his new Guns n' Roses tape.

Jessie suddenly jumped up and shouted, "Let's go swimming!"

"You swim all day. You're starting to look like a fish." She just stared at him longingly while he lay on his chair. He finally said, "You bring your suit?"

"Nope. So let's go skinny dipping. Your parents aren't going to be home for a while, right?"

"Right on." With that, Jessie took off her clothes, and, without giving Darrell a chance to look at her, she jumped into the pool. Darrell quickly shed his towel and suit and followed.

After a short game of dodging him, Jessie let him catch her. They embraced and kissed each other passionately. When they came up for air, she made her challenge. "How about if we race to the end of the pool and back?"

"You're crazy, but all right."

"Ready—on your mark—get set—" and without even saying go, she sprinted across the pool. After he realized that he had been had, Darrell took off after her. He soon caught up to her with his longer, more powerful strokes. It was close, but he flipped and touched the wall first. He maintained the lead until halfway back. He took larger gulps of air and strained more for each stroke. He didn't even notice her, but Jessie pulled even, and just nosed him out to touch first and win.

After she got a little of her breath back, Jessie shouted, "I beat you! Whoa! I really beat you!"

"Don't get so excited. It's not like it was a real race."

"What do you mean? Of course it was a real race."

"No, it wasn't. Besides, you took a head start."

"You caught up, though. No excuses now. Just admit that I beat you." Jessie didn't really care about winning, but she wanted him to admit it to prove Marilyn wrong.

"I was smoking earlier, anyway."

"I said no excuses. You really can't handle that I beat you in a race. Does it bother you that a girl beat you?"

"No." But Jessie saw that she had hurt him. She didn't mean to put it that way, but now she realized that Marilyn was right. She knew it was a painful question, and she never should have asked. Things were just fine the way they were, and she just wanted to have fun that night. She hated to fight with him. "Come on, baby. No more competition, okay?"

"Fine with me," he said. They continued to swim playfully, and when Jessie got tired, she pulled herself up to sit on the edge of the pool. She let Darrell look at her naked body for as long as he wanted. When Darrell pulled himself out of the pool and sat next to her, she saw that he was aroused.

"Oh, you poor baby," she said to him. "You're so tense. You do need to relax. Lie down and let the doctor give you the treatment."

Darrell lay back as Jessie took hold of him. She gently caressed him to relieve him. "How come you never want to make love?" he asked her. "You like doing this, but you never want to make love with me. Is it because you don't think I love you enough?"

"You know the answer. I can't afford to get pregnant right now."

"Why don't you start using the pill like everybody else?"

"I don't want to. I heard that there are side effects, and I can't worry about that during swim season."

"Swim season's almost over. Are you saying after swim season?"

"I don't know. I have to think about it. I do love you. Don't you like this?" She squeezed him a little harder.

"Of course I do. But it's not the same."

"For me, right now, it is." She picked up the pace to match his rhythmic movement until he ejaculated. He toweled himself off, and then jumped back in the pool to cool off, and when he got out, he stood over Jessie and dripped water on her head.

"Your turn," he said. He picked her up in his arms and set her down on a patch of soft grass. Without a word, she spread her legs to let his head in between. He began exploring with his tongue until he found her spot.

Jessie closed her eyes and laid her head back on the grass. She shut out the world as she entered her own mind and body. Her equilibrium was lost for a moment, and she felt herself spinning in circles as if she were lying on a whirling disc. She spread out her arms to touch the cool ground and regain her balance, and she slowly stopped her turning. She was in touch with the world again, so she let herself go, and the rotations started once more. The whole world spun underneath her. Or was the whole universe spinning? The sun still shone on her face, and she tried to focus on the inside of her eyelids. Everything was a yellowish red with a bright ball of reddish yellow in the center. She looked farther inside her own eyes and only saw lines. Flowing lines forming patterns and then repeating them. Farther and farther back she went, trying to see her own imagination. She started to see pictures; she must be getting close. She stood on a diving board. She did a graceful swan dive into the swimming pool, but, just as she entered the water, the process was repeated as if it were a video loop. She never saw herself climb the diving board ladder, and she never went completely into the water. She did her effortless dive over and over again, until she willed herself to stay in the water. She broke the plane; she was in. There was no sound, only feeling and sight. It was cool, but somehow dry. There was only color, only blue, with dark and light patches. Go deep. It got cooler and darker. Go deeper. It got cold and dark. There was no air to breathe. Must climb. Must get air. Panic! Not going to make it. Got to make it. Just hold on—

Darrell knew that she had come when he heard her gentle moaning, and when her smooth thighs clamped around his head. Jessie opened her eyes and relaxed her grip on Darrell, but drew him on top of her to embrace him. "Thank you," she whispered in his ear. "That was wonderful."

Darrell helped Jessie up, and they walked over onto the pool deck and dressed in silence. They sat back in their lounge chairs and held hands. Darrell smoked another joint, while Jessie took a short nap.

When Darrell woke Jessie up, she saw that it had turned dark. The stars were out on a clear night, and a quarter moon played hide and seek behind the swaying top branches of an oak tree which loomed over the house.

"My parents are going to be home soon," Darrell said. "And I wanted to talk to about something before you went home tonight."

"Sure, what is it?"

"I think we need to talk about college."

"What about it?"

"Well, I know we talked about going to the University of Florida together, but I haven't gotten a scholarship offer from them yet, and I don't think I will. I think we ought to go to Virginia, where we both have scholarships."

"But, with your parents' money, you don't need a scholarship to go to Florida."

"Sure, I can go to school there, but I can't swim there. I need something more than just school. I need to swim."

"But I thought you said swimming wasn't that important to you anymore. And you know how important swimming is to me."

"I know, but I need to do more than just go to classes. Swimming might be the only thing to keep me going to class. I sometimes think it was the only thing that kept me in high school."

Jessie was starting to hear Marilyn's voice in the back of her mind.

"So you want us to go to Virginia?"

"I think we should. It's closer to home, and most of our friends will be going there, too. Besides, you can swim at Virginia."

"But Florida's a nationally ranked program. It's a chance of a lifetime." Jessie drew in a deep breath and let out a defeated sigh. "What if I went to Florida, and you went to Virginia? Would we still be able to carry on a relationship?"

"If you moved to a different city, it would be just as good as breaking up with me."

"What you're saying is, if I go to Florida and you go to Virginia, you'll break up with me?"

"Basically."

Tears started to form in Jessie's already misty eyes. "I love you, damn it. But it's like you don't want me to succeed. Why can't you come with me?"

Darrell tried to comfort her with his arms, but kept his distance with his voice. "I told you why. I'm just telling you like it is. I can't go to Florida with you. And if you want me, you know where to find me. I'll be at Virginia. Think about it and we'll talk later."

Jessie broke from his embrace, wiped her eyes and sniffled. She calmed her countenance and her voice as she spoke to him. "Take me home."

She showed no signs of accepting or rejecting his conciliatory gesture of putting his arm around her as he led her through the house, out to his car. The drive was totally silent. Darrell kept the radio turned off, just in case Jessie might have something to say. She didn't.

When the car stopped in front of Jessie's house, she sedately said, "I just don't understand you."

"And I really don't understand you, either," he replied. "I don't understand why you're not jumping at the chance to stay with me."

Jessie said nothing as she strongly yanked open the passenger-side door and stepped out. She paused a moment as if to say one more thing, but just slammed the door shut as her message. Darrell punched the accelerator, which squealed his tires, in his own exhibition of anger.

Too much water again. Marilyn liked her coffee strong and black because it perked her up in the morning, but every time she tried to make it, she goofed up on the mixture. She looked at the clock on her desk. It was 7:55. Her staff would be in shortly.

Her three aides walked into the office together: Carmen DiAngelo, Jennifer Martin and Stanley Fraser. They greeted her like an out-of-sync chorus, "Good morning, Marilyn."

"Good morning, everyone. I'd like to have a short meeting before I get started with my day's activities, so, if you'll just get settled in the meeting room. Stan, before we start, see if you can borrow some coffee from Representative Hogan's office down the hall. I know he's in. I seemed to have ruined our supply this morning."

"Yes, of course, right away." Stan eagerly went in search of the coffee.

The other two aides went to their desks first to get notepads and pencils, then took their seats around the table in the meeting room. Stan arrived moments later with a bag of coffee crystals in one hand, along with a filled cup balanced on a saucer in the other.

"Here you go. He had extra, so he said you could bring the cup back any time." Stan handed the cup to Marilyn and then put the crystals into the coffee maker for the others.

"Thank you, Stan," Marilyn said. "I'd like to start today with a discussion on the sports bill. I'd like to hear your views on what your research turned up to get this thing going in the right direction. I've had a difficult time wrestling with this one, and I'd like to hear some fresh opinions on how we might solve this problem."

"Marilyn," Carmen said first, "I've been looking into this like you asked, but, frankly, I don't see a problem here."

"Could you expand on that a little further?" Marilyn asked.

"Well, it seems that everyone has started saying that if a man beats a woman in a race or something, it's somehow discriminatory. I just don't see it that way. When one man beats another man in a race, nobody's discriminating against the loser. One individual beat another individual because one had to be slower. So the same is true of a race between a man and a woman. One is faster, and one is slower. Just because, in the majority of cases, men are faster than women, it's not some form of unfairness or prejudice or discrimination that can be legislated away. It's just a case of one individual besting another individual. We're not supposed to be men and women anymore, just individual citizens, right?"

"Thank you, Carmen, but I think your rationale is stuck in the past and won't help to accomplish any sort of progress here. There is a problem of lack of equal opportunities to win, due to historical discrimination in training and support apparatus. And we just can't ignore it anymore. So, what have you got, Stan?"

"I'm glad you mentioned training, because I feel that has to be the crux of our approach. I outlined a proposal here," Stan said. "I don't think anything real can be accomplished without an intensive training program. My suggestion is to create separate but equal leagues for women right now, under the same rules and guidelines. This combined with radical changes in school training programs to get women ready for the competition, and in a couple of years, we can legislate one league in each sport with equal numbers of men and women participants without any loss of quality."

"Very well thought out. Thank you, Stan. What about you, Jennifer?"

"Well, I do agree with Stan. I think training is the only way to achieve true equality. You, Carmen and I have been victims of all the past discriminations, and we were discouraged from participating in many sports. But the very young girls now will have all the opportunities of intensive training and our new supportive society that they will be able to compete equally. As far as waiting, however, I don't see any other choice but to immediately mandate that all teams and leagues have equal numbers of male and female players. Anything else would be unconstitutional."

"I think you're right, Jennifer," Marilyn said. "I thought that there might be some other way, but there really isn't. There are going to be some problems with this at first, but I guess we just have to work through them. I'd like you to work with me on the drafting of the bill, Jennifer, because I think you have a good grasp on what needs to be done. I guess we can break up this meeting. I have a few meetings with other representatives, so I'll be in and out of the office all morning. Stan, I need you to type up my notes for the committee meeting this afternoon."

"Okay," Stan said.

"Carmen, you're still working on the speech, right?"

"Right. It'll be ready before you go home tonight."

"Then if that's all, we can get to work," Marilyn said as she walked over to the door leading to her private office.

"Marilyn?" Stan inquired as he hurried over to her. "I'd like to talk with you privately, before we get started on anything."

"Sure, I have a few minutes. Come on in. Oh, Jennifer, after I speak to Stan, I'd like to speak to you privately, also."

"Okay," Jennifer responded.

Marilyn gestured to Stan to enter her office. "Have a seat." She closed the door and went to her desk. She reclined in her big, black, high-backed, swivel chair. She pressed the tips of her fingers against each other and formed a sort of pyramid with her hands, then asked Stan, "Now, what can I do for you?"

Stan squirmed a bit in his chair across from Marilyn's desk. He had a grin on his face, and he tugged at his collar and gulped as he prepared to speak. "I'd like to know why it seems you always choose Jennifer's ideas and proposals over mine."

"You mean today?" Marilyn asked. "I liked your idea, but I thought hers was a bit more feasible. Even in its rudimentary form, I felt it was more likely to win the support it needs, and it's more likely to be signed by the president."

"I'm not just talking about today. Every idea I've come up with has been shot down. I think I've come up with some damn good stuff, but you never use it, or you'll use it in a roundabout way where I won't get credit. It'll suddenly become Jennifer's great new idea. You'll even go so far as giving Carmen credit for things, and everybody knows that she's out in left field somewhere, in terms of current political climate. She never has a clue to what's really in the issues, and she never supports the president's positions, no matter what it is.

"But I've kept quiet, and I haven't made a fuss because I didn't want to appear selfish," he continued. "However, this is getting to be too much. I sometimes feel like you're discriminating against me because I'm a man. I never get any of the juicy stuff. About all I do is type for you, or get coffee, or give messages to so-and-so. If this is really some sort of reverse discrimination, I might just make a fuss about the whole thing."

"Whoa now! Don't get all bent out of shape," Marilyn said, trying to calm Stan down. "You're an important part of this team. I'm sorry if I haven't shown a lot of support for you, but there's a big reason why I haven't. I can't risk showing any signs of favoritism toward you. Even if it's unintentional, I could be charged with discrimination against the others. The society is concentrating on eradicating discrimination against women right now, and it's not an instant process. We're in a period of adjustment. And during this period, you may feel as if you're the victim of reverse discrimination, but you're not. It's just part of the correction phase dealing with past injustices. I see this adjustment period lasting a few more years, but when it's over, the dream will be realized. Everyone will *be* equal, and there won't be any discrimination, reverse or otherwise. But there's not much you can do now to make it arrive any quicker. It will get better. There's little I can do about it either. To tell you the truth, I *do* like your idea better. Providing equal opportunity should be enough. And the idea of intensive training will not only prepare young women physically, but also mentally. In the past, there's been no feedback in the developmental stages to tell them what their true athletic potential was. And they also didn't have the same incentives as young men. So, thousands and thousands of women never considered athletics or gave it up prematurely. There's an untapped resource of quality female athletes out there to make the idea of equal sexual representation in sports feasible. And you realized it, Stan. It is good work. But even *you* have to realize that it wouldn't be acceptable. The influential people are impatient. Frankly, I think it could cause chaos if implementation isn't eased into. But, like I said, there's little I can do. I have to come up with a bill that the president will sign. I've been struggling with this because I really want something positive to happen here. I mean, they could end up handicapping the male athletes. And I don't want to see that happen. I know that none of this is going to help the way you feel, but everyone has to do some sacrificing. I don't agree with everything that is being done, but I have to sacrifice my ego a little bit to make it all worthwhile in the end. So, I'm expecting you to do the same."

"But don't you think that if you spoke up and presented your different views that maybe the path chosen wouldn't be so radical?" Stan asked.

"Oh, no. This thing is just too big and too important for one person to jeopardize it. Besides, I feel it will eventually change for the better. Perhaps I've confided too much in you already. Everybody seems suspicious of everything these days. Everybody is being scrutinized to make sure everyone is part of the program."

"So what do I do in the meantime?"

"Well, Stan, I want you to go back out there and continue to do your job just as you have been. And I feel I should warn you that a charge of reverse discrimination can be construed as discrimination itself on your part. All I can say is that you are appreciated, even if I can't show it too much. Okay?"

"Okay," Stan said with his proverbial tail between his legs. He was so fired up when he came in, ready to finally stand up for himself, but now he had no steam. He couldn't risk being labeled discriminatory. He always thought of himself as a law-abiding citizen, and to be accused of the society's most hideous crime would be devastating. Maybe she was right, he thought.

"Thanks, Stan. And could you tell Jennifer that I'm ready to speak to her?" Stan nodded and quietly walked out of the office. Marilyn stood up from her chair and walked over to the window to gaze out. Why did she tell Stan all those things? She didn't have to tell him that she disagreed with the present system. She could have just threatened him with his job, and he would have meekly obeyed. This was his first sign of aggressiveness since he started the job with her. Marilyn kind of liked that. Besides, she had gone through the same thing when she first entered the work force. At least, she didn't ask Stan to sleep with her if he expected any recognition. That was one good thing about the way things were now, she thought. Sex wasn't in the picture to complicate things now. There was a knock at her door. "Come in. Come in, Jennifer."

"You wanted to see me, Marilyn?"

"Yes, yes. I just got my notice that you'll be leaving us for a while. Your duty time comes up in two weeks."

"Right. I'll be gone June and July."

"Are you looking forward to it?" Marilyn asked.

"Yes, I guess I am, actually. I'm a little bit scared, too, but I like the idea of being able to defend my country." Although she was sincere about that, defending against a possible attack by Canada was not exactly what she thought defending her country would mean. She just couldn't get used to the idea that Canada was the enemy now.

"What I needed to tell you is that when these duty times come up in the Congressional offices with small staffs, the representatives with large staffs have offered a replacement to work for you while you're gone. Before you leave, I want you to go to Representative Anne Sinclair's office and meet with your replacement. Go over with her what you think she ought to know about the way this office works, and brief her on any projects that you're in the middle of. I also want to say good luck. I hope everything goes well." Marilyn embraced Jennifer and became a little misty-eyed. She liked Jennifer, and almost felt as if she were sending her own daughter off to war.

"Thanks a lot, Marilyn. I'll be back before you know it."

Chapter Three

A constant stream of headlights glared into Jennifer's eyes as she looked out from the bus window. It was almost midnight as the bus rolled southward on the Garden State Parkway. Jennifer was on her way to 'boot camp' at the Coast Guard Training Center in Cape May, New Jersey. She tried to forget about the long day she had just finished and tried to concentrate on the new day that was about to begin.

Jennifer thought she would have been in Cape May already, dealing with all the military personnel and lifestyle, and she geared herself up for it, with some trepidation. She wanted this to be a positive experience, but she remembered the training film they showed her of the shock treatment new draftees got as they arrived at boot camp. The film was to prepare the ones who volunteered for service for the abrupt change in lifestyle, but Jennifer fully expected things to be the same when she arrived, whenever that might be. She started the day very early, taking oaths and signing papers at the induction office, but the bus that took her from D.C. to Philadelphia had arrived late to meet the bus to Cape May. So she spent the whole afternoon and most of the evening waiting for the chartered bus to return and take her and a few others to the camp. The Coast Guard was given the task of training and deploying the border patrol force. For Jennifer, four weeks would be spent at the Cape May Training Center, for intensive military training and indoctrination, and then four weeks would be actual border patrol duty.

Jennifer sat by herself on the bus. Although there were a few other people to talk to, she didn't feel like talking. She kept trying to think about what it would be like. She was trying to be a good citizen, but it was such a new experience for her. So many men had been faced with the same situation, but only a handful of women had gone through this type of training before the Ratification. It definitely was going to be physical, and she had to wonder if she could handle it. She never thought of herself as a strong person physically, although she always had been quite healthy and somewhat athletic. But had that perception come from her slender figure? And would her slight frame stand up to the rigors that were required of her? She was given a physical examination earlier in the week, and the doctor told her that she was ready. She also was told prior to departure about all the physical tests she would have to pass to go on to patrol duty—so many pushups, so many situps, and so on. What if she failed and was told to go home? It would be a disgrace. Disgraceful because the training and the standards were the same as they had been for nearly fifty years. And the standards were for the average man, and if an average woman such as Jennifer couldn't pass, it would mean the chauvinistic men were right all along. True, she could get out of going on patrol duty and risking her life by failing the physical tests, but she would be sent back home a 'PUP' (Physically Unable to Perform). She knew of others who were sent back PUPs. They were always treated differently when they returned—treated as if they were a disgrace, treated as if they were inferior, as if they somehow had rejected the equality that had been granted to them by the ERA. If a woman failed her physical tests, she was thought to be unequal, and unequalness in the land of equality for women had to be inferior, disgraceful, and must be purged from the system. People ended up being demoted in their jobs until they were out of sight, out of mind, and literally had disappeared. Jennifer used to have lunch with a friend who worked at the office of Management and Budget, who had been 'PUPed' a few months before. First, she complained to Jennifer how they kept giving her lower status job assignments when she was first sent back; then she was moved around within the office to different and lower positions, and, when Jennifer finally lost touch, she had been transferred to another federal agency. When Jennifer asked another friend where she might have gone, her friend said that she didn't know for sure, but that she was probably transferred to the Post Office and was delivering mail back in her hometown. At first, Jennifer didn't connect the events, but then she began to wonder. The big rumor among the federal employees who worked in the offices of government agencies in D.C. was that being sent to the Postal Service to deliver mail was the punishment for the people who were sent back from their guard duties a PUP. Everyone joked about the Post Office as if it were the 'Siberia' for PUPs. It certainly wasn't the most glamorous of the government agencies, Jennifer thought. But this wasn't Russia, she thought, and there were no Siberias here. At least, she didn't know of any at the moment. There was no proof, and there had been no accusations. So there was really nothing to worry about, but she wished she had talked to her own letter-carrier before she left.

The rural countryside outside the bus window faded gradually, and more houses dotted the landscape. Street lamps now lined the road like sentinels standing guard, as Jennifer pictured herself becoming—one post in a human fence separated by intervals of a few hundred feet, stretching across the Canadian border.

The bus made its way through Cape May and finally approached the camp. Jennifer only wanted the long day to be over, and hoped they would just show her the place to lay her head and go to sleep. Some of the others on the half-filled bus began to stir, most making sure they had their personal possessions close by. Voices also grew louder.

Jennifer could hear things like, "This is it," and "Finally." One person expressed Jennifer's thoughts when he said, "I can't wait to hit the sack. I have a feeling tomorrow's going to be one hell of a day."

The driver stopped the bus inside the gates of the camp and announced their arrival. "This is the end of the line. Coast Guard Training Center, Cape May. They will give you instructions where to go. Have fun."

Jennifer thought he sounded a bit sarcastic. The driver yanked open the door, and a short, stocky, uniformed man stepped on the bus.

"All right, you puppies, the joy ride is over!" the man screamed. "I don't want no loafing, and I don't want no talking. I just want this bus cleared in fifteen seconds. *Move, move, move!*"

He didn't sound like a very patient man. So everybody tried to hustle off the bus. As the new recruits stepped off the bus, the man yelled at them again.

"Let's go, let's go, people! Don't waste the bus driver's time, and don't you dare waste my time. I need my beauty sleep, and it's past my bedtime. Pick a yellow square. Stand on it. And face the bus."

Jennifer found a little yellow square painted on the street, and she stood on it. When they were all standing on their squares, they were in perfect formation. Well, as perfect as they were going to get. Jennifer had felt drowsy on the bus, but now she was keenly alert and wide awake. 'Thanks a lot,' she thought.

"I said no talking! The quicker you follow instructions, the quicker we'll get this over with. You will not speak until you are spoken to." The man paced back and forth in front of the recruits.

He introduced himself as Chief Petty Officer Walter Horne, who was in charge of processing them into camp. Jennifer watched him intently as he strutted around in front of the group, like an actor on the stage—like a bad actor overacting the part, she thought.

Chief Horne took them into a nearby building, and then led his troops through the jungle of paperwork, step by step, making sure that nobody "screwed up," or stepped on one of those infamous paperwork landmines. Jennifer shuddered at the thought of having this guy on her back for the next four weeks. She had an idea of what kind of people these military types were, but she was still amazed at how picky this guy was, fretting over every little detail. They even were told not to address their fellow recruits by their regular first names—they were given new ones, Seamate Recruit. Jennifer thought they must call them 'petty' officers for a reason. She hoped the whole month wouldn't be like this. After all, they weren't regular military. After they finished all the paperwork, they were separated into groups of males and females, and left in the charge of two assistants, who were only one rank above the recruits themselves.

The males were led by a baby-faced kid named Briggs to the berthing area. "All right, just follow me," Briggs told the men. "Stay in line and no talking."

Were they going to spend the whole month in silence, Jennifer wondered?

After the men moved out, the women were led by a tall, gawky female named Campbell who bellowed, "Okay, follow me. Try to stay in line and—"

"And no talking. We know," Jennifer said under her breath. Only the woman standing on her right had heard her, and she giggled. Jennifer turned and smiled as if to say, 'What a joke this is.'

Campbell led the women across the compound to another building that looked like an exact replica of the first. Although the company had not been told to march, or taught how to march, Campbell appeared to be marching by herself to the beat of some imaginary drummer.

"Company, halt!" Campbell ordered, and as she stopped, she took two more steps in place to officially conclude the march. The company just stopped walking.

Campbell took them inside to a large, open room which constituted an entire wing of the building. Two rows of austere steel bunk beds stood on either side of the center aisle, with twin sets of lockers at the head of each bunk. There was a row of windows on each long wall, and a rectangular radiator ran down the length of the wall under the window sills. From the inside, on the left of the double doors was the lavatory and shower room. An empty bulletin board hung on the wall just before the first window. Otherwise, the room was stark and vacant.

When everyone had gathered inside, Campbell gave them another order: "At ease, everybody. This is your squad bay. This is about the only place on the base where you can really be at ease and relax. Except, of course, when a superior officer comes in here, you drop whatever you are doing and jump to attention. And I mean *jump!* I know you all want to make the best of your time here, and I know what it's like. I just went through boot camp myself, and I'm here to help you through the next four weeks, since I've been through the same things you'll be going through. Sometimes it's hard to understand why the company commanders do what they do. I'll try to explain why they might do certain things if you need me to, so that, hopefully, it won't be so stressful to you. It might be hard to imagine at first, but the company commanders are really trying to help you."

"Why do they have to yell all the time?" Jennifer asked Campbell. "How is that supposed to help us?" Jennifer wasn't sure if she should expose herself like that, possibly being branded a malcontent, but if others in the group saw how she felt, she might be able to find out if anyone else felt the same way. Maybe someone from the resistance movement—if there was one—would try to make contact with her.

"Believe it or not, they do that for a reason," Campbell responded. "It's to see how you'll handle pressure. They want to make sure that you're fully prepared to handle those tough situations that you might come across in the field once you leave here. It'll all become clearer to you as you go along. If you just keep in mind that it's not a personal attack on you, but just a part of training, it won't be so difficult. But right now, I want everyone to hit the racks. Lights out will be in five minutes. Be ready to go tomorrow."

Campbell left the squad bay and left them unattended for the first time since they got off the bus. Jennifer spied an empty 'rack' and headed for it. The woman who had marched alongside Jennifer in formation headed in the same direction and took the rack above Jennifer's. Once they had put their bags in the lockers, the woman introduced herself: "Hi. My name is Deborah Mullins. Oops! I mean Seamate Recruit Mullins."

"Hello, I'm Seamate Recruit Martin, but please call me Jennifer." Deborah smiled as if she thought this new first name business was kind of silly. "Nice to meet you," Jennifer said as she offered her hand to shake.

"Same here," she said as she shook hands. Deborah then began to undress and put her clothes on one of the rack's posts as she talked to Jennifer. "I really like Seamate Apprentice Campbell. I think she's going to really help. It's like she's one of us."

That wasn't exactly what Jennifer thought, but she agreed for now anyway. "Yeah, I like her too." Campbell struck Jennifer a bit differently. It seemed to Jennifer that she was more like one of them—the chiefs. Chief Horne was playing mind games with them, and Campbell was just playing her part.

Even though Jennifer knew what the next few weeks were all about, she didn't like the game that was being played. Whatever happened to the good old honest approach, she thought, instead of all this deviousness and trickery? And then they send someone in to tell them not to worry, and they're only testing them? She didn't like it at all.

Jennifer stripped down to her Fruit-of-the-Loom briefs and undershirt. The undergarments were exactly the same as the men wore, including the briefs—sans pee-hole. It was just another part of the unisex clothing revolution that had taken place in the first few months of the Thompson administration. Brassieres or any special adaptations for one sex, such as pee-holes, were outlawed. "Now that's true equality," Jennifer had said in jest to Marilyn when the legislation passed.

"I'm so excited about tomorrow," Deborah said. "I can't wait. I feel so proud to be serving my country like this. Don't you?"

"Oh yeah," Jennifer said sarcastically, but Deborah just thought she was agreeing. Jennifer already worked for the government, and she thought she could best serve her country according to her abilities. This was not among them, she thought. It didn't suit her personality. She was a bit sensitive to critical abuse.

"Tomorrow will come soon enough for me, though," Jennifer said as she climbed into her rack. The lights flicked off.

"Well, goodnight, Jen," Deborah said before she climbed into the top rack.

"Goodnight, Deb." Jennifer hated her name to be clipped or mangled into a nickname. She settled into her own rack. Not too bad, she thought, for an instrument of torture anyway. She knew it wouldn't take long to drift into a deep sleep, even in a strange bed, but she was afraid she might sleep too deeply. She wanted to wake up on time. But surely, they wouldn't let her oversleep. But before she could worry about it anymore, she was out.

Chief Horne woke them up rather abruptly the next morning and had the women standing at attention in front of their lockers in a matter of seconds, awaiting further instruction. At first, Jennifer didn't think about the fact that there was a man in the room among scantily clad young women, mostly because of the way he carried himself. He wasn't leering at them and hardly seemed to notice their state of undress. But she wondered, is this allowed? Wasn't this one of the horrors that was to be avoided at all costs in the new society? Just think, a man might be sexually stimulated looking at the bare legs of a woman, or the outline of breasts covered only with a white, cotton t-shirt. What if Chief Horne were just using this opportunity to get his kicks? Jennifer then inspected his groin area for the telltale rising bulge. Nothing.

After telling them to meet him in front of the building in five minutes, Horne left the room. When Jennifer saw that he was gone, she spoke in hushed tones to Deborah, who was almost jumping into her clothes beside her.

"Don't you think it was strange for him to even be in here like that?" Jennifer asked.

Deborah looked puzzled for a moment then said, "Oh, no, he was just trying to treat us like everyone else. He probably did the same thing with the guys. So he had to come in here."

"If we're supposed to be treated equally, how come we're not all kept in the same squad bay?"

"That's what we're all working for one day, but some of the guys in the company might not be fully disciplined yet. We don't have to worry about the Chief, though, because he's disciplined. It's just a way to protect us from them."

"Or *them* from *us*," Jennifer said under her breath, as she didn't really want Deborah to hear that. And it didn't appear that she did.

Jennifer dressed quickly and headed downstairs with the others. The whole company was gathered for the first time, as they joined the group that had arrived earlier than Jennifer's group.

"Company, FORWARD, HUH!" Horne bellowed as he led the group to the mess hall for breakfast. Again the company walked along and tried to stay in line, for they hadn't been taught to march yet. But Horne and his assistants marched in unison to some unheard universal military cadence. They led their flock of disheveled sheep across the base in search of nourishment.

"Company, HUH!" Jennifer and the rest of the company correctly guessed that meant for them to stop. Horne rattled off his list of instructions. "You will walk in single file by row; there will be no talking; follow directions inside; take what you want, as much as you want, and you will finish everything on your plate. We don't waste food here. You will have fifteen minutes. When you are finished your scrumptious and delicious regulation military meal, take your tray to the scullery window. You will come back outside and

stand in formation with the rest of the company and wait for further instructions."

Jennifer felt relaxed when Horne was out of sight, and so did the rest
of the company. Some were starting to talk to the people next to them.

"This is what I've been waiting for all my life, Purina Military Chow,"
Jennifer overheard one person say, and the remark generated a few chuckles.
The sun was just about to come up, and it was unearthly quiet. Jennifer actually felt a little peaceful for the first time since her arrival, and she was about
to turn to Deborah and say something about not getting a chance to witness
a sunrise too often, just to say something positive about the experience so
far, but her line moved and Deborah was in the adjacent line.

Once inside, the steamy smell of scrambled eggs reached Jennifer's
nose first. So she decided to take some. She looked at the chipped beef and
passed. Pale, greasy sausage—two; yellowish hash browns, no; anything-but-
round pancakes—well, just one; fruit: bananas, grapefruit, apples. The apple
looked good. Jennifer took a carton of milk and followed the line again until
she got to the table.

A male recruit sat across the table from her. He was about her age,
maybe a little younger. She decided to talk to him, to see if she could find
out a little more about this place.

"You must have been in the group that came earlier. I didn't see you
on the bus," Jennifer said in a hushed tone. "Did they have you do anything
yesterday? Did I miss anything?"

"No," he said casually. "They just processed us in. They let us just
hang around the squad bay until taps. The SA was telling us what it was like
here, though."

Very impressive, Jennifer thought. He already has some of the military lingo down. He sounds like an old pro already. "Oh, yeah. What did he
say?"

"Well, one of the things he said was that we were going to meet our company commanders today, and he said that they were the two toughest in the place."

"Tougher than Chief Horne?" Jennifer asked, because it was hard for her to imagine anyone more uptight than that guy.

"Oh, yes. He said Chief Horne is just a pussy cat in comparison. Besides, we won't have to even worry about Chief Horne. He said that we probably won't even see him again after today."

"Really? I find that part refreshing." Others in the company had been talking amongst themselves, but what had started in whispers now was a noticeable din, which disturbed the ultra-sensitive ears of Chief Horne, who was seated across the room at the Chiefs' table. "Pipe down over there!" he bellowed. "You don't have time to chatter! Just chow down, and get out!"

The room fell silent for a moment. It only took a few moments, however, before the whispers started up again. Jennifer tried to pick up the pace and eat a little faster when she saw a couple of people finish. Between gulps, she introduced herself to the guy she had talked to.

"By the way, my name is Jennifer Martin. Seamate Recruit Martin."

"Hi, I'm Richard Runge." He offered his hand. Jennifer hesitated a moment and glanced around the room, specifically to see if Horne was looking their way. He wasn't, and so she shook Richard's firm hand.

Jennifer felt she might be able to form a friendship with her new acquaintance, but if anyone saw them right then, one might think something fishy was going on, when there was nothing piscatorial about it.

"I know this training stuff is going to be just a bunch of bullshit," Richard continued. "I just can't wait to get into the field."

"I just don't understand what they are so uptight about around here," Jennifer said. "I mean, we're basically a bunch of civilians trying to do our duty the best we can, and they treat us like incompetent lowlifes who aren't capable of doing anything we're not told."

"Don't worry, Jennifer. I think they're just trying to get our attention and let us know how serious this can be. Once they think they have our attention in a couple of days, it should get a lot better."

"Geez, I can't even enjoy my breakfast," Jennifer said between mouthfuls.

"I think we should hurry up and get out of here," Richard said. "We don't want to be the last ones out."

Jennifer looked down the table and saw that over half of the people were finished already. She still had an apple left.

"Chow down and get out!" came the call from Chief Horne from across the room. Jennifer 'chowed down'. She did not want to be the last one out. She remembered how he treated the stragglers out of bed that morning, and she imagined he would have some snappy insult for the trailer, even though there *had* to be one *last* person, anyway. She took three or four bites of apple before swallowing, which was an ordeal in itself. Not only was there more food than usual for her all at once, but it seemed to her that her throat was constricted, and smaller, making swallowing difficult. She felt akin to an animal during a feeding frenzy.

Richard finished a few bites ahead of Jennifer and left to stand in the line to deposit the trays in the kitchen. Jennifer finished and left just a bare core on her tray. She got up and stood in line, too. Chief Horne was reviewing the troops as they passed by, but, as she moved further along, she saw that he was reviewing their trays, and he was sending some of the people back to the tables. Horne stopped the guy right in front of Jennifer. It probably didn't help that he was a bit pudgy.

"Come on, you fat pig. You're not going to tell me that you've lost your appetite, are you?" Horne said to him, putting his own face in close proximity to the scared-stiff recruit's. The tray contained a couple of toast crusts and a small portion of grits.

"I—I didn't have time to finish, Chief Horne," the chubby recruit said, apprehensively.

"Don't be so greedy next time. Now go back to the table until you have licked that tray clean, understand? We don't waste food around here."

The recruit walked back to the table to finish. Horne let Jennifer pass without much notice. She was surprised he didn't make her eat the apple core. After she had placed her tray in the window to the scullery and walked outside with the rest of the company, she thought, 'Poor guy. They're playing with his head. They tell him he can take as much as he wants. So he takes what is probably normal for him, but then they only give him fifteen minutes to finish it. And of course when he doesn't finish in time, they tell him to take extra time to make sure he finishes it. Why couldn't they just give us thirty minutes to start with?'

She hooked up with Deborah outside in formation. She didn't tell her how silly she thought it was. Deborah had seemed to always think that everything was as it should be. Normal. Nothing out of the ordinary. Jennifer was afraid that if she started complaining about everything she hated about this place, Deborah might think she was some sort of subversive counter-revolutionary, not willing to just go along and play her part. She wasn't quite sure what kind of person Deborah was yet. She might be the subversive counterrevolutionary. She had a good feeling from her first impression, but she also could be a 'mole'. There were rumors and lots of talk about different types of surveillance, and you could never know who might be watching you at any particular time. And that's what Jennifer hated about the whole situation. Why should she even question the integrity of a sincere and genuine person like Deborah, and suspect her of some kind of deviousness? But she did try to follow Jennifer around ever since she got there, she thought. She just had to be careful.

When the whole company was gathered together, including, finally, the chubby recruit, they were led to another building across the compound where they were to be fitted for uniforms.

The uniforms weren't much different from the unofficial unisex uniform of the new society, which consisted of plain trousers and shirts—no neckties, no lace, frills or ruffles, no pleats, no bright colors or adornments of any kind. Designers were given strict guidelines to follow, which would insure the asexual integrity of the person who wore the garment. It was easy to see how important such a practice was. For instance, if a designer produced something a little frilly that men would not want to wear, it would let the concept of inequality slip back into the society, which had so thoroughly eradicated it. So while the troops got the same type of prosaic trousers and shirts that were completely devoid of style, at least now they were all the same color to show that they were all part of the military family.

After they received their uniforms, the recruits were led to the barbershop. Everyone had short hair already, as was the only socially acceptable style, but they still were given the standard military buzz-cut, just to show discipline and to keep tradition. Jennifer didn't like her new 'do', not because she was still chained to the concept that part of her femininity would be lost without her hair, but because she didn't like to feel bristles on top of her head. She had been quite comfortable with her short hairstyle, and she thought they were going a little overboard this time.

The company next was introduced to its pair of trainers, the Company Commanders. The man, in full Coast Guard dress uniform, struck an imposing figure. He was tall and thin, with thickly muscled arms and shoulders. The chiseled features of his face and the bulging veins and tendons in his neck gave no impression that there was anything soft about him, whether it was in his body or his demeanor. Yet his lower body, around his waist and legs, made him look somewhat fragile. His slightly graying hair was short and thinning. (One would think there would've been a mad rush to eliminate male-pattern baldness; it was so unequally dispensed.) He wore black patent leather shoes with metal taps on the soles that clicked on the asphalt when he walked up to his new troops.

The woman looked diminutive next to her colleague, but she was the same height as Jennifer. Her skin was dark complexioned, and her jet black hair was straight as a pin. Her noble facial features were counterbalanced by wire-frame glasses that made her look more like a stern school teacher than a drill instructor. But her in-charge countenance was absolutely all business and no-nonsense.

"All right, listen up, people!" the man began in another yelling, booming voice. "I'd like to introduce myself. My name is Chief Strickland, and I fully intend to become your worst nightmare."

"And I'm Chief Kaminski," came the high-pitched, but weathered voice of the woman. "It is my job to make you miserable."

"Chief Kaminski and I are going to be on you every minute. You can count on it. And even if we are not around, we might still be watching you. In fact, you'll never know who might be watching you, waiting for you to fuck up."

"We are not going to let up," Kaminski continued for him. "We are not going to give you a break, because if you're taking heavy shit in the field, you're sure as hell not going to catch a break out there. We have a month to train you mangy people to not get killed in the field, or to get your buddies killed by you breaking down under stress."

Jennifer had no doubt that Chief Kaminski was quite serious about her reasoning for being tough on them. Just in case something did happen, they did have to be prepared, but Jennifer couldn't take it seriously at all. She figured that she would go to her station, and she would do a lot of walking and a lot of standing around. There was no way that there would be any action, though. Canada wouldn't attack the U.S., or vice versa. There was absolutely nothing to gain for either side, she thought. But she had to play along with the mind game for now, because, after all, if they were going to play war, they needed an enemy.

The twin chiefs spent the morning teaching the recruits how to walk —Your left, yo' left, yo' left, r-r-i-i-i-i-g-h-t, righta left—Forward huh, to the rear huh, column right huh, to the left huh, right oblique huh. Company huh.

Of course, whenever anyone misstepped and broke formation, the company was stopped and conditioned to never do it again by doing more pushups. It was Jennifer's introduction to what other recruits called 'being cranked'. She survived that session and now couldn't wait for lunch, whether she had to gobble her food or not. She just hoped there was enough food for the rest of the company.

But while Kaminski and Strickland stood in front of the company and instructed them on the finer points of marching commands, Jennifer was surprised to hear another voice behind her. Who would dare speak without being spoken to, especially since it was drilled into them not to?

"Gee, I'm so glad that I'm short," said a male voice, softly but possibly audible to the back section of the formation, which had been arranged according to height. "I've got a great view back here. You've got a nice ass."

What? Jennifer thought. Who would say such a thing out in the open like that? It sounded to her as if it was the person standing directly behind her, and she quickly turned her head to see who had made the crude comment. She saw the chubby recruit from breakfast. He just smiled at her and puckered his lips as if to kiss her. She quickly turned back to face front. She didn't know what to do. First, she couldn't believe he had the gall to risk getting thrown out, arrested, or even worse, shot on sight for uttering such a blasphemous remark. She half-expected the unseen 'spies' to swoop down on the guy and dispose of him before he could contaminate anyone else with his sexist attitude. She was sure someone else must have heard him also, but no one was turning him in. But the remark was directed at her. It was up to her.

Then she thought that maybe he wanted to be nabbed. It raced through her mind that he regretted not getting out of the country when he could, because deep down he was such a chauvinistic pig. He probably tried to change, but a leopard can't change its spots, and now he's cracking. If she turned him in, it would guarantee his downfall. Maybe he just deserves another chance. She would try to talk to him privately and find out his motivation. Then again, she thought, what if he was a plant, and was trying to test some of them and their reactions to wrong thinking?

She just had to wait for some sort of clue before deciding what to do. When the company finally went to the mess hall for lunch, Jennifer also realized that the guy behind her would be sitting next to her at every meal. While standing in line, she casually glanced back, pretending not to look at anything in particular, and she saw that his name tag said Finkel. Gary Finkel, she would later find out.

After they were seated, she fully expected him to start talking to her, if not to say something else dirty, then at least to introduce himself. But he didn't say a single word to her, and she paid no more attention to him.

Even though they were still not given permission to talk during meals, Jennifer joined Richard and a woman named Lisa Hopkins in conversation. They mostly talked about how rough their first cranking session was. Even though she didn't have much time to get to know anything about Lisa, Jennifer liked her instantly. She cracked a couple of jokes that provided one of the few light moments since everyone arrived, while everybody else complained about what they didn't like so far.

Jennifer was one of the last ones to finish, but she had enough time without rushing too much. She was walking down the long, narrow corridor to exit the mess hall when she heard that voice again.

"I'm such a lucky guy to have such a hot-looking lunch mate every day," Finkel said from behind her. Jennifer turned around, scowling at him, and was about to tell him off, but another recruit was coming down the hall, then a couple more approached. She didn't know what to do just yet. So she decided to wait for a better opportunity. She turned back around, moved along down the corridor like a good soldier minding her own business, and joined the rest of her mates in formation.

The twin chiefs returned and took the company back out for more marching drills. To Jennifer, it seemed as if everybody took turns screwing up, including her, which meant getting cranked some more. She couldn't believe her own mistake. She went right when the command was left. And the chiefs were there ready to pounce on her. For her punishment, she was told to lie on her back and keep her feet six inches off the ground, while she was harangued. She wished she had some other recourse against her blatant humiliation, but she thought it would be best to slip back to her more anonymous position in formation.

After their marching session, Strickland and Kaminski told them that for the rest of the afternoon they would be turned over to the physical fitness (PF) instructors for a pre-PF test, exactly like the one that they would have to pass to graduate, to see how much work they needed. They marched back to the squad bay to pick up their PF gear that was issued with their uniforms: shorts, sweatshirts, sweat socks, sneakers and towel.

Jennifer went to her locker to get her things, and Deborah was at the locker next to her. To Jennifer, she looked a little pale, and a bit haggard, not the same eager and trusting soul that she seemed to be earlier. Maybe all the pettiness and ridicule was getting to her, too.

"After what we've just been through today, I can't believe they're going to give us a physical fitness test," Jennifer said to her. "The way my arms feel, I don't think I could do one more pushup. How about you?"

"I don't know if I'm going to be able to make it through the day," Deborah said, on the verge of tears.

"Are you all right?"

"I don't know. I mean, I'm getting cramps. I think I'm about to start."

Jennifer knew what she meant and didn't want to say. Jennifer had just finished her period a couple days before she arrived in boot camp. She always had a fairly easy time of it, without cramps, but she was never under this kind of physical and emotional stress before.

"Maybe you'd be allowed to go to the infirmary," Jennifer told her.

"NO! I mean, I don't want to do that. That's the last thing I want to do. They'll drum me out, for sure. They'll think I'm weak. I have had them pretty bad a few times before. But I'll be all right, I guess," Deborah reassured her and tried to force a smile through her clenched face. Jennifer put her arm around her for support. How could she ever have doubted her? Jennifer wondered. Deborah was trying so hard to impress, while she was only trying to get by.

"You two are the sorriest excuses for soldiers that I've ever seen," Lisa said from behind them in a Kaminski-like shriek. Although they didn't want to hear that voice as long as they could help it, it was a good impression and made them laugh when they turned around to see who it was. They helped each other roll their gear into a bundle. Jennifer could see the color returning to Deborah's face now that the pressure had eased.

But the pressure returned in a matter of seconds when Campbell shouted, "Come on, people. You don't have all day. You have exactly two minutes to get out of here and be on the street!" She looked at her wristwatch impatiently.

As everyone scurried to finish and get out the door, Jennifer said to Deborah and Lisa, "Who does she think she is, giving orders?"

"She's just passing them on from Kaminski and Strickland," Deborah explained it away.

"Maybe Kaminski is grooming her to replace her one day. Wouldn't that be grand? A Kaminski clone," Lisa said. They giggled some more as they went out the door with the rest of the company. Jennifer realized that when they went out that door, they were leaving their sanctuary, and they had to be extremely careful about what they said.

Jennifer thought that she definitely could make a friend of Lisa. She wasn't sure if she thought exactly the same way about things, but she probably could sound off about the pressure of the place in a joking manner with her.

She thought it might be her only defense to relieve the stress that all the bull-shit and 'head games' caused. Jennifer still worried about whether she could survive the whole ordeal in one piece.

When the company regrouped in the street, they marched off to the gymnasium. There, the chiefs left them in charge of two civilian PF instructors and disappeared for the next couple of hours. But if the recruits thought that they would be getting a brief respite from the military discipline, they were mistaken and were quickly brought back to reality.

"My name is Bob Simmons, and this is Rebecca Watson," the instructor said as he motioned to the other. "If you have any questions, you can call us 'coach'. We are not military, but you are, so we expect you to act accordingly. We are in charge of you whenever you come into this gym. You are to obey us as you would your chiefs."

Great, Jennifer thought, two *more* surrogate parents! Simmons was a tall, blond, boyish-faced former pro baseball player with quite visible scars on his left knee. The sight of Watson, though, really awed Jennifer. She was a few inches shorter than Simmons, but she outsized him muscularly. She was a weightlifter and bodybuilder, who didn't look like she had an ounce of fat on her pumped-up body. She dressed in shorts, and Jennifer noticed her calf muscles rippling as she rocked back and forth on her heels and toes. She made Jennifer feel a bit inadequate. Here she was worried that she could even pass the physical tests, and if she couldn't, she would only have herself to blame. It wasn't because she was a woman that she wouldn't pass. The average men who had been recruited by, or joined, the military over the years passed the same tests that she was about to take. She considered herself an average woman, and she should be able to pass the tests. But looking at Watson didn't make her feel very good about herself. If only she had kept up some kind of exercise program, any kind instead of none at all.

The coaches led the group in stretching, demonstrating each type first. Jennifer was especially impressed at how limber Coach Watson was despite her muscularity. She was beginning to wonder if she was some kind of Super Woman. The stretches seemed more like exercises themselves, or torture would perhaps be a more fit description, as Jennifer worked up a sweat and gritted her teeth against the pain of loosening and flexing long forgotten muscles and tendons. Now that the complicated stuff was finished, they got down to business.

The recruits paired up to do pushups first. While one person did them, the other would check for proper form and keep count. This was one time Jennifer wished that she had larger breasts so that she wouldn't have to go down as far to touch her chest to the mat.

Feeling the effects of her earlier cranking sessions, Jennifer only completed seven. She would need twenty, a lot of improvement, to pass. When she announced her score, she expected to hear a comment of derision, but was surprised to hear Watson offer some encouragement.

"Don't worry. You've got four weeks to get in shape, and you'll have plenty of help," Watson said.

Jennifer's spirits also were lifted when she heard a familiar voice call out his score. "Finkel, four."

"You better get with it, Chubs," Watson needled him. "We don't need any dead weight around here."

Situps were next. Jennifer had to hold the feet of her partner, Tim Shackleford. Even though she didn't consider him very attractive, a strange sensation came over her. It had been a very long time since she was in physical contact with a man, and she enjoyed the feeling of his hairy legs brushing up against her arms. When he was in the up position, his knees spread slightly and her eyes were suddenly drawn to his groin area. His loose-fitting gym shorts allowed her to see part of his underwear and some pubic hair. She wanted to catch a glimpse of the ever elusive—no! She mustn't think about it. She knew she was in serious trouble if she couldn't stop thinking about sex in this day and age. She tried to concentrate on the count. Nineteen—

Twenty—Twenty-one—

  Shackleford finished 42 situps, with 40 being the minimum. Jennifer thought this could be easier than the pushups because she could rest on the down side, and breathe (an all-important step that she seemed to forget doing pushups). They switched places after one male recruit finished 75. There was also a female who stopped at 58.

  Shackleford clamped down on Jennifer's ankles with his huge hands. She was a little self-conscious now about what he could look at. He definitely would be able to see the smooth underside of her slender thighs, and the very bottom of her meager backside. So what if he looked, she thought. She even slightly parted her legs to invite a view, but he seemed to stare blankly. She also thought, wouldn't it be something if he just jumped on her bones right then and lay on top of her. Not for sex, but to embrace. That was one thing she particularly missed lately. She remembered it as a very special feeling, but couldn't remember why.

  Jennifer completed twelve regulation situps. Another big improvement needed, she thought. She had to stifle a laugh, though, when she heard that Finkel couldn't complete one.

  The recruits were quickly hustled through the other events without much chance to catch a breather. Jennifer passed the minimum standards for the long jump and the vertical leap. She wasn't impressed with that accomplishment, however, as she dismissed the standards as too easy. Most did pass also, but a few did not. Deborah was among the small group of unfortunate ones. She looked to be in a frazzled mental condition. On the pullups, she couldn't do one.

  Jennifer completed only three, but the minimum was four. After she finished, she found Lisa and watched the others have their turn. They watched one woman complete seventeen perfectly executed pullups.

  "Who the hell is that?" Jennifer asked. "I think she passed everything with flying colors so far."

"That's Marcia Sabatella," Lisa responded. "I met her on the bus ride up here, and I got a chance to talk to her. She was big into sports in high school. She was a state champion in track, I think. I'll get her to come over."

Lisa motioned for Marcia to come over. Even though she was obviously very athletic, what impressed Jennifer the most was that she didn't really look it. She was Jennifer's height. And she wasn't beefy muscular like Coach Watson. 'She must have had good training and stayed in shape,' Jennifer thought. Marcia made her think at least that it wasn't so hopeless for her. Jennifer had four solid weeks to train, and if she concentrated, she was going to make it.

"Marcia, this is Jennifer Martin," Lisa introduced her.

"Hi," Marcia said in a delicate wisp of a voice. "I hear we have a mile-and-a-half run next."

"You're kidding!" Jennifer said. "I already feel a bit light-headed where I could fall on my face if I'm not careful."

"You do look flushed," Lisa said. "Probably a lot like me. I'm exhausted. This is more than I expected."

"I was kind of looking forward to it," Marcia said apologetically. "It's my best event."

"That's right; weren't you state champion?" Lisa asked.

"Well, I had the Pennsylvania state high school record for the mile. A 4:37," she said quite humbly and shyly. Jennifer didn't want to belittle her accomplishment by asking her if it was the girls' record or the overall record. But, even if it wasn't the overall, it must've been close, she thought. Marcia was twenty, but looked even younger to Jennifer. Despite her athleticism, the closely shorn brunette head and unisex clothes, a spry, girlish exuberance clearly shone through. The new society's attempt to disguise and confuse masculinity and femininity didn't work on Marcia. Whatever the essence of femininity was, it warmed Jennifer's heart to think that it hadn't died out just yet. It still existed in at least one person, because she could see it, she was sure of that, in Marcia.

The coaches gathered the group outside the gym. They didn't have a regular track to run on, but they were told the course to follow that was marked off in bright orange cones and equaled a mile and a half.

"You'll have twelve minutes to complete the run," Simmons said. "It doesn't matter if you get to the finish line crawling on your hands and knees, as long as you do it under twelve minutes. You have five minutes to warm up before we'll start. I recommend that you do some extra stretching on your own."

Twelve minutes didn't sound too difficult, Jennifer thought. All she had to do was run about a seven-minute mile. But then again, she had no way to judge time, and she had never run a distance like that which she could remember. So she went over to stretch next to Marcia to get some advice.

First of all, she tried to copy Marcia's stretches. She definitely knew what she was doing. "Do you have any suggestions on how to run this thing? Is there any strategy?" Jennifer asked her. "I've never done this before. Do you start off fast and coast at the end, or save it for the end?"

"You should pace yourself a bit," Marcia offered. "But you should really just find where you're comfortable. If you're pushing too much and you're breathing too hard, back off a bit until you're comfortable. But if you're too comfortable and it's too easy, push it a bit. It'll keep you from lagging. You'll do just fine. Just remember, this isn't a pressure race; it's a run."

"Yeah, thanks. I'll keep that in mind."

Coach Watson called them to the starting line. Then came the call, "Ready, set, go!" Marcia and a number of male recruits jumped quickly to form a pack at the front. Lisa ran near the front of the next group, which was a bit crowded, but Jennifer stayed on Lisa's heels. That group looped around one building and backtracked toward the start line. Jennifer could see that she was in the middle of the pack and that there were quite a few running slower than she was. The course broke off away from the road heading back to the gym, and Jennifer was suddenly on a long, desolate road that was cut out of a field of sea grass as they headed toward the beach on the New Jersey shore.

The seldom-used gravel road was pockmarked with holes that required a great deal of concentration to traverse. Jennifer fixed her gaze on the patches of ground immediately before her, on which she was about to trod, lest she stumble and sprain or even break her ankle. She was gradually losing ground to Lisa. She couldn't pick up the pace, as she had trouble maintaining the current one. The sun was still high overhead on a clear day, and the sweat rolled generously off Jennifer's sparse scalp. She felt pain in her lungs as they stretched to a capacity that never had been needed before, or that she ever thought possible. She recalled Marcia's advice, and she slowed to a jog until she felt comfortable again, enough to push it once more. She had to fight the strong urge to stop completely as she slowed. A good number of others quickly passed her, until she was almost alone and isolated. She glanced back and could still see a few more approaching. The course turned again onto another barren road that paralleled the beach, but this one was paved and much smoother going.

Jennifer's lungs functioned more normally again, and she got more comfortable, despite now aching leg muscles. She developed a rhythm, with her breathing synchronized with her steps. She kept the rhythm as she slowly increased the pace. She looked down the road and saw that she was actually gaining on somebody. But when she recognized the person, she wanted to stop in her tracks, or turn and head the other way. It was Finkel. They were almost the only ones in sight on that stretch of road, and Jennifer was afraid that he would say something else to her. But she put her mind back on running, and she was set to pass him on his left shoulder.

She could hear him, wheezing and huffing and puffing. She turned it up a notch to bypass him as quickly as she could, before he could say anything. But when she came into his field of vision, he put on a burst of his own to catch up. "Oh no you don't, cutie," Finkel said as he was fighting for breath. "You're not going to beat me."

With no one else in earshot, Jennifer finally got up the nerve to say something back to him to find out what exactly was on his mind. "And what would be so bad about that?" Jennifer coaxed.

"I don't want no woman showing me up."

Jennifer had to fight the urge to stop cold and check to see if all was still right in the world. She couldn't believe her ears. Maybe Canadians still held feelings to speak that way, Jennifer thought, or people in other parts of the world, but not here. It was supposed to be different now. People were known to disappear for speaking such blasphemy.

"Unless you didn't realize it, there are at least five women ahead of you right now who will definitely beat you," Jennifer said as she ran harder to push him to his limit. She felt a sense of power over him now. She probably could break him any time she wanted, she thought. And she could deliver the KO punch just by telling him that she already had beaten him in every event so far. Finkel actually looked dazed by Jennifer's comment.

"Maybe I just don't want you to beat me." His statement knocked Jennifer for a loop yet again, though.

"And what could you possibly have against me?" she asked, flabbergasted.

"I don't have anything against you," Finkel said between gulps of air.

"Are you trying to get yourself kicked out of here? Because if you are, you're doing a hell of a job," she said, trying to vent some of her anger.

"Maybe I am. I know I surely don't belong here."

"I don't know what your problem is, but whatever you're doing, keep me out of it. I don't even know why I've been so nice up to now, but if you give me any more shit, I'll give you your wish and turn you in in a heartbeat." And with that she nearly sprinted away from him. She turned another corner on the course heading back to the gym, and as she turned, she glanced back long enough to catch a glimpse of Finkel puking on the side of the road. She hoped her threat would deter him from any more comments because she wasn't sure if she could actually do it. She knew that one of the problems of their new society was that it was too easy for a woman to accuse a man of an impropriety, an act of harassment or discrimination. She knew that she would be believed without question, even if it was just her word against his. So she wanted to give him the benefit of the doubt that he would straighten himself up, before she had no choice.

Jennifer also felt a burst of power from her confrontation with Finkel, and she resumed a steady pace. She now saw the finish line in the distance. Coach Watson shouted encouragement to the runners passing by, or was she just yelling? It was hard for Jennifer to distinguish sounds.

"Come on, sprint! One hundred yards to go. Not much time left," Watson shouted. The last phrase jolted Jennifer's fading will to go on. She came this far, and she wasn't going to fail by just a few seconds, she told herself. So she poured it on and ran as hard as she could. The only problem was she didn't feel as if she were going any faster. She felt halfway between collapsing and floating off the ground. Richard, Lisa and Marcia cheered her on from the sidelines.

"Come on, Jennifer! You can do it, Martin! Don't give up! Push! Push! Push!" She couldn't distinguish the voices.

Then another one reached her. "Ten-forty-one." It all came to a merciful end when Simmons announced her time, but she didn't know which muscles she had to use to stop. So she turned off the motor that ran her brain, and her body soon followed suit. She didn't quite fall, but she quickly searched for a soft patch of grass, just in case she did.

"Don't sit down. You'll cramp up," Watson said, raining on her parade again. Even resting had to be done in proper military fashion. So she stood back up, though she was doubting that her legs would allow it. "Walk it off to cool down, until you catch your breath. Breathe slowly, in your nose and out your mouth." They were always right, weren't they? After she followed Watson's advice, Jennifer felt much better. Alive again. Yes that was it. She survived.

"Come on, encourage your mates who haven't finished yet," Coach Simmons added. "Let them know they're not alone. Help them along, and don't let them stop."

This was a change, Jennifer thought. Was he actually saying it was okay to form some kind of human bond toward these other people? They weren't going to suppress their natural responses for a change.

Jennifer saw that Deborah was still giving it everything she had, despite her physical anguish. The group that completed the run crowded around the finish line and wildly cheered for the few stragglers. Jennifer was sure that part of the reason for that kind of response was that it was the first time the recruits got a chance to really break loose since they got to camp. Jennifer wholeheartedly cheered for Deborah as she trudged down the stretch. She almost jumped out of her skin when Deborah's time was announced at 11:50, beating the minimum by just 10 seconds. Jennifer immediately ran over to her and hugged her. She was the only thing that kept Deborah standing, but as Jennifer kept complimenting her on her achievement, she slowly regained her faculties. Finkel didn't even finish under twelve, but did get spared the ignominy of being last. One other male and one female recruit finished behind him.

"Attention, everybody," Simmons said. "This was your first day of training, and most of you did really well. The rest of you have three and a half weeks to get your shit together." Simmons wasn't berating this time, but rather jovially motivating.

"And congratulations are in order for Seamate Recruit Sabatella, who established a new course record in the mile-and-a-half at Seven-oh-five. I believe it was the first time it was established on the first day," Watson said, chiming in.

"Way to go, Sabatella," and other flattering commendations were offered by the company. Jennifer and Deborah went over to shake her hand.

"Nice going, champ," Jennifer said to Marcia.

"Thanks. I just really felt good today. But you all did wonderful, too. And you don't run track," Marcia said, deflecting praise. The boisterous compliment trading continued as the males and females separated and headed for the showers. It was the first time that Jennifer really felt good since her arrival. She almost forgot about the chiefs. Maybe they had mellowed a bit, too, Jennifer thought, now that the initial shock treatment was complete. But no such luck. After dressing, they were turned back over to Strickland and Kaminski. They led the company back to reality and more marching drills before chow. They did spare the cranking a bit, but not the verbal assaults.

After supper chow, the company settled down some for the rest of the evening in a classroom for a lecture on military protocol, such as whom to salute, and which ass to kiss, and so on. How to stand at attention, and how to 'square away' a bunk and a locker.

When the company finally got back to the squad bays for the night, it was almost taps, lights out at twenty-two hundred hours. Jennifer just had time to jump into her rack. As she nestled in for the night, she stayed awake only long enough to say to herself, 'I survived!' And she hoped that the rest of the days weren't all like this one.

Chapter Four

Jennifer didn't enjoy surprises, as she was a creature of habit. And although she didn't like this "boot" camp any better than in the beginning, she eventually got used to the routine of the place. After the first couple of days of breaking-in the camp, or being broken—it was hard for her to tell—she settled into a comfortable groove. She knew exactly what was expected of her, and she had performed well. Following orders wasn't so difficult, she thought.

Most of the days were almost identical, and each day that passed meant that she had to wait one day less to get back home.

Every day, except Sunday, started with calisthenics. All the troops in the entire camp were roused at predawn and herded to a mosquito-infested field to exercise. They weren't allowed to swat the buggers when they landed on various parts of their anatomy, either. That was to demonstrate personal discipline, Jennifer figured. So the 'Zeroes' dive-bombed with impunity, with nary an anti-aircraft gun (or even repellent) to deter the bloodsuckers. Jennifer had shown weakness a few times, especially when one hummed in her ear, nuzzled her lobe, then chomped it.

After the infest fest, the recruits showered and dressed for the day before heading to breakfast. Jennifer still didn't enjoy meals very often. She thought they weren't given enough time to eat, and she always ended up gobbling her food. Also, she wasn't used to eating three large meals a day, and she felt herself gaining weight. It would've probably simplified things if she skipped a meal here and there when she wasn't so famished, she thought. But she felt obliged to eat at every meal, and with no snacking allowed, she dreaded getting pangs of hunger during a rough training session.

Every day after breakfast, the company returned to the squad bays to clean up. They faced daily inspections, and thus attended to the tiniest details: dust on top of door frames, a strand of hair on sinks or toilets, beds made according to regulation, and, of course, everything had to be in its proper place. The company commanders gave some authority to a few members of the company to organize these group cleanup efforts. Those so chosen could dole out the individual tasks within the company. Seamate Recruits Robert Morrison and Marcia Sabatella were given the rank of Recruit Company Commanders (RC's) who had authority only over their own group. Tim Shackleford and Emma Garraty were their assistants, or ARC's. A recruit from each squad bay was given the title of Master-at-Arms (MAA) and was in charge of the daily cleanup efforts. Each thing an inspector found wrong or unsatisfactory was called 'a gig'. During the first week, the female squad bay got no fewer than 20 gigs for an inspection, which wasn't acceptable for Kaminski and Strickland. The woman who was MAA ended up bickering with the others when they complained about the job that they were assigned. And on the last day of the first week when the squad bay got 30 gigs, she was relieved of her 'command'. Jennifer then had her chance at the leadership role when Kaminski selected her as the replacement.

Actually, Jennifer felt uncomfortable having power over others. Even if they followed her orders without question, she didn't want to be hated. But she was given a big responsibility by the chief, and she did want to show her that she could handle it. She decided to let the women offer to do any job they wanted first, and if any choices overlapped or were left vacant, she would make the final decision on who did what. She thought the system could work, but she didn't have much of a chance to prove it. After three days of only slight improvement, Jennifer was relieved of her command. Kaminski said she didn't blame Jennifer, but rather, she ripped the company for not pulling together.

"You people are not working as a team around here," Kaminski implored. "You've got a little more than two weeks to go before we turn you loose to your duty stations, and you're way behind where you should be at this point."

Instead of being demoted, Jennifer was given a new job, company watch commander. She would have the task of assigning the recruits to stand various watches, which she felt better suited to her, as she was experienced with organizing Marilyn's schedule. The job of MAA now was bestowed upon Lisa Hopkins.

At first, Jennifer was surprised, but she wholeheartedly agreed with her choice. Lisa did a bang-up job for her. On mostly her own initiative, Lisa took charge of cleaning the head. As a matter of fact, if it wasn't for the near-perfect job on the head, Jennifer thought, they might have failed the inspections altogether. Jennifer thought Lisa was a good leader. Everybody liked her, and she had that inner confidence, knowing exactly what needed to be done and how.

After the stress of daily inspections, however, the company usually could be more at ease the rest of the day, which they spent attending classes or training. The subjects of instruction ranged from how to stand guard properly, to map reading and navigation. On other occasions, they were also dispatched to perform manual labor tasks around the camp, or they went to PF training in the gym. The evening hours usually were reserved for individual chores, such as preparing uniforms for personal inspections the next day. It certainly wasn't idle time, but the recruits could work at their own pace, unsupervised, ironing pants and shirts, polishing shoes, boots and brass. There wasn't much time to actually relax, but Jennifer got used to the schedule and the work load, and the pressure gradually eased.

Sunday was Jennifer's favorite day. First, there were no calisthenics, and nothing was scheduled for the day, which gave them their only free time of the week. There was nothing to do for recreation; they weren't allowed to keep books or to play sports. But, having nothing to do was what Jennifer and the others enjoyed most. Jennifer did like to go to the chapel services, however. She didn't consider herself very religious, but she enjoyed attending because it was quite peaceful, and it was sort of a haven from military lifestyle. Even the squad bays were not completely safe sanctuaries from chief petty officers. And the chapel gave Jennifer the chance to sing in the choir, which she hadn't done since she was 10 years old. It wasn't a complicated choir. It was more like a group sing. Jennifer spent some of her free time writing letters to Marilyn, and her mother in Virginia Beach and her father in Ohio. While it wasn't encouraged to keep in contact with parents (future generations wouldn't have the same opportunity, considering they wouldn't even know their progenitors), it wasn't outlawed yet, either. Jennifer followed the current custom of calling them by their first names instead of the vulgar, archaic and sexist terminology, 'Mom' and 'Dad'.

All in all, Jennifer felt more and more comfortable with each passing day there, learning and absorbing the training, but still waiting for it to end so that her life could get back to normal.

Everything was still running smoothly as the recruits headed into the middle of their third week. Occasionally, the twin chiefs got on their backs when they screwed up, but, at that point, they were generally screwing up less and less, and the pressure wasn't the same as the constant browbeating of the first few days. As a matter of fact, they were given more breaks and privileges as time went on. They actually were given permission to talk at meals. They sang cadence when they marched, a little recruit-penned ditty extolling the virtues of their fine company. They got a chance to show pride in themselves as a unit that way. There were even a few cheerleaders in the group, who encouraged the others to sing loud and proud to show everybody who was the best company in camp. One of the companies in the fourth week really had impressed them when they marched by, effectively drowning out Jennifer's company as they strutted in perfect step. Everybody agreed that they were going to work as hard to be as good as that company.

Besides their own resolve to work harder, the company still had the chiefs around to knock them down a peg, to show them that they still had a long way to go. Just that morning, the chiefs berated the company for their showing in the daily squad bay inspections. The women's squad bay got five gigs, and the men got seven. It was worse than the past few inspections, and that caused the outburst. The women in particular, under Lisa Hopkins as MAA, had turned in inspections of one, zero and zero gigs over the past three days. Kaminski and Strickland sounded like bells tolling doom, saying, "There should only be room for improvement every day," and "You can't afford to backslide this late in the game."

For Jennifer, the difference over the first two weeks was that she thought the chiefs were right now, It was criticism, but the company knew how to take it better, and they could use it positively to really improve. The chiefs *were* right that they *should* buckle down a bit, Jennifer thought. She changed the way she looked at the chiefs' tactics. She now saw their abuse as a friendly reminder to keep focused.

Jennifer was in a good mood that day anyway. She felt herself getting a little stronger, and she was learning many new things. She was coming back from an afternoon class as she headed up the stairs to the squad bay with her fellow recruits. She had just passed an important First Aid and CPR test, which had worried her very much at first. But now she was joking with Lisa and Deborah about a lifesaving scenario that they had to act out for part of the test. Lisa tried to perfect her imitation of the timid way Jennifer approached the victim, who was actually a CPR dummy. Jennifer showed more of a Southern accent than she realized she had in the pressure situation of the test.

"Are you all right? Are you all right?" Lisa imitated Jennifer's exaggerated drawl, and she shook Deborah's shoulder to portray the way Jennifer had shaken the dummy's shoulder. Jennifer and the others around them laughed at Lisa as she pretended to be too dainty to touch a dying person.

"Oh, come on. I didn't do that," Jennifer replied good-naturedly. But all thoughts of laughter stopped immediately when they entered the squad bay and saw the look on the faces of the people who had walked in just ahead of them, now standing with their mouths agape.

Jennifer, Lisa and Deborah looked around the room and joined the look of disbelief and staring in shock. The squad bay looked as if it had been hit by a tornado.

A white tornado, to be exact. That's what the fourth week company, who also experienced one, called it. Lockers were overturned, and their contents were strewn across the room. Bunks were dismantled and piled at the far end of the squad bay. The mattresses were found in the shower room in another haphazard pile. Sheets and blankets were scattered in the rubble and were covered with soap powder and black shoe polish. The polish was the favorite implement of the vandals, as it was smeared, and in some places caked, on the walls and floors. Everything in its place was now in some other place and in ragged condition.

Before their collective thoughts could ask the question, 'Who could have done such a thing?' the answer came when one recruit said, "Strickland and Kaminski must have been really pissed at us."

"You think they did this to punish us?" Jennifer said to no one in particular, and no one in particular answered her.

"Well, I guess we'd better start cleaning this mess up," Lisa said to her crew. They started by picking up the things in the middle of the floor so that they could at least walk through. Lisa's plan was to collect items in individual piles close to where each person had slept. One group made sure each pile had all the pieces needed to assemble their living space. Mattresses were being unloaded from the shower room and placed to mark where the bunks would go. Still, not much was actually accomplished when Kaminski strode into the disaster area.

"Stop what you're doing right now!" Kaminski shouted over the din created by the beehive of activity.

"Attention in the squad bay!" an alerted recruit screamed at the top of her lungs.

"At ease," Kaminski instructed after they had jumped to attention. "Now, nobody told you that you could start cleaning up. I thought you'd like to take in the view a little longer so that you could see what your life is going to be like for the next week and a half if you don't show some teamwork and improvement each day." Kaminski paced slightly before speaking again. She couldn't go far without shuffling her feet in debris. "I want you to put everything back the way you found it when you walked in here. You have five minutes. When I come back, I want to see everything not in place. Then, you'll have exactly two hours to get things shipshape again. And if you're not finished by then, we could start all over again, if you'd like," she said, then turned and left the squad bay.

Jennifer thought Kaminski must be going a little batty. First they had their squad bay demolished, and they tried to fix it up, but now they were told to demolish it again. In frustration, Jennifer threw a pillow that was handy, and hit another recruit in the face.

"Sorry, Mary," Jennifer giggled when she realized Mary wasn't hurt. In mock anger, Mary threw something back at Jennifer, who ducked out of the way. "All right, this is war. Let's total this place," Jennifer said, leading them on. Soon, the softer projectiles were hurled across the room in an all-out battle, which re-created the original bedlam and disarray. The women laughed and enjoyed it as long as they could to release the tension, for they knew now what was in store for them. Besides, what better way to create a mess?

Kaminski strolled back in, and the recruits jumped to attention.

"Carry on. Okay. You've got exactly two hours to get this place presentable again. Move it."

"She must be nuts. This could take all day," Jennifer said to Lisa after Kaminski left the room.

"I agree with you," Lisa said. "But we've got two hours to show Kaminski what we are made of. And that we're not quitters. Right?" Jennifer saw a twinkle in Lisa's eyes at that moment that said she was ready for this challenge, and that she really thrived on it. Jennifer wanted to quit when she thought of the task before them. But she received inspiration when she watched Lisa at work. She thought she should have thought more about not letting the company down, but, more importantly to her now, she didn't want to let her friend down.

"Okay, listen up, everybody," Lisa said. "I know this seems like a monumental task right now, and it's going to take a monumental effort. But we can do it if we work together. We not only have to work hard, but also very fast. Okay, this is what we have to do. First, we need somebody to ferry loads of everything that is soiled and machine washable to the laundry room, and— " She proceeded to map out a strategy to keep everybody hopping. Lisa found someone who said she had a good idea how to reassemble the beds, and she showed two crews of people what to do. Lisa then told them to work on opposite sides of the room and have a race to see which crew could finish their row of racks first. Others were already righting overturned lockers. Then an old fashioned firehouse bucket brigade was formed to ferry the heavy mattresses out of the shower room. And, after clothing, sheets, blankets, pillows and personal items were picked up off the floor, Lisa, Marcia and Emma formed an armored column of push brooms, one behind the other, to sweep away the unsalvageable debris. It took those three passes just to make the floor manageable again. Jennifer, Deborah and a few others were dispatched to get on their hands and knees to scrub the shoe polish off the floor. The usual crew went off to police the head.

"You know whom we have to thank for this wonderful mess?" Jennifer said to Deborah, who was a few feet away, still scrubbing as if the floor had an unquenchable itch.

"Chief Kaminski?" Deborah responded.

"Well, she and Strickland were no doubt the brains of the operation, but I was thinking about the muscle."

"What do you mean?"

"I mean, Kaminski and Strickland led us to the First Aid class, and then came back for us only an hour later. I don't think they had time to do this kind of damage. Their two shadows, however, disappeared around lunch time, and I haven't seen them all afternoon."

"You mean Campbell and Briggs?"

Jennifer shuddered when she heard those names, and she scrubbed the spot that she was working on a little harder. "It had to be."

"You know, I think you're right," Deborah said as she slopped more cleanser on her stain. "What a rotten thing to do. And they're supposed to be helping us through all this."

"Exactly." Jennifer was surprised that Deborah agreed on what finks the assistants were. She thought she would say something like they were only following orders.

"But, you know, they were probably just following orders."

"Yeah, but I bet they enjoyed themselves trashing this place." Because she didn't have any evidence to back up that statement or to obtain a conviction, she let it go. But she felt betrayed by Campbell, who tried to be buddies with the group, and who said she wanted to help them, and then turned around and wreaked such havoc on their lives. Even if she was ordered to do it, did Campbell have to be so coldly efficient like a ruthless Nazi follower of Hitler? Well, maybe she was going overboard with it, but Jennifer didn't understand it. They were doing just fine. Was all this just to teach them some lesson about teamwork? She knew that they could accomplish more working as a team than working as individuals. But does that mean they weren't working as a team before? She just wasn't convinced that this was supposed to help them instead of being a punishment kick meant to hurt them.

Jennifer had to leave a few stubborn spots so that the crew could cover the whole floor and then move on to the walls. They had to try for the overall effect of looking clean, even if it meant leaving certain areas incomplete. Time raced on and certainly would not allow a complete job anyway. Better to do a thorough, satisfactory job for now.

Lisa, in particular, hated to leave the job unfinished, but she urged her workers to move on to different areas, hoping to at least satisfy Kaminski enough so that she wouldn't have them start all over again.

Jennifer constantly glanced up at the menacing face of the clock watching over her as the deadline approached. She looked up again and saw Kaminski's face where the clock was, grinning devilishly with hands spinning wildly on the tip of her nose. Blink! The specter vanished. Jennifer had to wonder if she were losing her grip on reality. She visualized the image again, and it just made her laugh. So she figured that she must be okay.

The recruits went as far as they could go in two hours, and Lisa ordered everybody to finish what they were doing and clear the deck so that it could be swabbed, which would be the finishing touch. An amazing transformation *had* taken place. The squad bay no longer looked like a combat zone, but more like a slightly disheveled bunkhouse again. Jennifer stood close to the door, huddling with the others on a dry spot on the floor. She heard the clicking of heels in the hall outside the squad bay. The heels of jackboots? No. The heels of patent leather shoes? Yes. The heels of repression? Maybe. The heels of chief petty officers? Definitely. Jennifer instinctively stepped back as the doors swung open.

"Attention in the squad bay!" Jennifer yelled, along with two other jumpy recruits. Both Strickland and Kaminski rambled in to conduct the inspection.

"Carry on," Kaminski said. "Hmm, this doesn't look like the same room I left awhile ago." Hmm, a positive sign, Jennifer thought, but she waited nervously with the others as the chiefs toured the room, with Marcia and Lisa in tow. The chiefs said little, but scanned this and that, craning their necks to see flaws in the aura of tidiness. When Strickland passed an unmade rack, he looked to Lisa for an answer.

"We're just waiting for a few loads to come back from the laundry, Chief Strickland," Lisa said ever so deferentially. He nodded a detached affirmation and continued on. After completing the rounds, the chiefs gave the squad their conditional approval.

"You've done a good job," Kaminski told the group. "At least, you've shown me that you can work as a team. It's not perfection, mind you, but I do expect that after tomorrow's inspection. Now, I want you assembled below in five minutes to get some chow. If the men's squad bay is satisfactory, they'll be joining you. Carry on."

The chiefs vacated the room to conduct their next inspection, and the women remained completely silent for a few moments until the chiefs were thought to be out of listening range. Then the women spontaneously burst with joy and relief, shouting congratulations and trading high-fives, hugs and backslaps.

"We did it," was the chorus as they left the squad bay, which they didn't want to see again for a very long time.

With the urgency of the cleanup operation, Jennifer had forgotten all about dinner, even though it was past 1800 hours. She even failed to realize that the men were going through the same ordeal. When the entire company got to the mess hall, Richard related to Jennifer the chaos that was the men's squad bay. The same tactics were employed by the vandals, except that pieces of their bunks were found on the ground just below one of their third-story windows. The men also were able to satisfactorily reconstruct their squad bay.

Although Jennifer couldn't rationalize the need for such a contemptible outburst, she felt good about passing another one of their tests, however, overcoming an obstacle that was fully intended to trip her up.

While she was intent on keeping herself in line, Jennifer was surprised to learn that two other recruits apparently had been tripping on their own, without any outside assistance. One night, when the entire camp seemingly slumbered peacefully, Jennifer was awakened by the sounds of a scuffle. She opened her eyes and turned her head in time to witness another recruit being yanked out of her bunk by two persons wearing military police armbands. With catlike swiftness, the woman was ushered out the squad bay doors, while crying, "No! No! I didn't!"

Before Jennifer, or anyone else, could get up to do anything, she heard the voice of Chief Kaminski say, "It's over. Nothing for you to concern yourselves with. Go back to sleep."

Sleep was the last thing Jennifer wanted to do right then. That scene had spooked her, as she wondered what the recruit possibly could have done wrong. The next morning, she first wondered if it had been a dream, but then, she confirmed the event with Deborah and Lisa, although no one knew the reason. And indeed, one recruit, Patricia Wilson, was missing from the group.

When Kaminski spoke to her that morning, she only told Jennifer to cross Wilson's name, as well as Seamate Recruit Barry Updike's, from the company's watch roster. All Jennifer could say was, "Aye, aye, Chief." She was only able to obtain more information when she spoke to Richard at mealtime.

"You know what happened to Wilson and Updike?" Jennifer asked him.

"Well, rumor has it in our squad bay that the two of them had sex on the midnight watch out at the southwest gate two nights ago."

"Oh, my god!" Jennifer sat totally stunned. She knew that the southwest gate was on an isolated part of the camp, and that if sexual activity could take place somewhere in the camp, that would be the best place. It actually wasn't even an entrance gate. The fence that defined the perimeter of the base stopped at the beach in the southwest corner. A guard was posted there to keep civilians from wandering onto the base by accident.

"Do you remember if you scheduled them for watch out there that night, back-to-back?" Richard asked her.

"Come to think of it, I did," Jennifer recalled. "Oh, my god!"

The event seemed to have a chilling effect on the whole company, especially Finkel. He did not say another word for the rest of their stay in boot camp. Although, he did express himself nonverbally one time. Jennifer had turned around suddenly and had seen Finkel look at her while his hand was on his groin. Then he would smile devilishly. But everyone seemed to be preparing for the company's upcoming graduation. No one wanted to screw up, especially only a week away from getting out.

The last week was still filled with many obstacles to graduation, and Jennifer was by no means confident that she would join her mates for the ceremonies on Saturday. If she failed any part of her PF test, for instance, she would be transferred to the third week company for more training. A few fresh faces had already joined their company from the group that had just graduated.

The PF test was the biggest obstacle, and Jennifer remained very worried. She felt that she wasn't making much progress toward the magic numbers of 40 and 20, the minimum number of situps and pushups required. But Marcia spent a lot of time with her and put her on a private training workout, which included strength-building for her arms, chest and abdomen. Jennifer still wondered whether it would be enough in time.

Another obstacle for Jennifer was learning to shoot guns. For the past week, the company attended a series of classes that showed them how weapons worked, how to clean and care for them, even how to take them apart and put them back together. But Jennifer had never handled a gun before, so she even handled the unloaded weapons in the demonstrations with extreme caution, and even awe. But now, on Monday afternoon, she was expected to load into her gun an explosive, lead projectile that would travel twice the speed of sound and pierce an object of her choosing on a simple finger command. It actually frightened her. She didn't think her fear related to her femininity, though, because she thought it should frighten any sane person. But the female instructor vehemently indoctrinated the class, addressing the women especially, with the idea that the gun was the true instrument of equality. For many years the blatant symbol of masculinity, and therefore men's domination over women, the instructor rambled on, mastery of this weapon was imperative and crucial to gaining true equality with men. And rejecting this gift of fire, so to speak, would be tantamount to rejecting their own equality. Jennifer wondered what the men in the class thought about after hearing this tirade about losing their blatant symbol.

Jennifer dutifully learned what she needed to know to pass, fully expecting to forget everything she learned when it was all over. She understood that the true purpose of the instruction was to teach her to kill when necessary, but she wanted no part in having that detestable knowledge in the back of her head for future reference. She intended to eradicate the malady from her system at the earliest possible convenience. Now was the time to robotically go through the motions, and perhaps contain the infection. But theory and fear butted heads when the company finally went to the rifle range to shoot.

Just trying to follow the basic instructions, Jennifer still qualified for the distinction of 'sharpshooter' with the .45 caliber pistol by getting a high score. She also passed the minimum score for the M-16 rifle.

At first, Jennifer really beamed over her accomplishment because she was proud to have handled another challenge, although she wasn't sure what she could do with her newly acquired skill. Had she been duped? Had they really taught her to kill? They were so safety-conscious that, on the surface, they took great pains to make sure that no harm came to anyone, but the use of such a powerful force had to have some purpose. The more she thought about it, the more the luster of her accomplishment tarnished.

But Jennifer continued to meet each challenge as they arose, and that was the most important thing to her at the moment. As things were winding down, she had no more trouble with Finkel; the watch schedule ran smoothly and she grew stronger every day.

Jennifer made it to the next-to-last day, the eve of the big PF test, before her confidence began to crack a bit. She and her bunkmate, Deborah, showered together before they hit the rack for the night, and Jennifer confided her few remaining doubts as they reflected over the past four weeks. "I'm really nervous about the PF test tomorrow," she said. "I feel as if I'm getting stronger, but it's not fast enough. Do you know, I have yet to do forty situps? My highest is thirty-seven, and I haven't been able to practice pullups at all."

"Oh, you'll do fine," Deborah encouraged her. "Tomorrow your adrenalin will be pumping, and it'll help you over the hump."

"But, besides that, I think I'm about to have my period."

"Oh." Deborah looked around to see if anyone else could hear. She seemed to be embarrassed that Jennifer had said it right out loud like that. Even though they were in a women's shower room, women didn't talk about it much anymore. "Well, I certainly sympathize with you. I'm just glad that I'm not set to start again for another week, which is after I'm out of here."

"Do you have any pads left?"

"Yeah, a couple."

Jennifer wanted to borrow them if she could, rather than go to the source of supply for the squad bay—Campbell. She just didn't want any help from her.

In the new society, the pads were only allowed because, technically, they could be used for any other purpose to absorb liquids. Truth was, they never were used for any other purpose, but that was the reasoning Jennifer remembered being used when it actually came up in a floor debate in the House. They only came in generic boxes marked absorbent pads. They were sanitized for their true, intended purpose, but Jennifer laughed at the notion that they be used on other things. She conjured up a comical image of a man using one to wipe up spilled milk, or something.

"You know, I can't believe that all this is almost over," Jennifer said as she turned on a bone-chilling stream of water and quickly adjusted it to a steaming, but comfortably warm, setting. "The day after tomorrow, we'll never have to look at this place again."

"Yeah." Deborah almost sounded dejected as she stepped under her own shower head.

"Don't tell me you're going to miss this place?"

"No. I definitely won't miss *this* place, but I *will* miss the gang, you know."

"Oh yeah, sure, me too," Jennifer said as she shampooed her still-bristly hair. "I've met a lot of nice people here, especially you."

"Same here. It's just that they're probably going to split up the company when we leave here, and I don't know if I'll ever see you again after Saturday." Deborah also worked up a lather as she spoke.

"Well, I'm glad that I met you. To tell you the truth, I don't think I could've made it this far without a friend like you. This part of it has been really great because I kind of stay to myself at home."

"Me, too," Deborah said. She rinsed her head and then lathered up her body with a communal bar of soap. "You know, I envy you."

"Me? Why?"

"Because you have such a slender figure, and you look athletic. You're not short and dumpy like me. You've got such nice, small breasts, not like these melons I have to lug around all the time." Deborah lifted them with her soapy hands as she spoke about them. "I wish I could be your size."

Jennifer glanced down at her own chest and wanted to say, 'Breasts? Where?' She almost didn't think of them as breasts because they were so small. What she saw when she looked in a mirror was a kind of a flabby chest. Her aureoles were almost as wide as the breasts themselves. In pre-ERA bra sizes, she would have been a 34A to Deborah's 37D.

"Why? You have nice breasts. I've always kind of wanted mine to be a little bigger."

"No, you don't. They seem like a real handicap these days. You're lucky the way you are. Yours are perfect. Mine always seem to get in the way of everything. With a simple thing like running, I'm so self-conscious about bouncing too much. It's like I have to think about them all the time. They're always there. You know, I was thinking about getting reduction surgery when I got back home."

"Really?"

"Yeah, I asked the doctor who gave me the physical. The government's got this program now for breast reduction surgery for anyone who wants it."

"Ouch! That seems like a lot to go through for something that doesn't seem all that important."

"But, it is important to me," Deborah said as she turned off her shower head. "I think I will feel so much better about myself, like getting rid of excess baggage."

Jennifer didn't want to encourage her, but she stopped short of discouraging her. She probably couldn't change her mind anyway, she thought, but that kind of thinking really bothered her.

Deborah finished her shower quickly, and Jennifer told her that she was going to be out in a bit. She took an extra-long shower to really relax and be fresh for the next day, but she also mulled over in her mind what Deborah had just told her.

It was the first time she had heard about it. The state was sponsoring unnecessary surgery so that women could feel more—what? More like a man, she thought? If being more equal to a man meant being more like a man, she wanted no part of it. Jennifer suddenly realized what had been bothering her about the revolution. It wasn't the idea of equality so much because equality to her meant the same opportunities under the law. But, somehow, things got mixed up. Suddenly it seemed that to be equal meant to be manlike. For a long time, long hair was thought to be feminine. Someone thought that it was something that made women different from men. So they made women get rid of their long hair. They also couldn't wear frilly, colorful clothes because men wouldn't wear them, and, therefore, made them different. They couldn't even wear special underwear anymore to hold up their breasts because men didn't have them. And now, Jennifer finds out, women shouldn't have breasts either! Men can't have babies, and they took that away from women, too. Slowly but surely, the government was taking away everything that made women unique. Women seemed to be losing their femininity by attrition.

Jennifer stood under the steaming spray, letting the pulsing water strike the back of her neck and shoulders. She lathered up one more time and noticed a pink tinge to the soap bubbles around her thigh, confirming her fears. She turned the shower handle for a brisk, cold rinse. When she finished her shower, she toweled off and went to back to her bunk to find Deborah. Jennifer was an only child, but she felt as if she were going to a big sister for help.

With the pad in place, she felt more secure and relaxed when she hit the rack at taps. She also felt womanly. Since they hadn't come up with an answer for it, it was one of the few things left that was strictly for women only. Jennifer thought back to when she had menstruated for the first time, and her mother had to explain what it was. And she told her to think of it as her friend.

"Whenever your friend comes," her mother had said, "she's bringing you good news, telling you, 'You're not pregnant again'." It sounded silly to her later, but, being pregnant at 11 or as a soon-to-be teenager, was definitely a bad thing. She also remembered how that fairy tale advice made her feel better, especially because she had thought something was wrong with her, like she was sick or dying. So she wasn't pregnant, again. Kind of a shame, Jennifer thought for the first time. She thought about her mother again as her conscious and unconscious thoughts mingled and intertwined, and she drifted into a happy, dreamy sleep.

Jennifer and the rest of the company awoke peacefully and at a leisurely pace that Friday morning. The chiefs no longer performed the task of waking up the company as they had done in the first two weeks. Being in charge of the women's squad bay, Marcia announced wake-up time by simply turning on the lights, and there were no calisthenics for the first weekday that month. So the group slowly rolled out of bed when they felt the urge. Sort of. Jennifer and most of the others were in the habit now of waking as soon as the lights went on. With a half hour before breakfast, Jennifer washed thoroughly and tidied up, making her rack to inspection perfection, hopefully for the last time. She put on a fresh uniform as she nervously joked with the others who were milling around. Today meant only one thing to everyone in the room—the PF test.

Jennifer wished she had something to do to take her mind off it because she figured the less she could think, the better off she would be. But, as far as anyone knew, the test was the only thing scheduled for the day. After breakfast they came back to the squad bay to rest and digest, Jennifer supposed.

The company had a 90-minute break before they were to report to the gym, and there were no chief petty officers to be seen. Jennifer appreciated the absence of any more stress before the test, but, somehow, she found it hard to believe that it was planned for their benefit. Maybe they didn't want them to be tired or have any excuses for failing, she thought.

She didn't need any excuses, however. When the company reported for the test, Jennifer felt fresh and ready physically and mentally. Her adrenalin flowed and pumped her up when she needed it. And she posted personal bests in each event. She pushed 26 pushups, and pulled seven pullups. And when she reached 38 situps, she thought she was at the end of the line, but she even surprised herself by gutting out four more to pass. Jennifer didn't get any of the severe cramps that she feared might do her in, and the only effect she noticed was a little lightheadedness after the sprint. It grew worse during the mile-and-a-half run, but when Jennifer figured she would finish in plenty of time, she let up a bit and cruised into the finish, still beating her best time by five seconds. Despite the advice of the coaches, she collapsed on the grass after the run, more of as a release than of exhaustion, and she told herself, "It's *over*. I did it!"

So did most everyone else. And those who failed one or more events found out, to everyone's surprise, that they could rest, come back after lunch, and retry the failed events. Everyone who had to do this passed the second time as they could concentrate on just one or two events. Even a somewhat trimmed down Finkel passed on his second try at situps, as he just did get 40. They obviously benefitted from not being worn out from previous events, but Jennifer felt glad for everyone because they wouldn't have to face the prospect of staying an extra week, or getting 'PUPed'. And now she really looked forward to going to her duty station and performing the job for which she was trained.

Everyone was in a jovial mood the rest of the day as things wound down. That evening, the recruits got their civilian clothes back, and then hacked their way through the paperwork jungle once again, but this time to be processed out of boot camp.

CHAPTER FIVE

The ceremony was glorious. The whole camp turned out in a parade just to honor them, the graduating company of the Border and Coast Guard. Dress uniforms, precision marching, a military band, salutes and tributes. In her commencement speech, the base commanding officer made it sound like 'a farewell, to arms'. She said that they were being sent to fight the Second Revolutionary War. The band played, and the people bowed and prayed.

Jennifer was almost overcome by emotion. The place did not seem threatening anymore, now that she had nothing to fear from it. She had rank—Seamate Apprentice Martin, equal to Briggs and Campbell. Even her superiors, the petty officers, the chiefs and the officers made her feel as if she belonged. She was in the Guard, for now anyway, and she was one of them, just doing her job. She had to admit she was going to miss what she called the 'adventure' of the place. Company Whiskey-One-Seven-Two gathered on the New Jersey shore for a group photograph and was officially disbanded. The group was to be split into squads of ten and shipped out to duty stations, where they would be attached to new units. But, for now, they still would travel as a group.

They were flown from Cape May to Portland, Maine, where they boarded a bus for Fort Kent, Maine, a U.S./Canada border town. Each person carried sealed orders to be delivered to the new commander, who would then inform each person which sector to report to. Jennifer's group would be relieving another group just like themselves, temporaries in effect, serving a month out of the year.

So Jennifer found herself on another long bus ride to a somewhat unknown destination, but it was different this time. She didn't dread going. She actually looked forward to it. She approached it very pragmatically, too. She was going to perform a job, a very uncomplicated job at that. Nobody was going to invade the other. And everybody on the bus knew each other this time, having lived together for the past four weeks. People were laughing and having fun, enjoying the first truly unsupervised time in a month. A few people organized a group sing-along, and they tried to get everybody to remember their favorite childhood camp and traveling songs. Of course, they sang a rendition of "100 Bottles of Beer on the Wall." Kind of corny, Jennifer thought, but it was fun. They had left Cape May at noon and arrived in Portland at three, and then the bus ride to Fort Kent was five more hours. So they had lots of time to kill.

Jennifer sat in a window seat next to Richard, who told her about his adventures in college at Ohio State University.

"I was so broke my freshman year that I couldn't afford the bus ride back home to visit my folks," Richard said. "So I rode my bike a hundred-thirty miles from Columbus to Wheeling, West Virginia."

"I assume we're not talking about a motorcycle here. You mean an actual bicycle?"

"Yeah. I was on this racing team for a bicycle club on campus, and you know, we'd race twenty to thirty miles a pop. So I thought one-thirty would be no big deal because I wouldn't be racing. But it was a killer."

"I'll bet. Couldn't you ask your parents for bus fare?"

"Well, I didn't want to, for some reason, and I wanted to surprise them."

"You must have. They were probably surprised that you weren't roadkill or something." Jennifer stretched out her arms and legs stiffly and tipped like some sort of dead animal onto Richard's shoulder. He smiled and playfully pushed her off.

"Actually, they didn't think biking it was a big deal. They just said, 'Why didn't you tell us you were coming?'"

"That must have been fun." Jennifer admired his sense of adventure and daring.

"Actually getting there wasn't all that great," Richard said. "As far as Zanesville wasn't bad, but from there it seemed like it was all uphill. Going back to Columbus was really fun, coasting downhill."

"You rode back, too?"

"I had to." Richard didn't elaborate. He paused a moment and said, "Yeah, the club was really great. It wasn't actually affiliated with the school like other sports, but we had a sponsor, and we got to travel to races around the country. San Diego; Boulder, Colorado; Spokane, Washington, and Indianapolis. Really big races."

"You know, this is the farthest I've been away from home," Jennifer said, gesturing to the passing landscape beyond the bus window. "I grew up in Norfolk, Virginia. Then I went to college at Georgetown. And I worked briefly in Richmond before I moved to Washington, D.C. No big trips or anything. I just seem to stay in the same general area."

"So, pretty boring life, huh?" Richard teased.

"No, I love my job, and I had lots of fun when I was a kid."

They proceeded to trade stories of happy childhood memories. Jennifer felt close to Richard. The more she found out about him, the more she liked him. She felt that they were very good friends, very comfortable around each other. He was nice and seemed to be well adjusted to the new society, she thought. Men were supposed to be only interested in sex, or so she had been told for years. But this one wasn't. He seemed perfectly content to live in a sexless society. It's what they had been working for, but didn't it contradict everything she had been taught? By keeping men so segregated most of the time, the government was saying that men weren't ready yet. But, in Richard, she found the awaited end-result—men and women living in harmony without sex to interfere and spoil things. The thought of her relationship with Richard, or ones like it, fortified her resolve to see the revolution through. There was something good at the end worth working for, and they were it.

After a brief rest stop in Bangor, about halfway through the state, the bus rolled on. Inside the bus, it grew quieter and the conversations lagged. Most people grew weary as the day dragged. It had been a long day, Jennifer thought, considering it had started a world away, which was already becoming long forgotten.

Richard decided to take a nap. Jennifer intently watched the flowing countryside. Outside of Bangor, it was raw wilderness. They rolled through and past a few small towns, but 95 percent was forest, low mountains, lakes, streams and valleys of golden dandelions. Jennifer silently mouthed the magical names on the passed road signs. 'Passadumkeag', 'Mattamiscontis Mountain', 'Mattawamkeag', 'Squa Pan' and 'Aroostook'. Sunset in the tidewater flatlands of Virginia was a dull, gradual graying most days, but this sunset in the mountains was spectacular to Jennifer. The hills in the west were cast in long, purple shadows, while the tops of the hills in the east were in brilliant relief, with the trees on those hills throwing their own shadows, giving the scene amazing texture and depth. As the sun sank further, the resplendent green Maine summer faded into a subdued indigo. Then the landscaped turned black against the still light sky. When the sky also faded, nothing remained distinguishable. Only faint starlight and the bus's headlights kept the group from being swallowed by the night. There was no other traffic heading north, it seemed, and Jennifer counted only three cars heading south.

When the bus finally rolled into Fort Kent at eight-thirty, half of the people were dozing, but eventually were roused by the commotion made by the other half.

"We're here," Jennifer said.

"Where's here?" a groggy Richard asked.

"Fort Kent, the end of the line!" the bus driver announced, inadvertently answering Richard's question.

Fort Kent was not a military installation itself, but it had one on the western edge of the town. It was not the northernmost point in the continental United States, but it was extremely close. The base was new and small, but growing with the expanding hostilities. When the bus stopped inside the camp compound on the southwestern bank of the St. John's River, the natural boundary between Maine and Canada, a uniformed man boarded the bus and introduced himself as Commander Wilson T. Rogers, the commanding officer of Bossy Mountain Station.

"I realize you all must be tired from your trip, but if you'll bear with me for a minute, I'll take you to your quarters, and you can get squared away for the night. Tomorrow we'll ship you out to your stations. So let's move it out," Rogers finished.

This is an officer? Jennifer thought. He was authoritative, yet courteous, not at all what she expected after the treatment she had received in boot camp. Jennifer's impression was the higher you went up the military evolutionary scale, the less human they became. But it was her first real exposure to brass. Rogers was a young 35, and looked as if he could have been an old college chum of hers. It was not the image she conjured up when she heard the word 'officer'.

As she filed off the bus, Jennifer caught her first glimpse of Canada. She saw three clusters of lights on the other side of the river, beyond a well-lit bridge with sentries pacing in front of closed gates on either side. The light clusters were the border towns St.-Francois-de-Madawaska, Clair and Caron Brook, as she later found out. But this was the way it was going to be, she thought, us on our side and them on their side, and never shall they meet.

Rogers divided the group by gender and led the males and then the females to their separate-but-equal quarters. Jennifer snatched the closest available bunk in the stark, wood-frame barracks and fell off to a restless sleep.

In the morning on Sunday, after a skimpy breakfast (compared to the boot camp mess hall where they at least had choices), the new soldiers filed one-by-one, into Commander Rogers' office to present their sealed orders. It was a very formal but brief ritual. Each person walked in front of Rogers' desk, stood at attention, saluted and handed the orders to him. He read off the name, opened the envelope, perused the contents and announced the assignment. "Seamate Apprentice Martin, Jennifer," Rogers read and briefly glanced up at her to attach a face to the name. "You have been duly assigned to squad three, which will be subsequently detached to Depot Mountain Station. Dismissed."

"Aye, aye, commander." Jennifer saluted and marched out of the office.

The squads had been formed by Strickland and Kaminski, according to how they thought each group would work together. Rogers had each squad assigned to a station.

Jennifer was puzzled by the chiefs' judgment, however, when everyone discussed their assignments afterward. Almost none of her friends, the people she thought she worked best with, were assigned to her squad. Lisa was assigned to squad one, with Marcia as her squad leader. Deborah was assigned to squad two, with Robert Morrison as squad leader. And Emma Garraty led squad four. Among the people she considered friends, only Richard was in squad three with her. Tim Shackleford was their squad leader. And, to top it all off, Finkel also was in her squad. She hoped that he wouldn't be a problem. He hadn't bothered her in over a week, and he quietly went about his business.

The rest of the morning was spent standing in line as different departments in the camp doled out supplies and equipment. At the armory, the recruits signed out M-16 rifles and .45 pistols with a holster and a box of ammunition. The sea-bag that each person carried from boot camp containing extra clothing was traded for a backpack with a one-person tent and a blanket, and room to carry only one extra uniform. They also received an emergency mess kit, a pocket knife, a butane lighter, an electric lantern, insect repellent and emergency toilet paper stacked in flat sheets.

This should be fun, Jennifer thought. She had no idea what was in store for her, but she felt as if she were being sent on a big summer camping trip. She had gone to summer camp once when she was thirteen, but everyone stayed in cabins. She never had actually roughed it and gone 'camping'.

They were being shipped out that afternoon. Right after lunch, Jennifer said goodbye to the gang. "Lisa, I don't know when or if I'll get to see you again, so I want to say this before you go—you really helped me a lot by keeping me loose, making me laugh and being a great friend. I don't know if I could have made it without you. Seriously."

"Seriously? Well, thanks. And if you ever, *ever* need help again—come see Marcia here. I'm sure she'll be free. You know me. I'll probably be way too busy."

"You have already helped me tremendously, Marcia. If it wasn't for that extra training, I might still be in New Jersey."

"Oh, you never give yourself enough credit," Marcia said meekly.

"May I say something?" Deborah interjected. "I'd just like to say it has been a pleasure to serve with all of you. This has been the biggest thing in my life, so far, and you've been a part of it. It's like we've been through hell together. It's quite an experience that we've shared. I just hate to think that I probably won't be seeing my new friends anymore."

"Maybe we could try to organize a reunion five or ten years from now," Lisa suggested. "We could try to get the whole company back together and maybe share a *good* time, for a change. And the four of us should stay in touch."

"That would be nice," Marcia said. Jennifer thought so, too. It would be nice, but a sense of sadness also struck her. Everyone always seemed to say the same thing, in high school and college. But it never worked that way. Somehow they lost touch, despite the honorable intentions. When she spent a major portion of her life with the same people, she also wanted to continue the same way. This time probably would not be any different. The four weeks she already had spent with these people didn't even seem like that. That was a month out her 28 years, but it seemed like another lifetime altogether. Jennifer was beginning to forget that she had a life to go back to in Washington. But how would it look a few years from now? Would that month get smaller and smaller? Would it diminish the importance she now placed on the events and people? That's what saddened her. It happened before, and it would happen again.

But Jennifer hugged everyone or patted them on the back as they were sent off into the wilderness, until it was time for her to be sent off.

Jennifer and her squad piled into an olive green, topless truck with their gear and waited for the driver to get her paperwork in order. When they finally got rolling, they sang a verse of the Whiskey Company march song, as the first two squads had done. Shackleford led them:

"I don't know but I been told! Whiskey comp'ny's strong and bold! We follow orders do or die! Whiskey comp'ny's marching by! Walking tall, heads held high! If you hear us coming, step aside! We do pudah just for fun! We are number one! Sound off! One Two! Sound off! Three Four! One Two Three Four, one-two—THREE-FOUR!"

They sang as they rolled through the compound and out the main gate. They sang for the benefit of the people in camp to show they had company spirit. After they were out of earshot, they grew quiet as they settled in for the long drive to their station. Well, almost.

They passed a couple small towns, and then the truck turned onto a deserted road to nowhere. The road was used by logging companies and wound almost aimlessly through the Maine forest, parting the green sea of pine trees before them. The truck stopped at the foot of Depot Mountain, elevation 1,300 feet. The driver got out and assembled the squad at the side of the road.

"Is this it?" one squad member asked as she jumped off the truck.

"This can't be it. There's nothing here," Jennifer said.

"It's up there," the driver said, pointing up the hill. "Just fall out and follow me." She led them to a path in the forest that went up the side of the mountain. The squad, in full backpack, huffed and puffed as they ascended the peak. The driver was a Seamate like the squad members, but she was a Coast Guard regular, and she enjoyed needling her part-time, 'weekend warrior' counterparts. Without a pack, she hiked at a brisk pace.

"Don't tell me you're tired already. Come on, down there. Pick it up a little. Don't lag so far behind," she playfully goaded.

"No wonder they wanted us to be in good shape in boot camp," Jennifer said to Richard, while breathing heavily.

"Is this what we're in store for this month?" Richard quizzed. The path was new and not yet well worn, and he pushed sappy branches away from his face and kicked aside scrubby bushes.

When they reached the summit, they were greeted by First Class Petty Officer Henry Galloway. He was a boatswain's mate by trade, which more accurately meant jack-of-all-trades. Galloway was 47 and had a leathery face with deep wrinkles. He was an old salt, actually, an old sailor out of water. He could have retired from the Guard with 25 years in, but retire to *what*, he would have asked. He was rather intrigued when he heard about this newly created station. He was the only permanent personnel assigned to the post. He was his own boss here and in charge of the temporary troops.

"Ah, Janoff, I see you brought me a new crop of boots."

"Yeah, Boats, got some nice, fresh meat for you," the driver said as if she had just delivered a meal to the mountain grizzly at the zoo. "Sorry I

can't stay and chew the fat this time; I got to get my truck back. Some big inspection tomorrow. You know how that goes."

"Yes, indeedy. Maybe I'll catch you next month," Galloway said as
Janoff disappeared back down the path. "Well, I guess you swabbies should
get settled first. You bunk in those two tents. The males can take that one,
and the femmes get that one. After you get yourselves squared away, we'll
have a meeting in the mess tent over here to introduce ourselves, get ac-
quainted and let you know what I expect from you."

The compound was a small, oblong clearing in the woods on top of
the hill, with the two berthing tents on one side, the mess tent and a supply
shack attached to it on one edge in the middle, a latrine on the opposite edge,
and a lookout tower with a tool shed underneath on the other end.

Jennifer walked through the tent flap into her new home for the next
month. Five simple canvas cots were arranged around the center support
pole, each with a flat pillow at the head and a footlocker on the ground at
the foot.

"Whew, is it musty in here!" exclaimed Seamate Tasha Farland.

"It is kind of stifling in here," Jennifer said, "but I wonder what it's
like in the winter."

"I just thank the powers that be that I'm not here in the winter," said
Annie Callihan. The five women stowed their gear, then figured out how to
raise the heavy canvas flaps that served as walls. They turned their tent into
a summertime screened enclosure with a canvas roof. After completing that
task, they walked over to the larger mess tent for the meeting with their new
CO.

When Galloway said he would let them know what he expected from
them, Jennifer expected a list of things they couldn't do. No talking, no goof-
ing off, or no fun. But he surprised her when his introductory speech was
not exactly superior to subordinates, but rather benevolent teacher to eager
students, delivering his words in a friendly, good-humored, easy-going man-

ner.

"I realize you folks aren't regular military," Galloway began, "so I don't really expect you to act like regulars. Personally, I don't think you'll work at your best under those conditions. Now I do expect you to act with a certain amount of decorum, but I'd like you to be able to relax a bit. No need to be so rigid and serious around here. This isn't boot camp.

"This isn't your typical military installation, either. It's an outpost, and it's lacking a few of your basic amenities, like plumbing. You won't be able to bathe every day or wash your uniforms much. That's one big reason there won't be any personal inspections. I don't really care how you keep your living quarters. That's your personal living space for the next four weeks. So whatever it takes to get along, do it. As far as the compound area, I'll gladly call your attention to any glaring problems.

"There's going to be a lot of work to do, and there's no use complaining about doing some task because everyone will be involved in each job we do anyway. I only ask for everyone's full cooperation. If I get that and one-hundred percent effort, there'll be no problems. That's the only thing I really insist on. I need everyone to pitch in and work together. Just do your job, and the month will be over before you know it."

He went on to outline the tasks that they would be performing during their stay on Depot Mountain. Each person would stand a two-hour watch in the tower, scanning the countryside for any suspicious signs of troop movements. They would have the use of a pair of large and powerful binoculars mounted on a swiveling stand in the tower. The watchstander would be overlooking the St. Lawrence River valley, and on a clear day, a person actually could glimpse that majestic waterway. The watches ran twenty-four hours a day, and after someone stood a two-hour watch, that person had 18 hours off before standing the next one. It was a very rigid schedule because of the limited personnel. Once the schedule was set, there was no switching with other people to get a longer break.

The squad members also had a regular workday besides, where they would perform a variety of jobs. The main project on the hilltop was the digging and building of bunkers and pillboxes, which would then be landscaped and camouflaged. With one-inch guns and machine guns, the border could be protected for twenty miles on either side of the mountain. The main purpose was to slow down an invasion force until regular troops arrived.

Every so often, on an irregular basis, a group of seven squad members (minus three watchstanders) patrolled the forest surrounding the hill for six hours. They were to look for any signs of infiltration by the enemy along the border, but Jennifer thought it was more likely that they were looking for people who were trying to *leave* the United States. She hadn't heard about people still wanting to leave, but she figured there must have been some who were unhappy with the way things were turning out. But she saw no signs of anything her first few trips out. Because the border in this section was an imaginary line drawn between the two countries, the recruits needed to use their navigation and map-reading skills that they had learned in boot camp. One person was designated for mess duty each day, which basically included preparing meals and cleaning up after meals. It was an easy job. Breakfast consisted of fried eggs, fried potatoes, toast and canned juice. Lunch and supper were always the same. The meal consisted of each recruit's concoction for stew, served with bread, milk and a choice of fruit for dessert. Mess duty was the preferred duty because the mess person was excused from the more strenuous workday tasks, and if a watch happened to interfere with a meal, Galloway filled in in the kitchen.

When those jobs were taken care of, the recruits generally had free rein of the place. A nearby lake and stream provided the gang with some recreation—swimming, canoeing and fishing. If somebody wanted to go swimming after working hours one day that person didn't even need to ask permission to leave the compound, just to inform Galloway that he or she was going. And any fish that were caught could be brought back to the mess cook to fix for the catcher's meal (fried, of course).

So, despite some hard labor, Jennifer thought it still was nice duty. She enjoyed the assignment so far, and being such a small group, she got to spend a lot more time with Richard.

One day during the second week, Jennifer and Richard dug a hole that eventually would become a concrete bunker. Jennifer chose to do the job because even though it was backbreaking work, she knew how to dig, and the other jobs weren't any better. Finkel ferried the loads of excess dirt in a wheelbarrow to another pair who landscaped a finished bunker nearby. Under Galloway's direction, another group mixed and poured concrete for a pillbox. Galloway walked by their hole to check on the progress.

"Okay, the depth is just right, now, you just have to square out the corners a little more."

"Sure thing, Boats," Richard said from the bottom of the hole. He leaned against his shovel and wiped the sweat from his brow. The sun was almost directly overhead and left the pit nearly shadowless. "Uh, is it okay if I take my shirt off?"

"Sure," Galloway said, "if you've got your t-shirt on. You know, you two are a mess. You should go down to the lake after work and get cleaned up."

"That sounds like a good idea to me," Richard said, taking off his dusty uniform shirt.

"I should make it an order for everyone to go down and wash their uniforms tonight. Everybody's got a dirty job today." Galloway walked over to check on the landscaping job.

Richard and Jennifer went back to work, attending to the details of geometric hole-digging. They squared the corners and took out some rocks and pebbles to make the floor smooth. Jennifer also took her uniform shirt off when she couldn't stand it anymore. The thing was, Jennifer thought, Richard probably felt a little overdressed still. He probably wanted to take off his t-shirt as well, but men weren't allowed to go bare-chested anymore because women obviously couldn't. And Jennifer felt a little underdressed. Just a t-shirt was cooler but she felt as if she were walking around in her underwear, which she technically was under the current society's guideline. She wondered if she would feel less comfortable if she had the type of figure known to distract a man, such as Deborah's.

There was a large rock, almost a boulder, that had to be cleared before their job would be complete. Both dug around the sides to try to get it loose. When Richard could get under the stone with his shovel, he pried it up out of the floor by jumping on the shovel handle. Both Jennifer and Richard had to grab it to lift it out of the hole. After they heaved it up over the top, they smoothed the cavity that was left. They tossed their shovels out, and then Richard climbed out of the hole and gave Jennifer a hand as she climbed out.

"You know you're beautiful when you're filthy," Richard said to her, glancing at her soiled uniform.

In spite of herself, Jennifer laughed at the sight of herself. "Well, look at you, Pigpen," she joked. Richard, like Jennifer, was covered from head to toe with a dusting of dry Maine earth. Jennifer knew he was just joking about her slovenly appearance, but she was surprised to hear a comment like that. It reminded her of an old sexist joke, "You know, you're beautiful when you're angry." It was very condescending and patronizing for a man to say that to a woman, as though she were still a sex object, even in her most unattractive states. It also could be risky for a man to even tell a woman that she was beautiful because it implied sexual attraction. But she was sure he meant nothing by it.

Richard picked up the rock and lugged it to Finkel, who was standing nearby, getting another load of dirt, and he plopped it down in his wheelbarrow.

"Here you go, Gary," Richard said. "I don't know what you can do with it, or where you can put it, but it's all yours."

"Thanks," Finkel said curtly as he carted off the load.

After the workday, everyone who was free headed down to the lake. Dinner was held back an hour so that everyone could get cleaned up after the grimy day. The squad members brought their uniforms to a small waterfall near the head of the stream to wash. Everyone was dressed in their PF gear from boot camp. It was basically the official swimwear for the country now gym shorts and a dark t-shirt. Tans were sacrificed for propriety. After they finished their chores, they laid out the wet uniforms on dry boulders and ran to the lake like kids on summer vacation.

"This reminds me of a summer vacation we took once to Minnesota to visit my grandparents," Richard said to Jennifer while taking off his sneakers and socks at the small pebbly beach. Vacant cabins and docks dotted the shore of the lake, which had been a semi-popular, but remote, recreation spot until the government took it over for military use. "There was a raft in the middle of the lake just like that one." Richard pointed to a large floating platform tethered in the center of the lake.

"I'll race you," Jennifer said and at the same time ran into the water until she could swim. Richard followed close behind. Jennifer was not a great swimmer. She thrashed and splashed too much, and Richard easily overtook her with a decent swimming stroke. She huffed and puffed and tried to catch her breath when she finally reached the raft.

"A little out of shape maybe?" Richard kidded her.

"I'm just not a swimmer."

"Well, come on. Get on up there." Richard boosted her up the ladder by putting a hand on her rump. It wasn't a sexual 'touchy-feelie', Jennifer thought. She knew what they were like. She had dealt with quite a few of them in high school and college, and that wasn't one, she thought. Jennifer was glad in a way that he wasn't overly frightened to even touch her at all because if she were a man, no one would have thought twice about the same gesture. And that's the way it should be, she thought. But who knew these days?

"You ever do any diving?" Richard asked her.

"Not much. I'm not really a water person."

"Well, I can show you then. We'll start with a simple one. This is called a cannonball. It's easy, but it makes a huge splash for a two-point-eight degree of fun. You just take a running leap, tuck in your knees really tight, and roll yourself into a ball. Then POW! Hit the water." He demonstrated, and then she followed. Richard laughed at her mock ferocity as she attacked the water. "That was great. You should have seen the splash you made."

Richard continued to show Jennifer his favorite dives for the rest of the afternoon, most of which Jennifer didn't even want to attempt. Richard was so much fun to be around, Jennifer thought, but she wondered what other people thought since she spent almost all of her time with him. There was supposed to be nothing wrong with a friendship between men and women, but it did seem rare, a kind of oddity. However, Richard was like a breath of fresh air compared to the other men she had met. The only other man that she had dealt with on a regular basis over the past couple of years was Stan. And she didn't really know him that well at all. He always kept to himself, never talking about his personal life or giving any kind of clues to his personality outside of work. Jennifer remembered how she and Carmen always would ask Stan to join them for lunch, but he came up with excuse after excuse, so Jennifer began to think that he was afraid to get too close to them. Maybe he didn't trust himself, Jennifer speculated, but it shouldn't be that way. Her relationship with Richard was the way it should be, unfettered by sexual baggage. But, for some reason, closeness between a man and a woman always was assumed to be caused by sexual attraction. Richard was a nice looking man, she thought, but she wasn't sexually attracted to him at all. She would know the difference, unless somehow her sexual desires were so suppressed by now that she wouldn't recognize it when it hit her. No, she could remember the feeling. She just enjoyed his company. He was fun. She liked the other women, but they just weren't as fun as Richard. If Lisa were there, she probably would have spent most of her time with her, and that thought comforted her and removed any remaining guilt she felt. She probably wouldn't get to see him after the end of the month anyway. So she was going to enjoy the relationship as long as it lasted. Besides, maybe it was just her imagination that suggested someone else might get the wrong idea.

Later that evening, Jennifer and Richard joined the squad around a campfire. Galloway sometimes held squad meetings around the fire to tell the group what was coming up the next day or two, but he used it as a way to wind down at the end of the day. He also would start coffee for the night watchstanders. After he spoke, the others in the group would talk amongst themselves. Annie Callihan had a nice singing voice, and she quietly sang folk songs to herself, but the others usually gathered closely around her to listen. She didn't seem to mind the audience.

That night, while Annie sang, Jennifer and Richard continued an earlier conversation with each other. They sat apart from the group a bit with their backs resting against a large boulder just at the edge of the clearing. The faint, flickering firelight still reflected and danced off their faces, distorting their familiar daylight lines.

"So, you mean to tell me that was the extent of your camping experience?" Richard questioned.

"Yup."

"Then you missed out on all the fun of *real* camping. You know, pitching tents, cooking over a campfire, surviving on only nature's resources. This actually reminds me of the big camp out I went on when I was in the Boy Scouts." Richard suddenly looked as if he had said a dirty word. "I mean, when I was in the *Scouts*."

"No, you were right. It was the 'Boy Scouts' back then," Jennifer corrected. She didn't want him to be overcautious about everything he said, like most people she knew. However, people were discouraged from using gendered adjectives.

"Well, anyway, we had this big camp out to help us earn our badges," Richard continued, "but, at the end of each night, we all gathered around the campfire and sang songs or roasted marshmallows."

"Mmmm—Marshmallows. Sounds delicious."

"You know, I still remember it as being good and a lot of fun, but if we had some right now, I can't imagine that it would be delicious. I mean, if you roast a hot dog or a marshmallow over an open flame, one part always got burned to a crisp while other parts would still be raw. But we always thought it was great back then. I guess because it was the first time we ever got to cook for ourselves."

"I know what you mean," Jennifer said. "I think it would still be fun, though. Do you think the Guard has a marshmallow requisition form?"

They both giggled. Then when the conversation lulled, Jennifer gazed up at the twinkling stars.

"You got watch tonight?" Richard asked.

"Yeah, unfortunately."

"I had one last night, and did you ever notice on night watch that glow just off the western horizon?" Jennifer nodded. "I finally figured out what that is. It's the city lights of Quebec."

"Really? I know it's in enemy territory and all, but I've always thought that Quebec would be such a romantic city." Now Jennifer felt as if she had said a dirty word. Finding something romantic meant falling in love, and therefore being sexually attracted to someone. "I didn't mean *romantic* exactly. I meant, you know, stylishly intriguing."

"No, *romantic* is a fair word. I know what you mean. Anyway, if you look due west with the binocs tonight, you should be able to see it. It looks like it'll be a very clear night. You'll probably be able to see the boat traffic on the St. Lawrence River, too."

"Is that what those moving lights were? I thought they might be cars at first, but some had red, green or yellow lights, and I really wasn't sure what they were."

"And you should notice that the ones with the green lights only move to the right because you're looking at the starboard side, and the red lights only move to the left because that's the port side."

"I'm going to have to take a closer look at that. Not that there'll be anything better to do up there," Jennifer said.

"You know, those binocs are good for astronomy, too. You should point it up at the sky and take a look around. It's really fascinating. The moon will be out tonight. You can see the mountains and the craters in nice detail." After talking about stargazing and the points of interest in the sky, Jennifer excused herself to turn in early so that she could be rested for her watch.

When she was awakened at 0345, Jennifer dressed in the dark and then went out to the dying campfire. She tossed a few more twigs on and poured herself a cup of old, pungent coffee. She didn't much like black coffee when it was fresh, but she drank it to stay awake. The previous watchstander had already hit the sack, and so Jennifer slowly climbed the creaky ladder to the top of the tower.

The 'crow's nest', as everyone called it, was always peaceful at night. The normal forest sounds didn't seem to carry upward, and all Jennifer could hear was the lazy breeze blowing through the tower and the occasional crackle of the radio behind her. There wasn't much to see at night either. She scanned the horizon with the binoculars anyway, and saw a wide scattering of lights to the north, which she knew to be such things as streetlamps and houses. Turning east, there was almost a void—no lights, no shapes. During the day, Jennifer remembered seeing another tower on a mountain top and wondered if Lisa might be stationed there, or Deborah, or Marcia. Maybe one of them was on watch tonight. Jennifer waved in the general direction, just in case. The south was another black hole. But, looking to the west, she could see the lights of Quebec, just as Richard had said. "Wow," she said to herself when she made out the boat traffic on the St. Lawrence, also as Richard had said. She didn't know for sure, but he must be right, she thought. Everything did seem to fit when she checked the map on the radio stand. She was only to make a report when she saw something out of the ordinary, but everything was always so ordinary up there that it could put her to sleep.

She took Richard's suggestion and turned the binoculars skyward to the setting moon in the southwest quadrant. She picked out the Big Dipper with the North Star about two thirds up from the horizon, and then she located Orion. But she couldn't even remember the names of the other constellations that Richard had told her about.

Jennifer killed the two hours quickly, gazing at the heavens. As she stood in the crow's nest, all of Canada lay out before her, with the United States at her back. They were supposed to be the enemy, but they didn't look threatening or fearsome, she thought. Ordinary people would be waking up soon, going to work, or just going about their lives as they chose.

Jennifer's watch ended at 0600 hours. The sun had not yet risen, but the eastern sky had begun to lighten. She climbed down from her post and woke her replacement fifteen minutes prior to six, and then she went back to bed. Thanks to a privilege Galloway gave to all midnight watchstanders, she didn't have to get up at dawn with the rest of the company. She could sleep until ten, which she did deeply.

Tasha Farland, who also had a midnight watch, was already awake, and she woke Jennifer at ten.

"Wake up, sleepyhead. Turn to."

After a sound, satisfying four-hour nap, she didn't feel refreshed, though, but more naturally groggy. She wanted to savor that feeling and not get out of bed.

"I'm up," she said with her face still buried in her pillow. She gradually sat up, and then dressed. The worst thing about the sleep-in privilege, she thought, was that she missed breakfast. But lunch was only two hours away.

She left her tent to find her work assignment for the day.

When she spotted Galloway crossing the compound, he called her over.

"Jennifer. I just got a radio message. You're wanted back at Bossy Mountain Station. Commander Rogers' orders. A truck will be coming for you shortly. So you can head down to the road to wait for it."

"Do you know what this is all about?"

"No details," was all that he said.

Jennifer had no idea what the reason could be. Then she wondered if she was being reassigned. "Do I bring my gear?" she asked.

"No gear. I was assured you'd be back this afternoon." Galloway turned and left Jennifer standing there with a puzzled look on her face. She headed down the path, and at the bottom of the hill, she saw Richard sitting by the side of the road.

"You have to go, too?" Jennifer asked.

"Yeah. You wouldn't happen to know what this is all about, would you?"

"No, I was hoping you'd know." The truck pulled up, and, with a short exchange with the driver to confirm their identities, they climbed into the truck, which turned around and headed back to Fort Kent. As soon as they arrived in the camp, Jennifer and Richard were led to Commander Rogers' office. They were instructed to see him one at a time. Jennifer's curiosity was greater than her fear at that moment, and so she decided to go in first.

"Seamate Apprentice Martin reporting as ordered, Commander Rogers."

"At ease." Jennifer stood at parade rest in front of Rogers' desk. "You may be wondering why you've been called here. So let me get right to the point. I've received a complaint about the way you and Seamate Apprentice Runge have been carrying on."

"'Carrying on,' Commander? We have not been 'carrying on.' But we are friends."

"I don't know what's going on up there, and I'm not sure I want to know, but I suggest you two put some distance between yourselves. Listen, this kind of thing seems to happen once a month with each new unit. I know it's a lot different up here from the civilian life you're probably used to. But that's the way it has to be around here, out of necessity. Men and women have to learn how to work together and live together."

"With all due respect, Commander, I don't see that I'm having a problem with that," Jennifer said.

"Look at it this way. You've got just over two weeks to go here. So just cool it for now— understood?"

Jennifer felt that he wasn't even listening to her and that she was being wrongly accused. But she was sure she must have sounded no different from a guilty person denying all charges. "But there is nothing going on between us, Commander. We talk, joke and pal around, but that's it. We're not doing anything illegal."

"Look, I don't like the fact that I have to be involved in people's personal lives. Personally, I don't care what you do, but I received a complaint, and I have to officially give you a warning. If I get another complaint, I have to order an investigation. And that's when it really gets messy. Just watch what you do from now on. Make sure you don't create any false impressions then."

"May I ask who made this complaint against me?"

"I can't tell you that."

"So it's somebody's word against mine. And you're telling me that I can't be friends with Seamate Runge?"

"Basically, for now, yes. While you're here on duty, keep a low profile. After you leave—" He didn't finish his sentence, but shrugged as if to say it wouldn't be any of his business anymore and that she could do what she wanted.

Jennifer didn't reply, but she knew that when she left the service, the situation would be no different. Women and men could not be allowed to be friends as a precaution, she figured. Against what, though, she mulled? A precaution against the chance that some people might fall in love?

"I don't understand this," Jennifer said. "I don't know what I did wrong, and you're telling me not to do it anymore, whatever it is." Jennifer became emotional and her thoughts frazzled because the logic of the situation had broken down.

"Look, you seem like a nice person," Rogers said. "I realize this must be a tough situation for you. You're not regular military. I'm not accusing you of anything. This is just military procedure. You just go back to your unit and concentrate on your job, and I'm sure I won't be seeing you back here. Fair enough?"

"Yes," she said, but she hardly meant it.

"Very good. Dismissed." Jennifer saluted Rogers and walked out of his office. She waited outside by the truck while Richard spoke with Rogers.

During the trip back to Depot Mountain, she discussed the situation with Richard.

"Can you believe they want us to stop being friends?" Jennifer said.

"I don't think he said that exactly, but I think Commander Rogers is right. I don't want to see you get in trouble."

"But, don't you hate him telling you that you can't see me anymore?"

"I'll still see you around the camp. I think he was saying that we shouldn't be together just by ourselves. We should join the group more. Besides, it's only for two more weeks."

"But, after that, I won't see you at all."

"I guess I never thought of that. It's been hard trying to think of the future for the past couple months. You know, I've really enjoyed the time that we spent together. I'm glad that we got to serve together."

"So am I. That's why I'm so mad," Jennifer fumed. "Aren't you pissed off that someone is saying that you're not trusted enough to choose whom you want to spend your time with?"

"Yes, of course, but, you know, we do have to be careful that we don't give any wrong impressions."

Jennifer left it at that. She couldn't understand why she couldn't get through to anyone. Was she the only person who thought the way she did?

When she got back to camp, she kept to herself the rest of the day while she decided what she should do. And that night she decided to act exactly the same, regardless of the warning. After all, she hadn't done anything wrong. She was just going to follow her normal routine.

The next day wasn't exactly normal, however. The squad went on a patrol because there was a report of infiltration activity in the area. Richard was one of the three who didn't go along because of watch duty.

The lucky stiff, Jennifer thought. The area received its first significant rainfall in the month that day, a heavy shower that had the group slogging through the forest muck and mud. The squad members were equipped with rain gear, but it didn't help much. They were soaked to the skin by the first hour anyway. They carried their M-16 rifles slung over their shoulders. All Jennifer thought was what a bitch it would be to clean them if they rusted. Besides all that, the low, misty, gray clouds obscured their easily identifiable landmarks, and they fumbled with plastic-coated maps trying to locate predetermined objective points. They were led by Mike Gresham instead of Tim Shackleford, who also had watch that day. Usually everybody tried to have fun with this duty, but everyone was miserable. Their hearts weren't in it. They plodded from point to point just trying to get it over with.

"Okay, we need to go about two hundred yards due west," Mike said. He wiped the water droplets off the map and then off his forehead. "All right. Let's go." Mike pointed in the general direction and led the way.

"Is your compass broke, Gresham? You're going northwest, not west," Suzanne DeLucci reminded, referring to her own compass.

Mike shook his compass to dislodge the needle and watched it resettle. "We're okay. Maybe our path was a little bit west-northwest. We'll just go a hundred-fifty yards west-southwest."

"Come on. Make sure you know where you're going first," Jennifer said. "We must be pretty damn close to the line, as it is."

Mike led the squad again through the dense pine trees. He looked back at Maude Ademley, who was near the back of the group, and said, "Will you tell those stragglers to hurry up. We're not going to keep waiting up for them."

Maude stopped and waited for Finkel and Tasha Farland to catch up. The two were having the most trouble with the heavy packs that the squad members had to carry on patrol. Every time the main group let them catch up, they fell behind 40 to 50 yards when they started again.

"Is it a hundred and fifty yet, Jimmy?" Mike said to Seamate Jim Snyder, who was assigned the task of determining distance traveled.

"I don't know. Pretty close," he said.

"What do you mean, you don't know? Is it or isn't it?" Mike shouted at him.

"Give me a break. There are no landmarks out here. Every tree looks like every other damned tree, and visibility is for shit."

"I think we better figure out where we are," Jennifer said. She heard a buzzing like an insect, and then an explosion with the sound of splintering wood. She looked up to see fragments flying from a nearby tree.

"Shit!" Mike yelled. And the calm, drizzling sound of the summer rain turned into the thunder of gunfire. The squad dropped to the ground and scrambled for cover. At first, they didn't know which direction the fire had come from, but they saw shadowy figures moving in the distance to the northeast. The main group of five squad members finally settled behind a cluster of trees, their faces pressed against the prickly bark.

"I don't believe this," Mike said. "We actually found the invading squad."

"What do we do?" Suzanne asked.

"We shoot back." Mike had his gun loaded quickly and he aimed in the general direction where he had seen the figures. He squeezed off a few rounds, and after a few seconds he was answered by another burst from the enemy. The other squad members then joined in the fracas by returning fire. Jennifer fired her weapon a couple of times, but the shots would have been quite high by the time they reached the target area.

"Maude, get on that radio and see if we can get some help up here," Mike said. "If this is an invasion, we're going to need reinforcements."

Just as she made the call to the watch tower, Tasha ran up to the group, minus her pack and rifle.

"Where's Finkel?" Jennifer asked her.

"I don't know. He was right behind me," Tasha said as she tried to catch her breath. "He may have been hit—captured. I saw the enemy. And when they fired at us, I ran to catch up. Didn't look back."

"You say he might have been *hit*?" Jennifer asked.

"I heard him yell out, like he was in pain."

"We've got to try to find him. He may be wounded," Jennifer said to Mike.

"He also may be captured already," Mike told her. "Besides, we have to fortify our position here. We can't move around and spread out for a search, or we'll be captured, too."

"Fine. You fortify. I'll go myself." Before Mike could stop her, Jennifer ran off in the direction that Tasha had just come from, and a hail of bullets hit a group of trees that she had just left behind. Mike and the remaining squad members fired back heavily to possibly prevent their pursuit of Jennifer.

Meanwhile, Jennifer ran through the trees almost aimlessly. She didn't know where she was going. It had crossed her mind, why was she risking her own life to help this guy she didn't even like very much? A guy who had shown her disrespect and vulgarity. But the thought of him lying somewhere in the dark, dank forest, wounded, possibly left to die, overwhelmed her. If there was something she could do, she was going to do it. Besides, he was a member of the squad, a part of the family. She had to do everything in her power to help him out. Jennifer didn't know much about war, but she understood that part about protecting your own. That was the force that propelled her through the forest.

Jennifer still heard the sound of gunfire, but they weren't shooting at her anymore. She was able to slow down and look around. She found Tasha's discarded pack and weapon. She picked up the rifle (she thought it might come in handy if something else happened) and stumbled on to look for any signs of Finkel.

"Finkel?" she probed in a loud whisper. "Finkel! Are you here, Gary?" Her eyes darted back and forth. Then she heard a low moan and labored breathing a few yards from her. When she got closer to the sound, she finally saw the prone figure of Gary Finkel. She saw the red stain of blood on his backside, and she wasn't sure if he may have been close to death or not.

Finkel was only semiconscious when Jennifer touched his shoulder to check on him, and he quickly regained his senses, especially pain.

"OWWWAhah, ow! I've been hit. I've been shot! Tell me the truth. Am I going to make it?" he mumbled.

"Of course, you're going to make it. You've been shot right in the buttocks, it looks like. Can you get up? Can you walk? Because we've got to get out of here fast."

"I don't know. Ahhhhh!" Finkel worked his way up to his feet. He attempted a couple of steps and limped severely. "Oooh! I don't know how far I can go, and I feel kind of woozy."

"Well, it looks like you've lost a lot of blood. Here, let's try and stop the bleeding first." Jennifer pulled her pack off and reached into the first aid kit for a field dressing. "Turn around and drop your pants," she instructed.

Finkel did so gingerly. With his shorts still on, a small round hole was visible on the back of his right leg. The bullet was still inside. Jennifer wiped some of the blood away, put a gauze pad and a bandage on top of the hole, and then tied the cloth ligatures around his legs.

"There. That ought to do it for now," Jennifer said. "But you've got to try and walk. We may be in Canadian territory right now."

"Maybe you should leave me here."

"What? I'm risking my neck just to come get you. I can't just leave you here."

"Then stay with me. Why don't we just stay in Canada, if that's where we are?"

"What are you talking about? Desertion? You've got to be kidding. We're going back, both of us."

"But I don't want to die."

"Are you delirious or something?" Jennifer asked. "I don't think you're going to die. We just need to get you some medical attention quick. Come on. What are you waiting for? What's the matter with you?"

Finkel looked more in fear than in pain. He appeared dazed and frozen, caught between choices, still standing in front of Jennifer in his briefs. Then suddenly he became more animated again.

"I don't want to die a virgin, okay?" Finkel ranted. "If I go back to the U.S., I'll die a virgin. Please come with me. Please be my first. My first and only. Then you can leave me here to die, and I can die a happy man." He grabbed her left arm and moved in as if to kiss her. Jennifer's instinctive response to the unwanted advance was a knee to his groin, and in the same fluid motion, a right cross to his incoming jaw that took him down for the count.

The sight of Finkel writhing on the ground with pain in three-part harmony was somewhat comical to Jennifer. But she didn't laugh. She had just beat up a wounded guy who flipped out and still had his pants around his ankles.

"Look, I don't want to hurt you, and I know you don't want to hurt me," Jennifer said. "But I've shown a lot of patience with you, and I'm still at a loss to figure out why you're doing all this to me. What have I ever done to you?" Jennifer looked up into the leaking sky and said, "Why me? Why me?"

"Because I love you," Finkel said, then coughed and spit blood from his mouth.

Jennifer stood stunned for a moment. "You what?" She looked at him in shock and disbelief, and then helped him as he struggled to his feet so that she might get a quicker answer from him.

"I love you. And I just wanted to get you to like me," Finkel repeated.

"You sure have a strange way of going about it."

"Well, I don't have much experience with women. I guess I thought you were like me, and I thought that you'd understand me."

"I don't know why you thought that. But we don't have time for that now. We're going back where we both belong, right now."

Finkel collected himself and headed south with Jennifer's assistance, leaning on her shoulder. They eventually did meet up with the rest of the squad and some reinforcement troops, who were a mixture of Guard and regular Army. Jennifer rode in the ambulance with Finkel and visited him often in the hospital those last two weeks. And from her conversations with him, Jennifer began to wonder if she was really right about 'belonging' in the United States. She was increasingly troubled by what was going on in the society, but she never could put her finger on what was 'wrong' with it, until now. She had agreed with the ideals of equality, but something was dreadfully wrong. Finkel was a troubled young man, but she was convinced it was part of what had happened to the society.

In the beginning, they were told that sex and love were not the same thing, and that sex debased and perverted the true essence of love. But in the effort to eradicate the problems of sexual inequality, somehow they had managed to kill love. They separated married couples; they separated children from their parents; they separated all males and females whether they could coexist or not. Basically, Jennifer felt that Finkel got all screwed up because he wasn't allowed to love. Or to be loved. As far as Jennifer was concerned, love in the United States was dead.

CHAPTER SIX

Jennifer tried to rejoin the comforting routine of her old life after returning from duty, but it wasn't easy after all the hoopla. Through no fault of her own, she returned to a hero's welcome in Washington.

After the squad members had returned to the safety of the camp, they were questioned about what happened. The official report after the inquiry stated that the squad confronted an invading force, held them off and forced them to retreat. Mike Gresham was commended for his forthright leadership under stressful circumstances, and Jennifer Martin was commended for courage and acts of bravery above and beyond the call of duty, risking her own life to save another. They both got medals, Gary Finkel received a Purple Heart, and the other squad members were awarded combat ribbons.

The story circulated to the media, and soon Jennifer was the subject of interviews by major newspapers, national television and radio. And when the news reached Marilyn in Washington, she recommended Jennifer for a Congressional Medal of Honor. The resolution passed overwhelmingly.

When her tour of duty ended and Jennifer arrived back in Washington, a ticker-tape parade was given in her honor as the country's first female combat hero, and she spoke live to the entire country, watching and listening on all the television and radio networks. She took it all in stride and remained humble, trying to downplay her involvement. She graciously thanked every-one for the support and admiration, but she didn't express the suspicions that had been nagging her conscience. She wanted to say while everyone was listening, "We might have crossed the line first. We invaded them, by mistake." But she would've spoiled everyone's party. What they were hearing seemed like what they wanted to hear. The masses were hungry for a female hero, and they were ready to devour this fresh-faced woman-next-door.

Jennifer had no way of knowing, for sure, which way it really hap-pened, but she was quite correct. A Canadian squad was also on a routine patrol in the area. They were regular military and were quite *certain* of their location. When they saw Jennifer's squad, they decided to scare them back over the line by firing a few shots in their direction. Finkel was hit quite ac-cidentally, and the Canadian squad didn't even know about him. When they chased the main squad back over the line, they ceased the pursuit. They re-ceived no injuries from the return fire, and while Finkel may have bled to death if not found, he was in no real danger from the Canadians had they stumbled upon him. The Canadian press reported the incident for what it was, a misunderstanding, but the U.S. government called it an act of aggres-sion and threatened retaliation. But, after the weeks following the incident, nothing further developed. And, despite misinformation, Jennifer uncom-fortably endured the attention and tried to slowly slip back to her previous anonymity at the Capitol.

However, by the middle of August, Jennifer was still the nation's dar-ling, and her life was anything but normal. Besides the cards, letters and phone calls from people she didn't know, she was flooded with dinner invitations from female Congress members, fellow Aides and other acquaintances, whose paths she happened to cross in her daily activities of delivering messages, photocopying paperwork and researching law books. She declined most and accepted a few. Mostly she had to repeat the same story over and over, de-tailing her experiences in the Maine wilderness. And, while walking to and from work, she would be greeted by strangers saying something such as, 'You. You're the one who so and so—and so and so.' She sometimes said, 'Yes I am,' and the person would have to shake her hand and say something such as, 'Way to go,' and eventually allow her to move on. Other times, out of frustration at the sheer repetitiveness of the situation, she would say, 'Sorry, you must have me confused with someone else.' Thankfully for Jennifer, occurrences such as these were gradually declining.

This day, as Jennifer walked along Rhode Island Avenue, only two people accosted her, which was for the better because she wasn't in an accommodating mood. She was on her way to the Institute for the Advancement and Preservation of Life for her monthly egg donation. More like egg seizure, she thought. Jennifer missed her last two periodical visits to the Institute due to her service obligations. All her tribulations of the past two months now seemed worthwhile for a chance to avoid the embarrassing and degrading procedure.

The building that housed the Institute at the intersection of Rhode Island and Florida was itself intimidating and foreboding. The black marble and black granite edifice, which could have been a creation of beauty, rather stuck out like a wounded phalanx in a city dominated by white marble and granite. It was starkly rectangular like a chiseled brick. Only the ground floor, where Jennifer and all other visitors known to her were ever allowed, had windows. From the second story to the top of the seven-story structure looked like a solid stone set on top of the building. In humorous and very discreet conversations, the Institute was referred to as the 'Baby Factory'. It was the place that most believed, but couldn't know for sure, where they eventually combined the frozen eggs with the frozen sperm to thereby perpetuate the post-coital society. Jennifer hadn't even seen a baby or any child in the past two years. She did remember seeing a television news report on the high schools' new androgynous teaching methods and how it helped reeducate the poor students who were exposed to the gross misinformation of the past (which, of course, meant everyone). But she hadn't seen any evidence that the government was using the technology of a 'womb-less' birth, which it said it had. She knew that the Institute had been allocated the funds to care for and raise the nation's children, and she was curious to see the 'new-age' babies and children and how differently they turned out, if different at all. Would they be in any way superior to anyone raised the old-fashioned way, by mother and father? Perhaps they were being 'born' in the deep, dark recesses of the upper floors at that moment, and were being raised there in a perfect, sexually-sterilized environment, she thought as she walked down the elongated side of the Institute.

The center of that side of the building was marked by a garage-style door where trucks could enter for 'deliveries'. Hospitals around the country acted as collection centers for the egg cells and sperm cells, which were then shipped to the Institute for safe keeping. Except for those directly involved, no one knew anything else about the process, such as what happened to the cells. Were they stored indefinitely? Whose cells got chosen for fertilization? Who made the decisions?

Being a D.C. resident, Jennifer was 'lucky' enough to make her deposits directly. At first, she had hoped that this would mean she could find out something more about the Institute, but she was stonewalled, like the black marble and granite. She once asked to see the Director of the Institute, but she was told it was impossible. She also was stopped by armed security guards when she pretended to wander away from the regular offices to locate a stairwell leading to the second floor. Their fortress seemed impenetrable.

As Jennifer was about to cross the driveway for the delivery entrance, a truck with hospital markings cut in front of her. And when the door rolled up to allow the truck passage, she could only see a long, dark corridor that the truck drove through and disappeared into, indicating to Jennifer that the loading dock was deep within the bowels of the building. The door closed quickly behind the truck, thus keeping the whole operation top secret.

When Jennifer walked into the pedestrian entrance on one end of the building (she knew that at the opposite end, there was a separate entrance for men), she announced her name to the receptionist. She then told Jennifer the room number and the directions to get there. When she found the right room, she walked into a typical doctor's waiting room. There was another receptionist behind a glass partition, and Jennifer gave her name once again.

"Please be seated. Your name will be called when they are ready for you," the white clad woman told her.

Jennifer sat down, picked up a magazine and thumbed through it. She looked around at the other women waiting nervously. When one of them looked up at her, she quickly looked away, not wanting to embarrass her by acknowledging her presence. By acknowledging the person, you had to acknowledge the reason for being there, and nobody wanted to do that.

When Jennifer's name was finally called, she was still apprehensive, but a little relieved. A female gynecologist (only females were allowed to be gynecologists, of course) led her to the examination room. Once inside the room, the doctor closed the door.

"Okay, strip down from the waist and jump up on the table," the doctor said.

Jennifer did so without hesitation. She had been through the routine before, and it was all very clinical. She just wanted it to be done with as quickly as possible.

The doctor snapped on a pair of rubber gloves as Jennifer placed her feet in a pair of stirrups at one end of the examination table. Jennifer felt quite uncomfortable, but also somewhat like an exhibitionist. For about 29/30ths of a month, the region of her body between her legs was hidden, out of sight, out of mind—unmentionable. But for one day a month, she displayed 'it' for another person to poke, prod, examine and ask questions about. She almost wished she could shock someone with her nudity, but the doctor was definitely the wrong person. Knowing her job and the sheer number of procedures she must perform, 'it' was not an uncommon sight.

"Okay, just relax and this will be over before you know it," the doctor said.

Jennifer lay flat back on the table and unconsciously looked past the overhead lights and ceiling, unfocused on any particular spot as the procedure began. She felt the cool, smooth, stainless steel, tube-like endoscope being inserted into her vagina. She felt her muscles involuntarily contract around the instrument. When the scope more closely matched her own body temperature, her muscles relaxed a bit as the doctor slid it deeper. After the scope was securely in place, the doctor flipped a few switches, and Jennifer saw out of the corner of her eye a television flicker on.

From all her previous visits, Jennifer knew that the doctor had used a television screen to guide her through the body to the ovaries, but she had never been in a position to see what the doctor saw. Jennifer turned her head to get a better view. From her understanding of the procedure, she knew a tiny fiberglass filament was being maneuvered through her body that allowed television pictures to be taken. While only feeling an occasional scratchy or tingling sensation, she saw exactly what was going on. Jennifer was captivated for a moment by the images. 'I'm looking inside my own body!' she thought.

The tiny thread traveled through tunnel after tunnel, occasionally appearing in a large cavern, searching for the right road deeper and deeper inside of her. The tunnel grew smaller and smaller, but the scope rolled on. Eventually, the tunnel tapered out again into another cave. The end of the line. Jennifer saw a milky white spheroid blocking the path. The doctor searched for a nodule on one side of the spheroid and took the scope in closer. The picture grew a little fuzzy, and the screen was almost a solid gray tone. Jennifer couldn't make out what was going on, but apparently the doctor could. She turned on the tiny vacuum and scooped up exactly what she had come looking for, a fantastic single human cell—the incredible egg.

After the endoscope was put into reverse and taken out of Jennifer's body, the doctor injected the prized catch into a small test tube, sealed it, labeled it, and instantly froze it by plunging it into a container of liquid nitrogen.

"That wasn't so bad, was it?" the doctor said, as always, it seemed. "Okay, you can get dressed now. Just make sure you make an appointment for your next visit with the receptionist on your way out." The doctor picked up the box containing the frozen test tube and walked out of the room.

Jennifer dressed quickly and also left the room. She wanted to get out of that building as rapidly as she could. Now that she had witnessed the actual seizure, as opposed to just having the procedure passively done to her, she felt clearly victimized. They plucked an egg straight from her ovary, and they could use that egg to create another human life, if they so chose, and she would never know who it was or where it was. What made them think that they had the right to take it from her, she thought? After all, it was her egg, wasn't it? She should be the one and only one to choose what to do with it, whether to use it to create another life, or not to use it at all. 'Could I just refuse next time? Shouldn't I fight to have my body left alone?' she asked herself. 'Would they actually jail me for refusing?' From what she knew, nobody ever tried to refuse. Everybody just went along. She went ahead and made her next month's appointment, but she told herself, 'Maybe I just won't show up next time and see what happens.' Jennifer was growing more frustrated every day, but she just didn't know much about rebellion.

Jennifer walked quickly out of the building. She felt like crying, but she fought it. She didn't want anyone to see her like that, especially if recognized. She wanted to go straight home and go to sleep. She wanted to be unconscious for a while so that she wouldn't have to think anymore. 'Maybe I should just get totally drunk,' she thought. 'I haven't been really wasted since college.'

She walked back down the length of the building, and she still couldn't keep her eyes off it. She looked up at it and couldn't help speculating again what went on in there, and what might be happening to her tiny egg cell amidst that massive, formidable structure.

As she was about to cross the street at the intersection of Florida and Rhode Island and leave it all behind, she heard yet another unfamiliar voice call her name.

"Jennifer? Jennifer Martin? Is that you?" the voice asked. She expected it to be another well-wisher/admirer who had recognized her from TV, and she almost lost it. She wanted to tell the clown to just leave her alone, but she turned around and, instead, saw a vaguely familiar face.

"Jennifer. It is you, isn't it?"

A wave of memories and recognition crashed over her. Now she wanted to cry tears of joy for seeing again such a wonderful friend from her past. "Paul? Paul Kennedy? I don't believe it!" Jennifer hugged him and patted him gently on the shoulder to let him know how happy she was to see him, but she did so quickly to avoid attracting too much attention.

"How are you? How have you been?" Paul asked.

"I've been good. I can't complain." Upon seeing his warm, comforting face again, she wanted to confide in him, to tell him exactly how she had been feeling lately, but she resisted.

"I know. I saw you on television not too long ago. That was really some ordeal you went through. I wanted to contact you again, but I didn't know how. And here you are."

"Here I am. I was just making my monthly—uh, visit," she said nervously, pointing her thumb over her shoulder back at the Institute.

"Me, too. Nice coincidence." An awkward silence followed. They had to get out of the shadow of that building, Jennifer thought.

"Say, can you walk with me back home?" Jennifer asked.

"Sure, sure." They crossed the street and walked back toward downtown.

"Wow, I still can't believe this," Jennifer said. "What's it been now, almost ten years?"

"Yes, I think so."

"So, what happened to you?" she asked. "I didn't see you anymore after our frosh year."

"Well, I was still at Georgetown. I graduated with a degree in Computer Science. I got a job with a computer company in California. But I've been with another firm in Boston the last couple of years, and I've been in D.C. the past six months working on special projects for the government."

That didn't exactly answer her question, but she accepted the response for now. She remembered having a date with him to go to a jazz club one night, and she sort of remembered getting quite drunk, but she couldn't recall how she got back to her room. She just knew that she never saw Paul again after that night, until now.

"I understand you work for the government, too," Paul said.

"Yes, I'm a Congressional Aide, if you can believe it," she said. "For Representative Marilyn Connors of Virginia. It really is kind of exciting, if you're into law and politics."

"No, I can't say that they are among my strong suits."

As Paul walked her back home, they talked more about their jobs. Paul was a computer programmer who mostly worked on programming tiny computer brains which were used to help large machinery run more efficiently. He spoke of chips and bits, bytes and megabytes, uploads and downloads, disks and drives, bugs and viruses. Most of it went over Jennifer's noggin, but she marveled at his level of expertise and his enthusiasm for his life's work. Back when she knew him, they both just were trying to find and define themselves. Jennifer started to remember how she cherished that time of discovery in her first two years of college. It seemed so long ago now, as if it were a different world entirely. And it was. Back then, everyone was in a different frame of reference. Jennifer recalled getting ready to go out with her girlfriends on Friday and Saturday nights, fixing hair, putting on make-up and perfume, fighting for mirror space, all in hopes of meeting that special guy later in the evening. While still other friends were preparing for weddings. She remembered how fun it actually was to look through bridal magazines with her engaged friends, fantasizing about the perfect dress, talking about rings, houses, babies. Now, there was absolutely none of that.

Seeing Paul again made Jennifer realize that she did miss those things—she did want to find the right man, settle down and have a baby. She almost couldn't believe the thoughts she was having again. It was as if they were coming out of hiding. Jennifer looked at Paul and wondered what would've happened if they had stayed together. Would they have gotten married? Would they have run off to Canada after President Thompson's election? She felt she could have, but their relationship had ended so abruptly. At first, she just wondered what happened. She waited for him to call, but he didn't. She tried to call him, but she found out from his roommate Tom that he had moved, though he didn't know where. After a while, she got a little mad and tried to put him out of her mind. She started going out with other guys. But Paul kept creeping back into her thoughts. There were no other guys like him, she thought. Seeing Paul again made Jennifer realize just how much she had missed him.

He still retained a boyish face and his piercing blue eyes. The only hardening effect that she noticed age had on him was his firmer chin. Otherwise, his features remained soft and youthful. Despite doing mostly brainwork, he still looked trim and fit. Most of all, Jennifer thought, the same aura of gentleness still pervaded his personality.

Jennifer didn't know how it happened, but it looked as if she were getting a second chance, although, she would have to be satisfied with just being friends now, if he wanted to be. She was still mad about being ordered to stop being friends with Richard. She wasn't in the military now, and Paul was really someone she wanted to be friends with. She could use a link to the past. If someone told her she couldn't, she would just have to raise the biggest ruckus she knew how. Friendship, as far as she knew, was not illegal.

"You know what we should do?" Jennifer said when they reached her apartment building.

"What?"

"We should play chess sometime."

"That sounds like a wonderful idea," Paul said. "I haven't played in quite a while."

"Me either. Remember those afternoons we used to play chess on the quad?"

"I sure do—fondly. I really enjoyed those times," Paul said a bit sheepishly. Jennifer thought he might be ready to blush.

"I just thought it would be nice to sort of relive a piece of our youth. I feel like I've already done a little of that, just seeing you again."

"Yes, yes, I agree. What do you say if we meet in Lafayette Square for a game of chess Sunday afternoon?"

"That would be wonderful. What time?"

"How about two o'clock?"

"Okay, I'll see you then. Listen, I'm glad that I bumped into you again after all these years. Just promise not to disappear again, okay?" Jennifer smiled at him.

"That's a promise." Paul smiled in return, and he paused, as if to say something else, but then changed his mind. He did say, "Bye now, I'll see you Sunday." With that he turned and walked back down the street.

Jennifer went upstairs to her apartment, cooked supper for herself, read the newspaper and watched some television. But, all the while, she thought about Paul and their chess 'date' on Sunday. Even when she went back to work the next two days, she couldn't stop thinking about him. Not too many times do people get second chances in life, she thought. Saturday was the worst day, however, because she had nothing to do except think about him. When Sunday finally came, Jennifer was relieved, but thrilled at the thought of seeing Paul again.

In the back of her mind, though, Jennifer wondered if he would show up at all, but he quickly set her mind at ease when she saw him standing by the chess tables. She joyfully greeted Paul, but resisted her natural urge to hug or kiss him. He also resisted. They picked an unoccupied cement table with a chessboard painted on top. Jennifer hadn't even thought of it, but Paul brought the pieces and set them in their proper places.

"Now, take it easy on me," Jennifer said as she settled in her seat. "I don't quite remember, but the last time I played chess could have been the last time I played you."

"Then I guess you don't want to hear that I helped program a chess computer once."

"You're right. I don't."

"Not to worry, though. My part in the project was definitely not my chess expertise, but my computer expertise. I did join a chess club when I was in California, but I couldn't keep up with it for too long, with my work. So we should be starting on fairly equal footing."

"Okay, let's get started. Let the pawns be damned."

Jennifer began with her most familiar Pawn-to-Q-Four. Paul followed suit, setting up a Q's Gambit Declined. (The terms 'King' and 'Queen' had been banished in American chess. While the origins of the pieces had gender, they were simply referred to as the 'K'-piece and the 'Q'-piece.)

It was a beautiful summer day, comfortably warm with a breeze gently tousling the greenery in the park. Lafayette Square was a quaint place to play chess, despite the distractions of the crowd. For now, Jennifer thought, the crowd was a bit of a necessity. The biggest distraction for her, however, was playing in the shadow of the White House.

By looking over Paul's shoulder, Jennifer looked directly at the north face of the White House. And, while looking at it, she couldn't help thinking of the person who resided there—President Thompson. She had to wonder if Big Sister was in there right then, perhaps even glancing out the window in Jennifer's direction, by coincidence.

'How did she get everybody to go along with her cockeyed plan? Why did everyone just accept her unorthodox proclamations, especially the women?' she wondered. Of course, it had been so simple. Big Sister had just given them what they had been asking for all along. Men didn't have to endure the burden and the hardships of childbirth, and, to be truly equal, women had to be freed from that burden, too.

"Paul, do you have any female friends?"

"Uh, I never really thought about it before, but I guess not. Not really. I mean, I work with some women, but I never see them after work. I share a house in Takoma Park now with three male roommates, and only one I consider a close friend. I just kind of tend to myself anyway. I don't meet a lot of people. And my work keeps me really busy."

"I'd like to be your friend, Paul."

"I'd like that, too. I guess there's nothing wrong with that."

"You said it." They continued to play at a leisurely pace while soaking up the sun and the atmosphere. But Jennifer also wanted to know more about Paul and how he felt about 'things'.

"How are your parents?" Jennifer asked the loaded question.

"M-my parents?" Paul looked a little surprised.

"Yeah. How are your parents doing? In a way, we've only known each other for a short time. I think you only mentioned them once before. They lived in Harrisburg, right?"

"Right."

"Well, I just wanted to know how they've been the past ten years," Jennifer pressed. "Were they um—separated last year?"

"Well, Bob, that's my father, died in Oh-Nine from a heart attack."

"Gee, I'm sorry to hear that."

"So, no, they weren't separated by the order. Sylvia, my mother, still lives in Harrisburg, and she's doing fine. I think she's getting tired of the winters, though. She's been talking about moving to Florida. I think she doesn't like keeping up the big house for just one person anymore."

"Did they—love each other? I really want to know, so I need you to be honest with me, Paul. If they would've been forced to separate, would they have fought it or maybe run away together?"

"Yes, they did love each other very much. In a way, I'm glad that my dad—" Paul swallowed hard on the old phrase as he remembered his father with emotion, "—didn't have to go through that. He loved my mother and this country dearly. It would've been so tough on him. I don't really know what he would've done. But I've heard some sad stories. I'm all for a fair and equitable society, but that order didn't seem very fair to me. It must've hurt a lot of people."

"I know what you mean. I feel the same way. I had a hard time justifying it myself. Did you vote for President Thompson?"

"Yes. I thought she was the right person at the right time, but now I'm not so sure. She seemed to be saying what everyone wanted to hear, but now—"

"Now everything seems a little out of whack, askew?"

"Right. The goals are admirable, but who's to say the means will even achieve the desired ends. It seems that—well, listen, I don't want to sound old-fashioned, but I don't know much about what women want. I guess it's not really my place to say."

"No, no. It is." Jennifer reassured him. "I happen to agree with what you're saying."

"Why all the questions, anyway?" Paul asked, only out of curiosity, not suspicion.

"Well, because I've noticed that a lot of things don't even get talked about anymore. I don't want that to happen to us. I want us to be able to talk about anything we want to with each other. Okay?"

"Okay. That suits me. Then I hope you don't mind me asking, what happened to your parents?"

"Sad to say that, over the last few years of their marriage, not only did they not love each other very much, but they didn't really *like* each other that much. They separated on their own."

"I hope you understand what I mean when I say I'm glad."

"I do, and me, too." Jennifer smiled.

As the chess game went along, Jennifer made a few early mistakes, but played on, hoping to catch Paul in a mistake of his own. She capitalized on one, but it wasn't enough to win.

"Thanks, Paul."

"For what?"

"Thanks for the game. I really enjoyed it."

"So did I. It was such a nice day for it, too."

"Now remember, I get a rematch."

"But, of course, Jennifer, of course. What do you say about next Saturday—same time, same place?"

"I got a better place in mind. How about we go down to the Georgetown campus? It'll be like old times. We can play at our old spot overlooking the Potomac, and afterward, we can walk around the campus and reminisce about old memories, old teachers, old classes, whatever. What do you think?"

"I think you're a genius, Jennifer. That would be perfect. I'm just sorry I didn't think of it first. You got a deal." Paul and Jennifer bubbled with excitement and anticipation. Paul collected his pieces in a little pouch. "I can't wait until next week. Now work isn't the only thing I have to look forward to anymore. Thanks."

"It'll be fun. I'll see you next week." Jennifer put a comforting hand on Paul's shoulder. With two feet of space between them, it was the closest they could come to hugging in public.

"Bye, Jennifer."

As Paul walked away, Jennifer just remembered that she had to go out of town during the week. But she thought she would be back in time to meet him again.

Jennifer had to accompany Marilyn on a home district visit to Petersburg, Virginia. Marilyn was up for reelection in the fall, but she had no competition. She did a little campaigning anyway, just to keep her visibility up, and she needed to spend a certain amount of time each year in her home district.

Leaving D.C. didn't stop Jennifer from thinking constantly of Paul and their next 'date'. That was the way she liked to think about it—her date— and it excited her. Their meetings were thrilling for her, and yet there was really no risk involved, she thought. But she also didn't talk about it with anyone, just in case.

Jennifer lived full-time in Washington. She gave up the idea of trying to keep an apartment in Petersburg. Whenever they made home district visits, Jennifer stayed in a guest room in Marilyn's house, as did Carmen. Her official residence needed to be used for something. Stan always stayed at the same motel, which always kept a vacancy just for him. Marilyn enjoyed their little trips. Without admitting it, she played the mother role to Jennifer and Carmen when they were in town. Marilyn always cooked the evening meal, and made sure the rooms were comfortable for her 'daughters'.

After Wednesday night's meal, Jennifer helped clear the table and load the dishwasher. She didn't realize that she was acting any differently, but Marilyn noticed a change.

"What's the matter, Jennifer?" Marilyn asked her as she handed rinsed dishes to Jennifer to load. "You seemed so quiet at dinner."

"Uh, nothing. That was a very good meal, Marilyn," she said trying to swing the conversation away from her. But it didn't work.

"Thank you. I mean it, though. You seemed to be inattentive in our meetings this week. Not that I'm complaining about your work, because you're doing a fine job. Are you feeling okay? Maybe you're coming down with something."

"No, I feel fine," she said, loading the last dish. She poured the soap crystals in, closed the door and switched it on. Over the noise, she said, "We'll be heading back to D.C. on Saturday, right?"

"Bright and early Saturday morning. Is that it? Oh, I know you hate these trips, but don't worry. Only two more days."

"I don't really hate them, but I guess everybody's a little more comfortable in their own place." With that, Marilyn seemed to understand and let it be. But Jennifer had to be careful. Her thoughts were safe, but if they were constantly occupied with Paul, it wouldn't leave any room for much else, and she wouldn't act naturally, meaning people were bound to notice a difference. The best thing was to avoid any probing questions.

Once back in Washington, Jennifer felt more at ease because she was left to herself, away from the people who could notice anything peculiar in her behavior. She was excited about seeing Paul again, and that was 'peculiar behavior'. Jennifer didn't see too many people excited anymore.

When the clock finally rolled around to one o'clock, Jennifer walked to Georgetown, passing the Washington Monument, the Jefferson and Lincoln memorials, and the spot marked as the future site of the Thompson Memorial. She wound her way through crowds of tourists, but noticed that they weren't quite as big as they used to be just a few years back when she was in college. People weren't excited about their country anymore, she wondered? Maybe. But there were no kids! Yes, that was it. So much had changed in a short time, but it was hard to notice the difference right off. There were no teachers frantically trying to keep their students from getting lost on field trips. There were no families taking tours of the museums, the monuments and the government buildings. Was a whole generation lost? She shuddered at the thought and quickly moved on.

Paul was early again, this time sitting on the steps of the Georgetown

Cathedral. He sat motionless in waiting, but when he saw Jennifer, Paul stood up, smiled and lit up like a friendly beacon enticing her to pull into his safe port.

"Hi, Paul. It's nice to see you again."

"Hello, Jennifer. Are you ready?"

"Sure thing."

They walked over to the battlefield, so to speak, almost in silence. That was okay with Jennifer. She thought, 'He's just the way he was back then, a little awkward, a little shy', and, he already had made her feel ten years younger.

Jennifer spread out a blanket on the same grassy knoll where they had played years before. Two mighty oaks stood atop the hill and provided generous cool shade. Paul set up the board and the pieces as the stately Potomac quietly ambled by in the distance.

"I think I'm ready for you this time," Jennifer said. "I studied, and just because I like you doesn't mean I'm going to go easy on you."

Paul seemed to blush at the comment, '*I like you.*' "We'll see. We'll see," he said.

Maybe, as part of the nostalgic mood, they opted for the venerable Ruy Lopez, a true classic opening. The two forces sitting on opposing sides of the board conjured up images of the Maine wilderness in Jennifer's mind. One squad against another squad, representing one country's colors against another country's colors. Sometimes you can move into enemy territory without being captured, as she did. But, eventually, someone *does* get captured. And there's usually retaliation. Then it escalates until checkmate. Finality. But wait. Don't forget about stalemate or draw. One or two pieces remain on the board for each side with no advantage to either, similar to their position at the start, but with a whole squad sacrificed for nothing.

"Have you served in the Guard yet, Paul?"

"No. I'm scheduled to go in November, though."

"Oooh, that's got to be the worst time. No matter where you end up, it'll be up north."

"I haven't really thought about it much because I know I'm not going to like it. I know I'm not an aggressive person. I don't even like the idea of fighting. But I'm willing to serve my country if they need me. It's just, I'm not sure they really need me. It all seems a little ludicrous, if you ask me. Even that incident that you were involved in, they made it sound like an all-out invasion. But how come they haven't sent anyone else yet? I keep hearing it that it could be any day now, but it seems like it could have all been just a small misunderstanding."

"That's exactly what I think." Jennifer told him all her feelings of that incident and of her experiences in boot camp. She finally got a chance to express her thoughts about the whole debacle. He really understood what was going on, she thought. She wasn't the only one.

Jennifer eventually won the chess game by making the fewest mistakes. It wasn't pretty, but neither of them cared about the outcome.

"Let's take a walk around the campus," Jennifer suggested.

"Okay."

Gothic architecture dominated the campus, especially the cathedral and the administration building, the dormitories to a lesser extent, and some of the older college buildings. Some obviously newer structures tried in vain to capture the old world charm that seemingly only age could produce.

"Did you ever have Professor Shipley?" Jennifer reminisced.

"Yes, I did. The Brit who still thought he was in London."

"That's the guy. He used to walk the campus like clockwork with a cane in one hand and an umbrella dangling off the other."

"Yeah, and you could set your watch by him, depending on where you saw him campus." They both laughed at the thought-to-be-lost memory.

"Remember Sheila and Tom?" Jennifer conjured again.

"Sure. They introduced us. Whatever happened to them? Did they end up getting married?"

"No, no. It's a long story, but, basically, Tom got Sheila pregnant in her sophomore year, and she ended up getting an abortion. Their relationship was pretty messy after that, and they broke up." Jennifer kind of shocked herself by nonchalantly and openly talking about sex like that. But it was the way she would have back then. There still was no better way to say it. Definitely not, she got 'p', so she had to get an 'a'. Or something like that. By omission, Paul would have guessed at the meaning anyway. So why bother? Just tell it like it is. And it also exhilarated her.

"That's too bad. They were a cute couple," Paul said.

Even that phrase, 'cute couple,' sounded foreign. Jennifer didn't know anyone else who would have cause to say it. This was getting more and more fun, she thought.

A rumbling of thunder caught both their attentions. Jennifer looked back over her shoulder and saw that a rainmaker had crept up on them and now hung almost directly overhead.

"We'd better get going," Paul said.

"Look, there's my old dorm building, Gregor Hall." Jennifer went over for a closer look. She looked up to the second story and tried to remember her old room. "That must be the one. They look like they're all empty. They must be getting the new crop next weekend." She just realized that the 'new crop' would be the first harvest of high school students who'd been in government care for the past year. They probably wouldn't be too much different from her in her frosh year, but it could be just the beginning of a radical change. Who knew how these experimental androgynes would turn out?

A few raindrops fell onto their heads as they looked up at the dorm.

"Shit. I have to walk home," Jennifer said. She didn't know if Paul had a car, but she knew he couldn't take her home anyway. "Come on, let's duck into the archway until the rain stops."

They did so as the water pelted down harder. They pressed their backs against the door as they tried to keep from getting soaked. Jennifer leaned back and hit the latch. She stumbled a bit as the door gave way.

"Look, the door's open. Why don't we wait inside?" Jennifer suggested because they were still being splashed by the rain in the archway.

"I wonder why it was left open," Paul said as he stepped inside and wiped the excess water off his face.

"Who cares? It's dry in here."

"It looks deserted. It doesn't look like there are even any summer students here."

Jennifer smelled fresh paint and spied a couple of work ladders and a paint-splattered blue tarpaulin in the main hallway. "They must have moved everybody out for renovations. But this sure does bring back old memories. Hey, since we're here, let's go up and see my old room."

"I don't know. Maybe we sh—" Paul tried to say, but before he could finish, Jennifer bounded up the stairs. He followed a little hesitantly. When Paul found Jennifer, she had found her old room.

"Well, here it is. Isn't it great?" Jennifer smiled and bubbled with pride.

"It looks a lot like the one I had in Sanderson Hall."

"I know they all kind of look alike, but this is where I spent two years of my life." Jennifer pointed to the blank walls and spaces and filled them with the stockpile in her memory. "My desk was here, right under my Stevie Appleton poster. I had a stuffed Tweety Bird doll on my dresser over here, with lots of make-up, hair brushes and stuff like that. And, of course, my Hoya blanket on my bed."

"I know, I know," Paul said.

All sorts of memories flashed back in Jennifer's mind about the room, but that wasn't one of them. "When were you ever up here, Paul? I remember seeing you in your room, but I don't remember you ever coming up here."

"Well, it was the night of our *date*," Paul said. "You were, uh, kind of drunk that night, and I helped you up the stairs."

"I do remember getting drunk, but I don't remember that. I must have been wasted. Thanks for seeing me home safely."

"No problem." Paul was relieved that she didn't remember.

"You know, I've had so much fun seeing you again that I almost feel like it's 2005 again."

"Me, too," Paul said wistfully.

"But I have to ask you something. I've been afraid to say something before because I thought it might ruin the chance for all the good times we had over the past week. But I have to know something."

"What is it?"

"Sit down with me, Paul." Jennifer sat him down on the bare mattress of the bed. She placed a gentle hand on top of his hand. He didn't seem to mind. "About our date. You know, that was the last time I saw you until just last week. What happened to you? I tried to call you, but I couldn't find you. I just need to know why you never called me again. Was it because you saw me so drunk?"

"No, no. It wasn't because of that, really. It wasn't because of you. It was all me. Um. I—ahem. This is going to be hard to explain." Paul was nervous as memories of that night flooded back to his mind. A side effect of the memories and a growing cause for his nervousness and discomfort was the fact that he sported an intense erection. He only could hope that Jennifer wouldn't notice.

"Did I do something really terrible? Did I say something obnoxious?"

"No, no. You know, I sort of put it out of my mind, I guess, because when I saw you again, I thought that we just lost touch somehow, and I didn't know how. But now I remember it all so clearly," Paul said.

"My God, what happened that night? I don't remember much of anything."

"Well, when I brought you home and helped you up to your room here, you, uh, came on to me, and I didn't know what to do. I knew you were drunk, and I didn't want to take advantage of you. It could've been just the alcohol talking. Well, anyway, when you passed out, I just left. I swear I didn't do anything to you."

When Jennifer finally realized what had happened that night, she thought, 'Wow, what alcohol can do to your inhibitions!' "But why didn't you call me the next day? Did you think I was a real jerk and not want anything to do with me?"

"No, of course not. I thought you would think that I was the jerk."

"But why would you think that?"

"Well, I didn't know how much you would remember. I thought that you would wake up the next day naked and figure that I must have taken advantage of you, and you wouldn't want to see me again."

"But you didn't do anything, right?"

"Right. Honestly."

"I believe you. And I would've believed you then. I knew you weren't the type of guy who would take advantage of women. That's why I loved you so much. You were the sweetest, gentlest man I knew."

"You loved me?"

"Yes, honestly. I had a big crush on you, and I thought I had let you know it, but I know I didn't come out and say it. I guess the alcohol just broke down all my inhibitions because I really did want to make love to you."

"You did?" Paul swallowed hard.

"Yes," Jennifer said with a smile and a gleam in her eye. "But, in a way, I'm glad it wasn't that night."

"I have to tell you, Jennifer, that I loved you, too."

"You did?"

"And I wanted to make love to you, too. I guess I never was very good at expressing my feelings. Talk about lost opportunities. I thought you must've hated me."

"And I thought you hated me."

"Then all that was just a misunderstanding? Just think of all the time we missed that we could've been together."

"Maybe it was all for the better. Just think if we would've gotten married. I couldn't imagine what it would've been like if they took you away from me, or took our children away."

"We could've left."

"Yeah, I guess we could have." For a moment, Jennifer thought she was talking about their actual past, that they did marry and they got separated. Because that's what it felt like to her now. They *were* separated unjustly and painfully.

"Maybe all our opportunities aren't lost. Since we're here again in the same room, we can take care of one," Jennifer said. "You know you forgot to do something the night of our date."

"What do you mean?"

"You forgot to kiss me goodnight at the end of our date. You could kiss me goodnight right now to make up for that oversight."

"I guess that's only fair. It's just like we're taking care of unfinished business."

"Right. "

Paul started slowly. He slid over closer to Jennifer. Then he put his hands on her shoulders. He said, "Goodnight, Jennifer. I had a great time. We'll have to do it again sometime. I'll call you tomorrow."

"Okay. Goodnight, Paul." Jennifer moved her head closer to Paul's. Paul also moved at the same time, and their lips collided in the middle. Jennifer's tongue parted his lips and searched for his tongue. Upon meeting, they intertwined. Soon their faces, their bodies and their hearts were locked together. With a nine-year interlude, they each had an unquenchable thirst for each other. They tossed and turned their heads, trying to find the optimum position to drink in enough of each other. They grunted and groaned. They pushed and pulled. They wrestled and sweated. They rolled over onto the bed. Because her lips couldn't quite consume enough of Paul fast enough for her desire, her hands moved to take in every part of his body. Following her lead, he did the same. Jennifer felt Paul's hard-on through his trousers, and he moaned his approval. Paul felt her breasts through her shirt. In an attempt to get a better hold of him, Jennifer found Paul's zipper and took it down for the count. She unbuttoned him and then reached down inside. For the first time in ages, she felt the warm, spongy flesh on top, the almost bony shaft in the middle and the fuzzy spheroids below. At the same time, Paul found his way underneath Jennifer's shirt and he felt her warm, gel-like flesh on the outside and the stiff, supple nipple in the center. They broke from their kiss and panted for air. They remained in frenetic motion, however, as they undressed each other without speaking. When Paul saw Jennifer's naked form for the second time, he thought it matched perfectly with the mental picture emblazoned in his memory. A light flashed outside the window, and the sharp crack of thunder pealed almost simultaneously. Instinctively, they jumped into each other's arms. When they made love, they wrestled and rolled in an attempt to sexually devour the other. And, it was as if they made love in zero gravity. They wore both on top, and yet neither was on top. Paul shuddered as he ejaculated inside of her, and then he continued to pump voraciously partly because he wasn't quenched. And partly because Jennifer wouldn't let him go. Then it happened for Jennifer. She finally had an orgasm through intercourse, and she collapsed in ecstasy. But she didn't have much time to savor the moment.

When they got a chance to catch their-breaths and their thoughts, they realized what they had done and had to come back to the present as quickly as possible.

"You know, of course, that this is the only time we'll ever do this," Jennifer said as she dressed, but with a look of satisfaction in her eyes despite her admonition.

"I know. I can't believe what I did. I raped you." Paul felt more shock now than pleasure.

"You did not rape me, no matter what anyone else says. I consented. We're in this together. We may have made the biggest mistake in our lives, but I don't regret it. Do you?"

"No, of course not. But, what if someone finds out?"

"We just have to make sure that no one finds out."

"But how do we do that? Do you realize what they could do to us?" Paul raved on. There was silence as they both paused to conceptualize the barbaric punishments mandated for their seemingly benign actions. They were chilled by the thought.

"Yes, I realize what they *could* do, but I don't plan on letting either one of us be deformed for life over an act of love. We'll run away together if we have to," Jennifer said. Then she thought what it would be like getting arrested, and certainly, being separated. "And if we can't do that, we still get due process in this country. How would they be able to prove that we did anything?"

"Video tape," Paul said succinctly. "The government has the technology right now. I know because I'm working on it for them. I just don't know how widespread it is."

"What are you talking about, Paul?"

"Have you ever heard of fiberoptic cameras?"

"Sure, like endoscopes and arthroscopes."

"Exactly. But, for the past six months, I've been working on perfecting the operating software of a system already in use for international spying. I'm talking about video cameras that can be hidden just about anywhere because the lens is as small as a single fiber of glass, thin as a human hair. And the fiber can also be any length. So a camera could be anywhere. This could be a camera," Paul said as he reached down to the floor to pick up a hair. "Well, it's actually a hair, but do you understand what I'm saying? It could've been. It could've recorded everything that went on in this room."

"I understand, but the government couldn't possibly have every room in the country hooked up to television cameras. The logistics would be phenomenal." Jennifer tried to assuage her own fears as well as Paul's. "The threat is the deterrent. You know, Big Sister is watching you, and all that crap. But they couldn't possibly watch everybody. You know, we were weak once, like I'm sure a lot of other people have been. We just have to be strong and make sure it never happens again."

"So, what do we do now?"

"I think the best thing is to not act suspiciously. We just go on with our lives as before. We don't do anything out of the ordinary."

"What about seeing each other again?" Paul pressed her.

"Well, we established a routine of meeting each other for a friendly game of chess. That's innocent enough, and explainable. We just have to settle for that kind of relationship. As a matter of fact, to show that there's nothing out of the ordinary going on, we should come out here again tomorrow to play another game."

"If you think so. I'll go along with that. I just don't want my thoughtless actions to jeopardize you in any way."

"Just don't worry," Jennifer reassured him. "Nobody's to blame. It just happened. And I'm glad it happened. We just have to be more careful."

"Okay, we'll meet tomorrow at the cathedral like we did today."

"Yep. And only play chess, like we did today."

"Right," Paul said.

They traveled home separately, and the next day, they journeyed back to Georgetown separately. While keeping a decorous distance between themselves at all times, they walked to the hill. They played a perfectly innocent game of chess, as planned. It would've been a flawless plan, however, if they had not been mystically drawn back to Jennifer's old dorm room by long dormant (and now erupting) biological urges. They couldn't even rationally explain why they walked in that direction after the game, why, upon seeing the building again they walked closer, why they checked if the door was locked, and why they entered and went directly to the same room, knowing full well the consequences. Of course, once there (they couldn't avoid it now) they made passionate yet unlawful love, fast and furiously, for the second time in two days, this time as if their world might actually end the next day. In fact, they planned on it.

CHAPTER SEVEN

The world didn't come to an end, and, in fact, both their lives returned to the monotonous, uneventful routines which they had grown accustomed to. Jennifer hadn't seen Paul in the four weeks following the electrical reunion of their souls. She didn't trust herself anymore. Paul was upset when she told him that they shouldn't see each other for a while, but he knew it was for the best. Apparently, they hadn't been detected, and there were no repercussions for their indiscretions, but it didn't make sense to keep tempting fate. They couldn't take any more risks like that in the future. They both knew their luck was bound to run out.

Paul immersed himself in his work, as he usually did when he wanted to forget emotional troubles and worries.

Jennifer, on the other hand, had an excess of free time due to a Congressional recess for summer vacations. She did spend an extra-long Labor Day weekend in Virginia Beach to visit her mother. The time away from Washington not only gave her a chance to relax, but also a chance to renew a relationship with a person who had been so dear to her. She tried to get to know her mother all over again and to take advantage of the relatively short time that they had together. Especially in recent months, Jennifer had missed her mother more and more, despite the legal dissolution of familial connection.

And when she was leaving to return to Washington, Jennifer hugged her mother deeply and with conviction in disdain of all eyes, and cameras, which may have been watching. The thought in her mind at the time was really a message to all unwelcome peepers. 'I'm hugging my mother goodbye. If you don't like it, you can just kiss my sweet ass.'

Once the session reopened at the Capitol, Jennifer also wrapped herself in her heavy workload. She still thought about Paul and wanted to call him, but she resisted. Things were going smoothly, she thought. There's no use risking chaos.

But the fabric of her security blanket started to slowly unravel, and the clock of the biological time bomb inexorably had begun to tick.

There were clues along the way, but she either dismissed them or explained them away with faulty rationale. At the beginning of the week, Marilyn took her aides out to a big dinner to celebrate the passage of a law she had drafted. Jennifer ate a lot of spicy food, and that night after she got home, she became violently ill and vomited up the entire meal. She thought it was something she ate, a disagreeable spice, or bad meat perhaps.

The next day at work, she was standing on a ladder replacing books in the law library as Stan handed her the volumes. She became lightheaded and dizzy. Jennifer lost her balance and fell off the ladder. Luckily for her, Stan was able to catch her, and she escaped injury.

"Are you all right?" Stan asked her after he quickly set her down on the floor. He didn't want to touch her for too long, although he was proud that he was able to save her.

"Yes, yes," Jennifer said as her head started to clear. "I guess I reached out too far, and I lost my balance."

"Maybe I should put the rest of the books up," Stan said.

"Yes, that would be a good idea."

Every morning that week, Jennifer's limbs were heavy and weak, and she had to drag herself out of bed each time. On Wednesday, she simply skipped her September donation appointment, partly because of the way she felt, but certainly not as part of any protest. However, Jennifer feared that, somehow, the doctor would be able to detect that she had participated in sexual intercourse recently. Possibly there were tiny abrasions, she reasoned. Then on Friday morning right after breakfast, she upchucked again. 'Maybe I'm coming down with something', she thought. Then another thought occurred to her. It had been six weeks since her last menstrual flow. 'It couldn't be that', she thought. If she were sick, that could've caused the delay. She remembered being a week late before, but she couldn't recall ever being two weeks late, and she always had been fairly regular. Jennifer thought back: 'Six weeks ago was August 2nd, and I slept with Paul on the 20th and the 21st. Oh no! It could be. But, wait. They took my egg before that, the egg that was set to be released that month. Only one egg is released each month. So I can't possibly be p-r-e-g-n-a-n-t. Unless, somehow, two were set to be released that month.'

Jennifer didn't know what to do. There was no way to be sure. She couldn't go to a doctor to have the test to confirm or deny her suspicions because they would be forced to report it. And she couldn't just do nothing and let her abdomen expand, which would be like wearing a neon sign blinking to the world, 'I fucked up,' or like wearing a scarlet 'I' for intercourse. It might be all in her imagination. But, even if she wasn't sure now, she could wait a few more days at least, a week maybe. And if her period still didn't come, she could be reasonably sure.

She had to talk to Paul.

First, there was one more day of work, and then she would try to see him that weekend. She dreaded going to work that day, but she didn't want to do anything out of the ordinary. Jennifer ached all over. Even each strand of hair on her head seemed to be in pain, dry and brittle enough to break off at any time. When Jennifer walked into the office, she tried to appear pleasant and normal. But she couldn't touch her morning coffee. Suddenly, the smell nauseated her. She worked by herself at her desk for most of the morning, and then went to a staff meeting at eleven o'clock. Jennifer thought she was getting better, but by eleven, she felt weak from not having any of her breakfast left in her stomach.

Marilyn was discussing some details of an upcoming subcommittee meeting when she stopped suddenly.

"Jennifer, dear," Marilyn said, slipping into that motherly tone, "you look as white as a ghost. Are you all right?"

"Yes," Jennifer answered timidly. "I think so." Her co-workers' eyes were now focused on her. The room started spinning and her nausea returned. "Uh, I'm sorry. May I be excused?" she said to Marilyn as she stood up, turned and ran to the washroom with her hand over her mouth. The washroom was adjacent to Marilyn's private office, which sat opposite the conference room. Marilyn, Stan and Carmen could still hear Jennifer's dry heaves.

When Jennifer returned to the conference room, they looked to her, but tried not to stare.

"I'm sorry for the interruption," Jennifer apologized. "I wasn't feeling well this morning, but I thought I'd be okay for work. I think I'm coming down with the flu or something."

"Have you been to a doctor?" Marilyn asked, still showing her concern.

"No. I don't really think it's that serious."

"Would you like to go see my doctor? She's really nice, and I'm sure she could fit you in if I tell her you're a friend of mine," Marilyn offered.

"No, no!" The last thing she wanted was to see a doctor, but especially her doctor. If she did a urinalysis and ordered the right test, she might discover her suspected condition. "If it's okay with you, I'd like to take the afternoon off. Since it's the weekend, I'll just jump into bed, bundle up and try to sweat out the virus. And I should be refreshed and ready to come back to work Monday morning."

"Sure, sure. Go on home. Take care of yourself," Marilyn said. "You probably know what's best for you."

"Thank you very much," Jennifer replied. She just hoped Marilyn didn't already suspect something.

Jennifer walked home slowly, thoughts of different case scenarios filling her head almost with each labored step. When she got back to her apartment, she crawled into bed and napped the rest of the afternoon, partly to rest physically, and partly to temporarily stop the thinking process.

And when she woke at 4:30, her first new thought was Paul. She had to talk to him as soon as possible, but she couldn't call him at work. Personal phone calls from a woman might be hard for him to explain. So she would have to wait until he got home. Paul actually worked in Bethesda and lived in Takoma Park, Maryland, both just outside the District limits. But, with D.C. area rush hour traffic, it could take him an hour or more.

While Jennifer waited for the time to pass, she cooked a supper for herself. After her nap, she felt refreshed and hungry. The nausea had completely ceased, leaving her only with a hollow stomach waiting to be filled. She ravenously ate to her stomach's content, happy that she seemingly functioned normally again. But she still wasn't sure what to make of it. She didn't know if the bug had just passed, or if this, in fact, confirmed her worst fear, that it was the morning sickness that comes and goes.

After she collected her thoughts, Jennifer called Paul. She was a bit startled when she didn't recognize the voice that answered the phone. Then she thought, just one of Paul's roommates.

"Uh, hello. May I speak to Paul, please?"

"Yeah, sure," the voice answered her, and after a brief delay, she heard the sweet, familiar voice of Paul.

"Hello?"

"Hi, Paul."

"Why, Jennifer. It's so nice to hear from you."

"I need to talk to you right away, Paul. It's extremely urgent."

"Of course, go right ahead."

"No, I can't on the phone. Could you come over right away to talk to me?"

"Are you all right? You sound upset?"

"Meet me and I'll explain everything. Can you meet me in Lincoln Park in an hour? In front of the monument."

"Yes, of course. I'll be there."

"Thank you, Paul. Bye."

"Bye."

Even though she didn't say anything, Jennifer knew that even that call was very risky. If anyone were listening, that person would know that she was meeting a man, and could then arrange surveillance and still find out the big secret. But Jennifer had to risk that because she couldn't wait any longer to discuss the situation. And Paul was a big part of it. He had the right to know her suspicions as soon as possible.

Jennifer waited calmly for 45 minutes, and then she had to get out of the apartment. Even if she were early, she needed to walk around a bit.

The crisp, September evening air refreshed her for a moment. The air also was amazingly calm and clear. Not only were there no clouds in the sky, but the lights, which were being turned on in the fading dusk, sparkled with astounding clarity.

There was little pedestrian traffic on the sidewalk outside her building. So, at the sound of footsteps behind her, she instinctively turned to see a figure in the darkness. From her quick glance, Jennifer saw a man bundled up excessively in an overcoat and a cold weather cap with ear flaps and a bill that kept his face in shadow. While the weather was cool, it was not freezing, and so it struck her as odd. And she assumed that it was a man, from the person's height and build. The government had not yet done anything about the difference in the average height of men and women. 'Could they do anything, and would they do anything?' Jennifer thought and then shuddered.

When Jennifer crossed the street to the park, she quickly glanced back again, and the shadowy figure followed. At first, she didn't want to be paranoid, but she also didn't want to be naive in thinking that she wouldn't be followed.

Jennifer continued into the park, stopping at the ERA monument. The man strolled slowly behind her, as if also admiring the monument. Jennifer suddenly recalled years before, how dangerous the park was for young women to be alone, even at this hour of the night because of the threat of rape. But the problem supposedly was taken care of. But just because she didn't hear about it anymore, did it mean it wasn't happening now?

Just as Jennifer's pulse raced with fear, the man passed her and was soon out of sight. Jennifer sighed with relief, then felt pure joy as she spotted Paul's familiar figure approaching. They did not embrace, despite their surging desire, and they barely glanced at each other, as they both stood in front of the ERA monument.

"Let's walk," Jennifer suggested, and they strolled casually in the opposite direction of the mystery man.

"What's up?" Paul asked, not hiding well his anxiety about the unknown problem.

"I don't know how to tell you this—" Jennifer paused, glancing skyward, seemingly searching for divine assistance. "But I think I may be pregnant," she continued in hushed tones, the last word in a soft whisper. And although the word was barely audible to Paul, he immediately understood it and its companion ramifications.

"Are you sure?" he asked.

"No, I'm not. There's really no way I can be without going to a doctor," Jennifer replied. "And you know I can't do that. It's just that I have the symptoms, and I'm two weeks late. I've never been that late before."

"Wow! From my understanding of the process, there are so many obstacles to actual conception that the odds are almost astronomical for it to happen after only one or two times."

"But it can happen after just one time. That's not the important thing right now." Jennifer's voice showed her desperation.

Now Paul looked directly at Jennifer. "Well, what are we going to do now?"

Jennifer felt her heart glow when Paul said 'we.'

"I want to leave," she said. "You know we can't stay. I'm sure you could imagine what would happen if we stayed. They would take our baby away, if they even allow the birth. They'll throw us in jail for rape, separating us forever, and, in the process, probably spay and neuter us like we're household pets." Tears rolled down Jennifer's cheeks as she whispered her emotional tirade. Then she self-consciously glanced around to check if anyone was in hearing distance. But it appeared as if they were alone.

"I agree," Paul said, still a little stunned about the whole situation. He saw the hurt in Jennifer's eyes and heard the fear in her voice, but he didn't know how to comfort her. Since things were still unknown, however, he asked what he thought was the next logical question. "What if it turns out you're not pregnant?"

"I want to leave anyway," Jennifer said plainly. "I've given this a lot of thought. I mean, don't you want to? What kind of life do we have here anyway? You know we can never really be together here. And that's what I want, to be with you, for always, now that we've been given a second chance. I want to be able to say 'I love you' freely, and to show it freely. We'll never have that here. Don't you want that, too?"

"Yes, yes, I do. I want to be with you, too." Paul was deeply moved by her declaration of love because he hadn't been sure that she felt the same way about him. But it was still a lot for him to take in all at once. "But I guess I never thought about leaving my home, my own country, for good."

"I know how you feel," Jennifer said. "I loved my country. That's why I got into politics. But it's different now. Something's not right here."

Paul and Jennifer continued to stroll through the park. It was risky being together, in the sense of drawing attention to themselves as a pair, but it still wasn't against the law for a man and a woman to talk to each other. And what they had to discuss could not be delayed any longer. If passers-by came too close, they paused in their conversation until it was clear, or pretended to talk about a chess problem.

"Well, how are we going to do it? How are we going to get out?" Paul asked, and they both thought about the dilemma for a moment.

"If it were a couple of months ago, we could have just gone to the Canadian embassy down the street and asked for political asylum. But it's been closed," Jennifer responded.

"I know. Since travel is still permitted to Mexico, we could each get a visa as if we were going on vacation and apply at the Canadian embassy there."

"It would take too long. It takes a few months to get exit visas these days, and I could be showing by then. Besides, we'd have to travel separately, or pretend to travel separately. I'd rather stay together, if at all possible." Jennifer gently exposed the flaws in Paul's plan. "And we can't have any paperwork involved, especially government paperwork. But I bet we could drive to Maine and hike across the border. With my experience up there, I think we could evade the patrols and get through."

"That sounds pretty risky," Paul said.

"It is very risky. It's probably the biggest risk we'll ever have to take in our lives, but I think it would be just as risky, if not more, to stay here."

"Wait, I got it. I think I know of a way," Paul said excitedly. "When I was living in Boston, my roommates and I would sometimes go deep sea fishing, and we would always charter a boat from the same guy. I got to be good friends with him. If I charter the boat as if I'm just taking another fishing trip, we could sail right on out of here. Just keep going out to sea, and then right up the coast to Nova Scotia."

"But the captain will be aboard running the boat, right? How will you convince him to take us to Canada?"

"From long talks with him I got to know him. I know he thinks like we do. Of course, he never came out and said anything directly, but I think, if we just tell him the situation, he'll understand."

"Whoa. You can't tell anybody anything," Jennifer interjected again. "It's too dangerous. He could turn us in."

"He wouldn't. I trust him. And I think you just need to trust me on this one because I know him."

Jennifer considered it for a moment. "Okay, if there's one person in the world today that I do trust, it's you. I think it is the best plan."

Paul smiled as the plan unfolded before them. The thought of being together with Jennifer for the rest of his life, anywhere, warmed his heart. "When do you want to leave?" he asked.

"I want to leave right now, but I suppose that's not possible. Can you make the arrangements for next weekend? I don't think I can wait any longer than that."

"Yes, I think so. I'll try to book the charter tomorrow."

"Can you meet me, say Wednesday, to make sure everything's all set and to also finalize our plan?"

"Okay."

"How about American University at seven? I know they're having a chess tournament there. We can even play if you want to."

"Sure," Paul agreed.

Jennifer stopped walking and faced Paul. She reached over and squeezed his hand. "Thanks, Paul," she whispered, and they parted, each heading in the opposite direction.

When Jennifer went back to work Monday, she felt much better as the nausea subsided. And again, she didn't know if that meant she wasn't pregnant. But it didn't even really matter now. The decision had been made. Her outlook brightened considerably at the thought of leaving the gray, lifeless world she was in now. She had to leave for her own sake. Even if she wasn't pregnant, the thought of her becoming pregnant in the future quickened her heartbeat. If she stayed behind, that joy never would be known. And her heart nearly skipped a beat when she thought that another human life possibly could be growing inside her right then. She had to leave. With those feelings, she felt as if she just didn't belong there. Of course, while waiting for the week to pass, she couldn't let anyone know that anything was out of the ordinary. She couldn't leave any hints that she was emigrating, defecting, abandoning ship, turning tail and running, turning traitor to the cause and the revolution. She supposed all those things were true, but she didn't care anymore. So she went about her business as usual, but acted a little grumpy in hopes of hiding the gleam in her eyes.

Jennifer bided her time until Wednesday when she could see Paul again. She decided to play in the tournament, partly to give her a cover, but also to take her mind off the plans that had been consuming her thoughts. But it wasn't completely possible. Chess usually takes total concentration to win, and Jennifer's concentration could not be total on chess at the moment. She lost in the first two rounds of a three-round Swiss tournament. After her early exit in round two, she went for a walk with Paul, who also had suffered the same fate in his game, to a secluded spot on the American University campus.

"Were you able to make the arrangements?" Jennifer asked when she was sure they were alone.

"Everything is set," Paul said. "We can take a leisurely drive up to Boston early Saturday morning, and, by the afternoon, we'll be on our way for our little 'fishing cruise'."

From the way he made it sound, she thought it was too easy somehow. If it were only a few years ago, it could've been just a leisurely drive, a getaway weekend or an impromptu vacation with her steady, and no one would've thought twice. Yet now, it was much more dramatic, a drastic measure, in fact, perhaps a race for their lives, and she could not leave anything to chance.

"We have to be very careful," Jennifer said. "I don't think we ought to be seen traveling together. So I guess I'll have to lie across the back seat of your car the whole time you're driving."

"That could get really uncomfortable on such a long trip."

"I have an idea," Jennifer said. "Bring some old clothes with you. You know, a few shirts to hang in the windows, maybe a few cardboard boxes to stick in the back. Just something to block the view so that I could sit up without being seen from the outside."

"You know, I never thought about what to bring along, but I guess we should travel light," Paul said as his eyes calmly scanned back and forth for any eavesdroppers.

"You're absolutely right," Jennifer said, not even looking at Paul, but also scanning the scene. "We should only take a few extra clothes. We can't leave any signs that we're going anywhere. We just have to be gone. We should take some money with us. They should still be exchanging currency. I think I can withdraw about a thousand without drawing suspicion."

"What if close my savings account and say I'm just transferring to another bank?" Paul asked.

"I don't think that's a good idea because you'd probably have to take it in a check to avoid suspicion, and once we cross the border, their banks might not be able to take it because our assets could be frozen once our departure is discovered. Once they get the request for the transfer of funds anyway, they'll know exactly where we are at that time, and won't release it. I think you better just take about a thousand in cash if you can. We'll just have to start over once we're there. If that's okay with you," she added gently, wanting to make sure she wasn't pressuring him into doing anything he didn't really want to do. But the look Paul gave Jennifer was the closest thing to a reassuring embrace he could get without making actual contact. The look told her that starting over together would be the best thing to ever happen to him.

"Of course, Jennifer. Whatever it takes," was all that he said.

They made arrangements to next meet on Saturday morning at 6:30 at a gas station down the street from Jennifer's apartment. There Paul could fuel up for the long drive, and Jennifer could find a way to sneak into his car. They pledged no more communication until that time. Jennifer was hoping to steal a quick kiss, but someone passed close by.

"I know. I've always had so much trouble with the English opening, too," Jennifer said, obviously more audibly than her discussions with Paul. "I don't think I've ever won when someone tries that opening on me."

Paul followed her cue as they started to talk about chess and walked back to the tournament site for the final game.

Jennifer tried to spend the next two days as normally as possible. There was no real packing to do, only mental packing of her memories of her native land that she hoped to never see again. But most of those memories were pre-ERA anyway, and were already relegated to a bygone era—of her high school friends, her parents, her college roommates and—boyfriends. Short as those relationships always seemed to be, she remembered each one vividly—the excitement after being asked out, the clumsy and uncomfortable first date encounters, and, more often than not, the disappointment afterward. Jennifer recalled the push and tug interplay between the two groups, young males and females. And the like-love questions of doubt and insecurity: Does he like me? Do I like him, or maybe him? Does she like him, too? Do I love him or like him? Does he really love me, or is he just saying that? And even though none of those relationships worked out in the end, that kind of vibrant interaction at least made her feel alive, unlike the past few years when she felt more like the walking dead.

On Friday morning, Jennifer's stomach was a bit queasy again. It could be morning sickness or just nerves, she thought. But when she went into the office, she tried to be cheerful, and not as melancholy as she felt. She wanted to leave with a good impression on her last day, for even if she didn't make it out of the country, this certainly would still be her last day.

Jennifer felt especially sad when she saw Marilyn, and when she thought about deceiving her, betraying her trust and friendship, such as it was for an employer and her employee, she really did feel like a traitor. So she tried to keep their contact to a minimum that day, lest she break out in tears. Marilyn was really a good lawmaker, she thought. She especially wanted to know how a law might affect people before she voted, but she, like Jennifer herself and so many others, was swept up in the engulfing wave of equality.

During her lunch break, Jennifer went to the bank to cash her last paycheck and withdrew a thousand dollars from her savings account. She had close to fifteen thousand dollars left because she had spent so little over the past few years. She didn't own a car, and it made no sense to spend a lot of money on clothes when they all looked the same. She had to leave it all behind because she didn't dare withdraw any more, for fear of setting off some sort of paperwork alarm that might tip someone off about her intentions.

When she went back to the office, Jennifer was like a soldier marking time. She didn't get much accomplished and mostly watched the hours and minutes tick away until five o'clock. But a little after four, Marilyn walked up to Jennifer's desk.

"Jennifer, I need a favor," Marilyn asked.

"Sure. What is it?"

"I need you to write a rough draft of a speech I have to make next week on the Fellowes Amendment. Here are some notes. I'll need it first thing Monday morning so that I can make revisions and such."

Jennifer just looked up at her and was about to say, 'I can't', but she didn't.

"You know I hate to make you work weekends, and I wouldn't if it wasn't somewhat of an emergency. Because, as you know, I'll be in Richmond this weekend attending a few functions," Marilyn explained to her. "Besides, you're very familiar with the amendment, and I like your style. Since it's such short notice, you don't have to stay late tonight, in case you made plans already. It's something you can do at home if you like. It just needs to be done this weekend because there's going to be big changes here next week. New personnel and everything."

"Wh—what do you mean, 'big changes?'" Jennifer stuttered, thinking wildly for a moment that Marilyn knew of her plan somehow, or was preparing for her impending arrest.

"Well, I guess I can tell you now," Marilyn said. "I've been given some new committee responsibilities, and it means we'll be extremely busy around here. But, don't worry. You, Stan and Carmen won't be burdened with all the new things. I'll be adding two new staff members."

"Uh, that sounds wonderful," Jennifer said.

"Don't worry. You'll get more details later. So, can you take care of that for me?"

"Sure thing. No problem," Jennifer said to reassure Marilyn, but it didn't make her feel any better lying to her.

"See you later," Marilyn said as she walked back to her private office.

Why did she have to say that? Jennifer wondered. She felt bad enough as it was. Now she would be thinking about everybody come Monday morning when she would not show up. Marilyn, Carmen and Stan would be going on with their lives, as usual, not really thinking about it, but expecting Jennifer to come through the doors as she usually did in her quiet, pleasant manner. Only she wouldn't walk in the door that day at all, or any other day. They would naturally ask each other, 'Where's Jennifer today?' They would call her apartment. No answer, of course. They might call the police. The search for Jennifer would begin. She didn't know where she would be at that particular moment, but she hoped she would be safe and sound in a Canadian hotel at the time.

When the clock struck five and the mass exodus of government employees began (being especially intense on a weekend), Jennifer made an effort to say goodbye to everyone without making it sound like a final farewell. Even as she stepped into the hall of the House Office Building, she greeted each passerby she knew by name (and even a few she didn't know) with a 'Have a great weekend!' or 'See you next week.' Almost everyone in the building knew Jennifer by sight. Her hero status, in these parts especially, had far from abated. But, as she walked quietly down the frenzied streets on a still warm Washington autumn eve, she wished that she would never be noticed again.

As she slipped back into her apartment and her anonymity, she solemnly fixed and ate her last supper in Washington. Almost unconsciously, Jennifer dipped her bread into her wine, and when she realized what she was doing, she paused and prayed, for the first time in quite a long time, for her safe passage with Paul.

After she finished her meal, Jennifer left the dirty dishes in the sink without even rinsing them, as much as she hated to. She had even contemplated writing the speech and mailing it to Marilyn so that it could still be on her desk Monday morning as promised. But if she were going to leave, things naturally would remain unfinished. She shouldn't pretend that she was going on vacation or something, and that, eventually, she would be back. There could be no return here. 'So leave things unfinished!' she finally told herself.

Jennifer was tired of thinking about the whole affair, and she thought the best way to stop thinking was to go to sleep. She climbed into bed at 7:30, but she could not sleep. She tossed and turned and naturally thought even more about leaving the next day. Then she tried to at least confine herself to good thoughts, especially about Paul. Jennifer tried to picture the two of them together in some as-yet-unknown house, raising baby, loving each other. She tried to picture them in a backyard, teaching baby to walk, watching her/him stumble in the lush, soft grass. Jennifer did doze off intermittently and would be hard pressed to separate conscious thought from dream. And, because of that, she thought her dreams were perhaps too strong, as if she were somehow transmitting a signal that others could pick up on Dream-TV. And she half-expected the Dream Police to knock on her door at any minute and burst in to end all her nonsense by taking her away, before she could infect anyone else.

Jennifer sat bolt upright in bed when she didn't know where she was—at home, in Canada, in jail, or in her childhood home. When the familiar items around her were slowly recognized in the mid-night dark, Jennifer looked at her alarm clock, saw that it was 3:30 a.m., and then realized what day it was: September 24th.

She still had time to kill, but she wouldn't get back to sleep now. She released some nervous energy by getting ready for her odyssey, first taking a long hot shower, dressing in two layers of her generic clothes and a flannel jogging suit, and then cooking a large breakfast of sausage, eggs, grits, orange juice and coffee. She couldn't finish it all, but she ate until stuffed because she didn't know where her next meal was coming from. She told herself, 'When facing the unknown, you've got to be prepared for anything'.

As six o'clock approached, she announced to herself and to no one in particular, "I'm ready."

Jennifer's plan was to look as if she were out for a morning jog. (After her training in boot camp, she promised herself to stay in shape. But, with people recognizing her and her waning commitment, she had been out infrequently by this time.) She would jog around the park, for effect, then down the street to the service station. She would stop in to use the restroom, and Paul would pull around to the restroom door after filling up with fuel and leave the back door open while he busied himself filling fluids under the hood. Jennifer would come out of the restroom and quietly slip into the back seat if no one were looking. Then off they would go.

As she jogged along, Jennifer thought about Paul's half of the plan. She wondered what Paul had gone through last night. She wondered what Paul might have said to his roommates, if anything, especially if he were asked where he was going so early on a Saturday morning. But, just taking off for a weekend couldn't be that unusual. So he probably had no trouble with them, she thought. And then she wondered briefly if Paul even would show up today. 'They' could have gotten him already, and were getting ready to pick her up at any moment. She tried to convince herself that it was only her imagination. 'Stop making scenarios,' she told herself. 'Let's just see what happens.'

When she jogged by the station, the designated rendezvous point, the first time, Jennifer didn't see anything. She checked her watch and realized she was a bit early. So she looped back around to pass by again in ten minutes. This time she saw Paul at the pump filling up his tank. Jennifer jogged in, just glancing at Paul and making sure that he saw her, got the restroom key from the attendant and jogged to the small building behind the main station.

While she was in the restroom alone waiting for the sound of Paul's car outside, Jennifer emptied her fluids and then nervously busied herself by washing her face to cool down.

When she finally heard a car pull up close, she peeked out the door, saw that it was Paul's car, and watched him open the trunk, the back door and the hood. Paul checked all his fluid levels and added what was needed to make everything appear as ordinary as possible. Jennifer then stepped outside, leaving the restroom key in the lock, scanned the station's driveway for a moment and jumped into the back seat, quickly closing the door behind her.

Jennifer felt a little relieved at this point. The windows were blocked as they had discussed, and she sat upright in the back seat to collect herself, completely unseen from the outside. While she waited for Paul to finish, Jennifer peeked through a couple of shirts that were dangling from hangers to view the street in the hazy, gray predawn light. Nothing unusual going on out there. Good, she thought. Just the city waking up on cool Saturday morning. But her eyes were suddenly drawn to man at the gas pumps. Her heart sank into the pit of her stomach as she tried to fathom the frightful sight. Pumping gasoline into a nondescript white sedan was the same man who had followed Jennifer into the park just a week before. With his back to her, Jennifer was still sure it was the same man. He had the same build, the same overcoat, bundled up with gloves and a cold-weather cap with ear flaps, despite the mild temperature. The air was crisp for a Mid-Atlantic autumn morning, but it was far from frigid. It was as if he were hiding his identity.

Even if he turned to reveal his face to Jennifer, it wouldn't have helped her to recognize him because she hadn't seen his face the previous time. But she was absolutely positive; it was the same person.

'Who is this guy?' she wondered. 'Is he following me, keeping tabs on me?' A few thoughts entered her mind. 'FBI? CIA? Secret Service? They must have found us out or overheard our conversations. They're probably getting set to nab us once we make a run for it.'

Jennifer started to think things were beginning to close in around her. 'Why do you have to do this now?' she wondered. 'What kind of criminals are we anyway? Just let us quietly slip away, and you'll never hear from us again.'

She jumped at the sound of a loud thud and drew away from the window instinctively. But it was just Paul slamming the hood down. He walked to the back to shut the trunk.

'Wait just a minute,' Jennifer told herself. 'Calm down a second. This doesn't necessarily mean anything. I'm just being paranoid. Even if it is the same man, seeing him again could just be a coincidence. He probably lives in the neighborhood. I was bound to run into him eventually.'

Paul climbed into the driver's seat. "Are you ready to go?" he asked.

"You bet," Jennifer replied anxiously. "The sooner the better." She took a last peek out the window, but she still didn't get a glimpse of the mystery man's face. He was inside paying the attendant for his gas.

Despite the camouflage on the windows, Jennifer nestled in, lying across the back seat as Paul pulled out into city traffic. After a few turns this way and that, they circled around RFK Stadium, crossed the Young Memorial Bridge and hit the Interstate Beltway northbound. Only once they got rolling on the freeway did Jennifer begin to relax and sit up to view the road ahead.

Paul glanced back over his shoulder at Jennifer and said, "Next stop, Beantown!" It wasn't exactly true; he knew that he would need to stop for gas at least once on the way, but it was his way of saying the plan was finally in motion.

They didn't say much as the miles rolled swiftly past (but surely not swiftly enough for either's taste) because they were both quietly concerned. While the trip seemed to have all the trappings of a leisurely weekend junket, they knew it was far more critical than that. The seriousness of the matter at hand pervaded the atmosphere of the cramped compartment of Paul's car.

When Jennifer suggested turning on the radio for some music, Paul apologized for not thinking of it, and he admitted that he hardly touched it anymore except to listen to the all-news station. The songs of the day (the only ones which were allowed to be played) just didn't strike the right chord with him. The ones which still had lyrics sang of the revolution or the praises of the 'movement.' Or any of the others were so lacking in any real emotion, they bored him to the point of nausea, being such a bland diet without much variety or depth. The troubadours couldn't sing about love and relationships anymore. What was left? Jennifer agreed, and they settled for an instrumental-only station.

They rolled along in harmony and melody with the rolling farmland of northeast Maryland and northern Delaware. They o'erleaped the majestic Delaware River, via the Delaware Memorial Bridge, and then droned along the monotonous New Jersey Turnpike.

Just outside of New York City, Paul stopped for gas at one of the

Meadowlands area rest stops. After fueling up, Paul went to buy some snacks for the two of them.

"Hurry back," Jennifer said to Paul as he left her alone in the car. She didn't know why, but Jennifer still sensed the danger of their situation. Their little trip could be over at any minute, and she didn't like the thought of being separated from Paul for any reason right then. But she couldn't go in with him. So it was necessary at that moment.

Jennifer peeked out the window again to keep an eye on Paul as he walked into the combination convenience store/gas station. But she recoiled in horror as she realized her worst fear. They were being followed. At the far outer island, gassing up a white Dodge, was the man from Washington, complete with overcoat and cap despite the warmer temperature of the day. Jennifer almost bit through her lower lip as she cried, "Oh no! What do we do now?" The sight confirmed her suspicion. This could not be a coincidence, she told herself. He definitely was following them. But why following? Why not arresting? Jennifer wondered. Even in the daylight, Jennifer could still not see his face. The bill of his cap cast his face completely in shadow.

Jennifer could make out that he was a bit stout, but not exactly hefty. He wasn't looking in Jennifer's direction, but just concentrating on filling his tank.

Paul returned with the food. But Jennifer wasn't interested. As soon as Paul got back into the driver's seat, Jennifer said, "Please hurry. Go!"

"What's up?" Paul asked as he sensed her urgency and started the engine. "Just go! Go!" she yelled impatiently, bouncing up and down, clearly agitated.

Paul quickly put the car into gear and merged back onto the turnpike. Jennifer debated whether to even tell Paul what she suspected, but, after 15 minutes back out on the highway, Paul asked her again, "What was the matter back there."

"I—I think we're being followed," Jennifer said nervously. "I just saw a man at the rest stop who was at the same gas station where we were in D.C. this morning. It can't be just a coincidence. Check the mirror and tell me if you see a white Dodge back there."

Paul glanced in the side mirror and checked the weaving cluster of cars and trucks behind him. "I don't think I see anything," he said.

Jennifer moved the boxes behind her to create a peephole out the back window. After searching for a few moments, she stated, "I don't see him right now either. But I'm not imagining things. Maybe we lost him for now."

"Even if someone's following us, what do we do about it?" Paul asked gently. "Do you want me to turn back?"

"No. We can't do that. I guess we see it through to the end, see what happens."

"Okay," Paul said, taking one hand off the steering wheel and offering it to Jennifer. "I'm with you all the way."

She took his hand and squeezed with all her conviction. As they settled in for the second leg, they shared the doughnuts and coffee from the rest stop, and occasionally checked behind them instead of focusing completely on the road ahead.

They skirted the big city via the Tappan Zee Bridge, and soon rolled into the Constitution State of Connecticut, which was the worst part of the trip for Jennifer. To avoid the roving eyes of the many toll booth operators that they would encounter, Jennifer lay across the floor of the car with a blanket pulled over her. And she could feel every pothole that pockmarked the Conn Turnpike.

She sat back up and breathed a sigh of relief as they passed the last toll and entered the Ocean State of Rhode Island. Paul was a little more familiar with the scenery now, but Jennifer was fascinated that, while certainly not mountainous country, the highway cut right through huge rock formations, creating cliffs of granite on either side. The southern part of the state seemed to be dotted with such outcroppings, as centuries ago Ice Age glaciers dumped these huge boulders in their present locations.

Now just past the capitol dome of Providence, their destination lay a mere 50 miles to the northeast. Once out of the city, they were back into the countryside, whizzing past quaint New England farmhouses which still stood, Jennifer thought sadly, despite the families which they symbolized having ceased to exist.

The traffic thickened as they headed into the Hub. "We're almost there," Paul suddenly announced.

Jennifer shuddered at the word 'almost.' She didn't want that to be their epitaph, "We *almost* made it." And she didn't care anymore if passing drivers saw her together with Paul. She climbed into the front seat, and held Paul's hand (out of plain sight, however) as he drove. They exited the Interstate and now wove their way through the streets of Boston. Jennifer noticed that they did draw a few looks from pedestrians and other drivers while they were at stoplights. But was she just being paranoid again? If she were driving alone, she could have gotten the same kind of look from people and never taken notice. They were probably just looking at her for the same reason she was looking at them, she told herself. Eyes naturally glance around. Something new comes into your field of vision, and you look to see what it is, then look at something else. She had no reason to think that everyone would know what she was doing from just looking at her. But she felt so different from everyone passing by on the street, seemingly contented, and she began to worry that people could see that she was different just by her looks.

Paul finally turned off Northern Avenue onto pier D in South Boston, looking for the docks of the charter fishing boats. Jennifer took a last look behind her for the Dodge before they parked. Still no sign. 'If he were following, we must have lost him,' Jennifer thought.

Paul parked the car and turned off the engine for the last time. "Let's go," he said as he looked at Jennifer, and they simultaneously jumped out of the car and hastily unloaded everything they had brought with them—the clothes, the boxes filled with a few blankets and overcoats, and, of course, the fishing gear, which Paul brought along to avoid his roommates' suspicion. Paul then led the way down the dock to a medium sized cabin cruiser named Shenanigans.

"Ahoy, mate!" Paul bellowed at the foot of the gangway.

"Ahoy there yourself, landlubber!" came a cry from inside the boat. A short, lean figure made his way out onto the deck and into view. "Come aboard, come aboard, Paulie. Just drop that gear where you may. I'll stow it in a sec."

When Paul had his hands free, he offered one to shake with the man in the captain's hat.

"Hey, Cap, you old sea dog, how've you been?" Paul greeted while beaming. Jennifer never had seen him so animated before.

"I've been just dandy. Kind of had a slow summer, though. You know how it goes. But I was thrilled when you called me, mate."

"Oh, by the way, this is an old friend of mine, Jennifer Martin. Jennifer, this is Cap—uh, Jim Flynn, captain of Shenanigans Charter."

"Pleased to meet you," Cap said as he shook Jennifer's pale hand. She was already feeling the effects of the bobbing deck beneath her feet, and she grabbed the rail for support.

"Didn't bring along your sea legs I see," Cap said.

"Jennifer hasn't been on the water much," Paul spoke for her. "But I told her about all the fun we used to have on your fishing trips, and she insisted on checking it out for herself."

"Not to worry," Cap said to Jennifer. "It does take a little time to get used to it, but once you do, it becomes second nature, and you'll be trotting around the deck as if you's on dry land. A lot of newcomers start out rough, but by the end of the day, they're reeling in the fish like an old pro. Tell you what, I'll guarantee your satisfaction or your money back."

"Thanks," Jennifer said, glancing back and forth between Cap and the pier.

"Listen, Cap. We'd like to get started as soon as possible, if you don't mind," Paul said, noticing Jennifer's anxious looks. He figured it was best to be on their way and explain later.

"No problem. Lucky for you I'm all provisioned and fueled up. Here, put these on," Cap said, handing them two life jackets. "Regulations while we navigate the harbor, you know." Cap then stowed their gear and went back into the cabin. He made a few final checks on the engine and then brought it to life with a few chugs and sputters.

Still out on deck and out of Cap's earshot, Jennifer turned to Paul and said, "Are you sure he's going to go along with this?"

"Positive. I just know he will, once we explain things to him. But, on the small chance he doesn't, we'll still go out for an afternoon of fishing, come back like nothing's happened, and then think of something else. Okay?"

"Okay."

Above the din of the now roaring engines, Cap shouted to Paul. "Cast off that aft line, mate!" Paul did so with the line securing the stern to the dock, and the boat pivoted at the bow. "Now cast off t'other one!" Cap shouted again. Paul ran up to the bow and cast off the line, freeing the ship completely from its berth. Cap deftly and expertly maneuvered the boat backward until he had room to turn it around.

Jennifer kept her eyes on the pier. She watched her homeland slip slowly away. As it was her first glimpse from that perspective, it wasn't exactly the sight she would have associated with her mental picture of America and her homeland. But that's what it was. She had made it out of the country, albeit only five hundred yards so far, simple as that. But she realized it wasn't that simple. God only knew how many more yards were left to go to finally be free from the dominion of the U.S. government, and to be in charge of her life again.

But, with one last glance back before relaxing and letting the docks fade from view, her dreams shattered yet again. She wasn't horrified, however, for she had been almost expecting it. But she let out a whimper and cried, "No, please, no."

Paul noticed her distress and said, "What's up?"

"Look," Jennifer said, pointing back to the pier. They could still make out the form of the mystery man from Washington standing next to his white car, looking out to sea in their general direction.

"Looks like you were right," Paul said calmly, not showing any alarm. He looked puzzled and thought for a moment. "You know, it doesn't really make sense. If he was following us, he had to have known what we were doing beforehand. And if that's the case, why did he even follow? Why not just cut us off, or be waiting for us at the dock?"

Jennifer looked at Paul. "I don't know what he's doing, but he has to know something. He came from the same gas station in Washington to right here."

"Strange," Paul said. "Do you think he sees us?"

"He must. He seems to be looking right at us. But he's not doing anything. Maybe he waited for us to run, and he called the Coast Guard or the Marine Patrol to intercept us and bring us back."

"Even if they did board us out here, we still say we're going fishing," Paul reassured her. "What can they really say?"

"They must know, have some kind of evidence," Jennifer said.

"Look, we can't even see him anymore. Let's just relax a bit and try not to speculate."

"Okay," Jennifer agreed. Now that the pier was out of sight, she fixed a seat on a coil of line to look out over the bow, to see what now lay ahead of them. Once she got comfortable, she even tried to take a nap, but as her stomach rose and fell with the bow bouncing over the waves, her nausea got worse.

Once they were completely out of sight of land, Paul thought he should talk to Cap about their ultimate destination. Paul knew that Cap would be heading for his favorite fishing spot off the coast of Maine. So they were headed in the right direction. It was just a case of convincing him to make a small diversion. Paul went over to talk to Jennifer.

"Jennifer, I think it's time we talk to Cap," Paul said as he gently nudged her from her attempted nap. "We just lay it on the line, tell him everything, tell him what we want to do, and ask if he can help us."

"Okay," Jennifer responded weakly. Paul turned to walk into the cabin, and Jennifer stood up to follow him. But she didn't get very far. She felt unsteady on her feet and grabbed the rail to gain her balance. Instead the nausea overwhelmed her, and she heaved over the side.

Paul turned back around when he heard Jennifer and went to her side, putting an arm around her.

"Are you all right?" he asked, trying to comfort her.

"Yes, I think so."

Paul wiped her face with a handkerchief and let her compose herself again. "Do you want me to talk to Cap alone?"

"No," Jennifer replied. "We're in this together. Besides, I think I feel a lot better now than I did ten minutes ago. It's only just before you puke that you feel as if you're going to die." She smiled at Paul, and made light of her illness, reassuring him that she was feeling better. "Come on," she said when she regained her equilibrium.

They left the outside deck and entered the small cabin where the captain's chair was located. Cap sat askew in the chair with one hand on the rudder control following the plotted course, and the other on the throttle, or getting a fix on their position with the LORAN-C.

"Excuse me, Cap," Paul began. "We—uh, need to talk to you—about something very serious."

"Sure thing. What's up?" Cap said.

Paul laid out the story for Cap, telling him everything about their situation, and Jennifer's possible condition in a straightforward tone, which still couldn't quite belie his gnawing fear and growing desperation. And Cap quietly listened while keeping a hand and an eye on the rudder. "You're our last and only hope, Cap. We need your help to defect. Can you find it in your heart to help us and take us to Canada?" Paul ended his plea.

Cap was silent for a moment as he looked out to sea. "You know, I knew something was up when you called me, but I had no idea it was this big. I've known you for a few years now, Paulie, and you were always straight with me, a really nice kid." Paul and Jennifer waited patiently but nervously for Cap's decision, as they held each other's sweaty hands.

"Now, when this equal rights thing came along, I thought it was long overdue, and I was all for it, mind you. They made a few changes in the rules here and there, and I tried to go along. I knew the rules and I lived by them. But, as God is my witness, you folks are no criminals." Cap looked directly into Jennifer's eyes. "And I can't in good conscience bring you back to the States, knowing what they could do to you. I'll take you wherever you want to go."

"You will? You will?" Jennifer screamed, gushing with relief and joy. She ran up to Cap and hugged him and kissed him on the cheek. "Oh, thank you, thank you, Cap. Paul said we could put our trust in you."

"Well," Cap said, blushing slightly.

Jennifer ran back over to Paul's side and hugged him. "We're going to make it. We're going to make it," she whispered. Paul kissed the top of her head as he held her. It was the first time they had embraced since they made love a month and a half before.

"You're a pretty smart fella there, matey," Cap said to Paul. "That was some plan. I don't know how you knew I'd have enough fuel to make it to the Canadian coast." Paul just looked back at him without giving any clues. "Well, anyhow, if you'll take over the chair for me, Paul, so's I can plot a new course for Yarmouth, Nova Scotia. That's the nearest port. Ah, but you probably already knew that. Just keep your nose on oh-one-five for now."

"Aye, aye, captain." Paul said, saluting as he took control of the rudder. Cap had let him steer on other trips, so he was able to keep on the current course without too much difficulty, following the swaying compass until Cap plotted the new course.

Cap was already poring over his charts, figuring their present position, and considering their final destination. Jennifer watched him intently.

While trying not to interrupt his train of thought, she had to ask him, "What are you going to do when we get there, Cap? Are you going to go back?"

"Well, I haven't had time to even think about that," Cap said. "You know, I might have just as much reason to not return as you do. If the authorities ever find out that I aided a defection, I could be in big trouble, too."

"I guess we never thought about what could happen to you," Jennifer said ashamedly.

"Never you mind about that. This might be just the push I needed to finally shove off for good from my tarnished homeland. I guess I had the chance to leave same as everyone else, even a better one actually with my own mode of transportation, but I never considered leaving my home, you know. I know the harbor and the bay like the back of my hand, and I was born and raised in South Boston. It was home, and I knew nothing else. You know, my father was a commercial fisherman, and every day he'd walk down the same pier where I dock now. And he always dreamed of having his own boat. And he sacrificed a lot to make sure I had this one. Well, anyway, I still had me old pals from the neighborhood around, but, you know—it wasn't much of a neighborhood without the families no more."

"I know what you mean," Jennifer said.

"I guess I told Paulie there pretty much the same thing one trip we had. You know, two Irish boys sort of bonding, or whatever you want to call it. I guess I was dissatisfied for a long time. I think it's time to start afresh.

I'm sure I can run my charter out of Canada, now, jus' as easy. Maybe I'll even find a lovely woman like yourself to keep me comp'ny."

It was Jennifer's turn to blush.

"I had a wonderful woman, you know," he continued. "She left me, though, quite a few years ago, when I was literally struggling to stay afloat—" Cap was about to ramble on, but stopped suddenly. "Are you all right? You look a little flushed."

"I'm doing better. I do feel a little warm, I guess, from all my excitement," Jennifer replied.

"Well, you get a little weak from not having anything in your stomach. The best thing to do is to go on deck and get some fresh air. I'll get you some soda water and saltine crackers to help settle your stomach."

"Okay," Jennifer said and headed out on deck.

"And the best thing to do is keep your eyes fixed on the horizon," Cap called after her.

Jennifer followed Cap's seemingly sage advice. She stood on the fantail and gazed across the horizon. There were a few other ships and boats in view, ranging from a huge tanker to a bobbing sailboat. One in particular caught Jennifer's attention. It was a medium-sized white ship, with a broad red stripe on the bow. After a few seconds, it registered in Jennifer's mind.

"We're being followed by a Coast Guard cutter!" Jennifer yelled back into the cabin. Cap rushed out to take a look where Jennifer was pointing.

"Hmmm," was the only sound he made after a few moments of staring off into the distance. He went back into the cabin to get a pair of binoculars. He aimed them at the approaching form of the ship. "Yep, definitely Coast Guard. Looks like a 210-footer. It could be following us, and they can board us at any time out here in international waters 'cause this is an American flag vessel. From what I heard about them, though, top speed is only about 18 knots. Twenty maybe downwind in the right current. We can do 22 easy, and probably 25 knots if I need it." He tried to calm Jennifer. Cap then rushed back into the cabin, and Jennifer followed. Cap relieved Paul, pushed the throttle almost to full and steered for the new course.

Paul put his arm around Jennifer to reassure her as she led him back to look out over the stern again. "Don't worry. Cap will deliver us safe and sound."

As hour after hour passed and the dunes of the desolate sea-desert rolled by, the chasing cutter came no closer, but also failed to fade from view.

Even as darkness came, they still could make out the ominous running lights of that great white shark of a ship looming just on the horizon, seemingly waiting to make the kill. Jennifer's hopes teetered on the edge of that horizon, and her nerves frazzled close to the breakdown point. She tried to nap in a bunk in the cabin below. She mostly prayed and eventually cried herself to sleep. In the wee hours of the still dark morning, Jennifer was awakened by a jubilant Paul.

"We made it, we made it, Jennifer! Cap's last fix puts us five minutes outside Canadian territorial waters. The Coast Guard cutter is more then five minutes away. We made it, we made it!"

Jennifer rushed topside to witness the passage out of international waters into Canadian territorial waters. With the current state of alert, the cutter could not approach any closer without risking attack by the Canadian Coast Guard or Navy.

Jennifer, Paul and Cap watched the five minute deadline pass, and after another five minutes, Cap took another fix placing them well inside the boundary. They erupted in jubilation and thankfulness for their newly acquired freedom. Then they quietly slipped into the harbor at Yarmouth, where they would apply for political asylum to begin their new lives. Their harrowing odyssey was over.

CHAPTER EIGHT

Immediately after asylum was granted, Jennifer and Paul were married. And while having the blood test, Jennifer asked the doctor to give her a pregnancy test, even though she was almost convinced that she was with child. The doctor confirmed that she was six weeks pregnant.

They had a small ceremony in a Catholic chapel with Cap as a witness. And while she had no wedding gown, Jennifer insisted on getting married in a dress. Paul also bought a dark suit and a tie, and they both reveled in the old-fashioned American garb, which, of course, was still contemporary in Canada.

There was no time for a honeymoon, however, for they had to concentrate on putting their lives back in order, getting jobs to support themselves and getting a permanent place to live. Cap had decided to rebuild his charter business in Halifax, and he bade them a fond farewell. Paul and Jennifer then settled on Ottawa as the place to begin their new life together. With her interest and experience in government, Jennifer thought the Canadian capital would be the best place to start. Paul didn't know what geographic area held the best opportunities for employment. So he agreed with the choice of Ottawa for now, because of its central location. If necessary, he was still close enough to the bigger cities such as Toronto, Montreal and Quebec, where he might find more openings for computer programmers.

With the cash they had brought with them, Jennifer and Paul were able to obtain a small but comfortable apartment in a quaint residential section of Ottawa. They rented some furniture and quickly settled in before they both started the job hunt in earnest.

Paul pored over the classified ads in the *Ottawa Citizen*, and while Jennifer waited for him to finish with that section, she scanned through the news sections, checking out the local news to get a feeling for their new hometown and country, or catching up on the international news of the past week.

Paul sat at the dining room table, circling ads and copying down names and phone numbers. Jennifer sat on the living room sofa with several sections spread around her. She flipped through one section, and stopped suddenly to read one headline in particular that caught her eye. It was to a small story buried near the back of the international/national section.

"Whoa! This is unbelievable. Paul, darling, you've got to hear this," Jennifer said with her nose still buried in the paper.

Paul looked up and murmured, "Hmmm?"

"Get this. It says, 'American Combat Hero Kidnaped By Canadian Agents, U.S. Charges.' It's about me—us."

"Really?" Paul's interest was instantly piqued. He walked over to the side of the sofa where Jennifer sat, leaned on the arm and peeked over her shoulder to read the story along with her.

"They're quoting a *Washington Post* story saying that I was abducted by Canadian agents and taken to an undisclosed location inside Canada. Is that hilarious or what? Hey, hon, you're not a Canadian secret agent, are you?" Jennifer and Paul both laughed at that ludicrous thought.

"Whoa, get this," Jennifer continued, still chuckling. "It says the U.S. is claiming that the abduction was done in retaliation for my part in the aborted invasion by Canadian troops this summer. There was no invasion. It was all a misunderstanding. I still think our platoon wandered over the line and didn't know it. There was a skirmish, but there was definitely no invasion."

Paul read the story further. "It also says the *Post* quoted a high-ranking administration official saying, 'The shining symbol of our great new society was taken to undermine the revolution.' So, tell me, how does it feel to be a 'shining symbol'?"

"Oh, please," Jennifer said. "I got enough of that patriotic malarkey back in July. You know, it is so amazing how they just bend the truth to fit their own purposes. I'll bet the U.S. has been wanting an attack all along so that they could fight. And when one didn't come, they invented one, in hopes of provoking one. Tensions flared, but still nothing happened, and things died down again. It seems as if they're taking a piece of the truth, the fact that I did leave, and creating an international incident as justification to start an attack themselves."

"God, I hope not," Paul said. "I'd hate to be the trigger for a war."

"Our leaving has nothing to do with it. They can't be that stupid to not know what happened to us. Maybe it was just convenient for them that we did leave. And now they're using it." Anger now surfaced in Jennifer's voice. The humor of the situation had worn thin. "Damn them. Why couldn't they just let us go in peace? They lost. We're gone. Can't they just forget about us and let us die?"

"They were probably embarrassed that we slipped away right under their noses," Paul explained. "They had to come up with some kind of story to save face."

"But who are we? We're nothing. We're two pawns in a three-hun-dred-million piece chess game. But I don't want to play."

"You may be underestimating your worth," Paul told her. "You are the first female combat hero, after all."

"They made that up. They invented me," Jennifer countered. "I just happened to be in the wrong place at the wrong time."

Jennifer continued to read to the end of the story. "The U.S. is demanding my 'instantaneous release.' Whoa. Love those bureaucratic words. Check this out," she said. "They even quoted Marilyn Connors, my old boss. She says, 'I will work tirelessly and relentlessly to secure Jennifer Martin's immediate and unconditional release.' Geez, I can't believe they got her to buy that bullshit story. She's way too smart to swallow that."

"Maybe there's something else going on here that we don't know about," Paul suggested. "I mean, what about that guy who followed us?"

As Jennifer tried to picture the mystery man again, a sudden, chilling thought came to her. "Whoa. You don't suppose that he was a Canadian agent? Maybe there was a plan to kidnap me after all, and they found out that I was ready to leave on my own. And that guy just followed us to make sure that we got away without any problems."

"It seems a little far-fetched," Paul said. "But if true, that's quite a scary thought."

"You're telling me." Jennifer ruminated some more. "You know, if I go to the Canadian government, I'm sure they wouldn't tell me if they had a plot to kidnap me. And I guess it doesn't matter much. I'm here now, and free. I'm not a prisoner. Maybe I should just go to the media and tell my side of the story. Maybe there'll be some way to get the story back across the border to let the American people know what's really going on. I don't want to go down in history as some kind of martyr."

"Well, I don't know if it's such a good idea for you to be seen right now. Maybe you should just write a letter to the editor of the *Ottawa Citizen* explaining things, telling them that you're here of your own free will, or whatever. Then see what happens."

"I guess you're right, Paul. I'll do that. It should be a good start." Jennifer gave Paul a thank-you-for-caring-so-much kiss, and he went back to scour the classifieds. 'He does seem to have the right idea,' Jennifer thought. 'We do have more critical things to worry about right now than becoming involved in an international ideological battle.'

But when she went back to reading her own paper, she did so almost absent-mindedly, skimming headlines without taking in the meaning and the relevance because she still had her mind on what they had been discussing. Jennifer thought about the series of events in her life over the past year that had led her to this foreign land she now called home.

The identity of the mystery man especially haunted Jennifer. She easily came to the conclusion that he was an agent for the U.S. government, but never once thought about him being an agent for the Canadian government. However, it did answer the question of why they were followed and not arrested. But that raised another question. Why would the Canadian government want her? She had a hard time swallowing that ideological rhetoric about undermining the revolution. But who was it who had planted the seed that a Canadian conspiracy might not be such a joke? Paul.

'No. Impossible,' she told herself. 'How could he possibly be involved in such a bizarre undertaking? But he did appear suddenly out of the blue, after my patrol duty, after I was praised a hero, and after all those years. He could have been among the first waves of emigres before the border closed. He could have been recruited for his computer expertise by the Canadian secret services. He did say he was working on spy cameras. But, really, for whom? After the incident on the Maine border was publicized, he could have recognized my name from his own past, and he could have been suddenly very useful to his superiors who dreamed up an elaborate scheme to kidnap a symbol. Could he have so expertly seduced me to convince me to leave with him?' Jennifer found it hard to fathom. 'Besides, it was my own idea to leave. The pregnancy couldn't have been planned. Or did it just happen sooner than expected? And he didn't seem as worried about being followed. And what about his 'friend' who conveniently had a mode of transportation out of the country?'

Rubbish. All complete nonsense, she told herself, and all for one very big reason. For every minute she had known him, Paul had been one hundred percent completely honest about everything. He was no actor. He was no bullshitter. He always had been, and always would be, just one thing—Paul. And that's what she loved about him. And, of course, another point in his favor was that he loved her. At least, there was one way to find out.

Jennifer playfully sneaked up behind Paul, still sitting at the dining room table. She wrapped her arms around his shoulders and nuzzled his ear. Paul warmly responded by caressing her arms, and then tilted his head back to receive a kiss.

"Mmmm. Let's make love," Jennifer suggested. "You know we haven't done it since we got here, which means, not since August. And now that we have the freedom to do it whenever we choose, we've got to use it or lose it, baby."

"I didn't think I should try anything because of what the doctor said," Paul replied.

"What did the doctor say?"

"You know—that you're—pregnant." Paul almost whispered the last word as though he still wasn't accustomed to saying it freely.

"Oh that," Jennifer said, looking astonished. "Silly. That doesn't mean that we can't have sex anymore. In fact, it should even be more special because we'll be sharing our love with one more. Besides, it's not like it will hurt our baby."

"Really?"

"Really. And just think, you don't even have to worry about getting me pregnant."

Jennifer led him up from his chair. Paul couldn't resist the come-hither look in her eyes. He almost had to remind himself, 'I'm married now. I'm allowed to do this kind of stuff.' He picked Jennifer up and carried her to the bedroom. When he placed her on the bed, he immediately began clutching at her clothes, disrobing her in a matter of seconds. He discarded his own clothes in a similar manner, and he almost pounced on top of her. He began as he had the two previous times, like there was no tomorrow. He seemed to move at the rate of his own pounding heartbeat. Paul began by kissing Jennifer's face, but he noticed that she wasn't really reciprocating as she had before, and, in fact, she seemed to be grimacing in pain.

"Whoa, whoa. Owww. Hold on a second," Jennifer said, most definitely grimacing.

Paul withdrew and almost jumped from atop Jennifer, then lay beside her. "I'm sorry. I'm sorry," he pleaded. "Did I hurt you? Did I hurt the baby?"

"No. It's not that. It's just that you were going a little fast, and it was a bit uncomfortable," Jennifer said. She thought it was strangely reminiscent of her very first time, losing her virginity, but she didn't mention that to him.

"I'm sorry," he apologized again. "I was just doing what we did last time."

"It's okay. I'm still kind of new at this, too," she said, trying to assuage him.

"I thought you liked it this way," Paul said, referring to their smoldering August weekend.

"I did. I did. But I guess it was just a little different situation. I think it was like we were starved for nine long years, and when we got the chance to eat, we gobbled all the food to just stop the hunger. But now we're not so hungry, but we still need to eat. We should just eat slower so that we can taste the food and enjoy the flavor. The mood is definitely different now, for me anyway. We're not trying to hide from anyone. We don't have to worry about getting caught. We're here alone now, with nothing to fear. Let's just, sort of, savor the moment."

"I don't know if I understand what that means," Paul said, looking perplexed.

"Well, we should just try it slower this time. We should try to get in touch with each other's feelings. Here, lie back for a second. I'll just gently run my hands over your body, and you let me know what feels good."

Jennifer and Paul took turns caressing and massaging each other, letting the other know what felt especially good. Then they embraced again and kissed ever so gently. At that moment, Paul knew exactly what savoring the moment meant.

Paul let his hand drift down between Jennifer's legs and gently caressed her where and how she had described to him as giving her the most pleasure. Jennifer moaned her approval. Then Paul let her slowly guide him into her. He allowed her to set the pace. When she moved up, he moved down. When she moved down, he moved up. They continued slowly, savoring each tingle until they moved in perfect harmonic rhythm. And as Jennifer approached climax, instead of going faster, she drew out each stroke longer and longer, arching her back higher and higher, her hands on Paul's buttocks pulling him deeper and deeper inside her. She tried to hold back as long as she was able, but when she no longer could, she let go in a spasm, almost shuddering in Paul's arms. Then she started again, picking up an almost frenzied pace to quickly build pressure for Paul. She stopped suddenly when he seemed to be on the brink and then pulled him deep inside her again, squeezing and holding until Paul finally let go, and his final few pulsing thrusts brought her to her second orgasm.

They lay together quietly, exhausted and spent. While in Paul's arms, Jennifer thought about the significance of what they had just done. For the first time as husband and wife, they made *love*. They shared their feelings for each other intimately with physical contact and they spiritually bonded, fast and strong, forever. At the same time, another thought came to Jennifer. 'I also fucked him. And it was good. I screwed him, humped him, banged him, balled him, got laid, got nailed, got hammered, got knocked up, did the wild thing, did the hootchie-coo, tickled the love thing, did the bump and grind, did the horizontal mambo, did it, went all the way, scored, got serviced, got down, got poked, got boffed, got the shaft, had intercourse, had sex, slept with him, copulated, had coitus, popped the cork, popped the cherry, hid the salami, romanced the bone, rode the May pole, rode the wild pony, and rode the mule all the way home.' They did all that and every other name to call it. The previous two times, they fornicated and procreated. So they did it all. But the phrase that meant the most to Jennifer was 'making love' because she felt as if they actually had created a new love, a new entity that was the 'family'.

Paul, who was enraptured in that feeling and enwrapped in Jennifer's arms, whispered into her ear, "Is this what it feels like to be loved?"

"This is it, baby," Jennifer said, then squeezed him again and kissed him.

As it was the middle of the day, they eventually had to get back to the business at hand, getting jobs. Paul called a few numbers from the ads after he recuperated, and he set up some interviews, while Jennifer finished preparing her resume. She planned to try a few government agencies and any business she thought might be looking for administrative assistants.

Later that night when Paul and Jennifer went to bed, they made love again, for the first time in the dark, secure in their feelings for each other and their new life. Jennifer adored the wonderful feeling of being able to do it anytime she wanted now. She felt so secure having someone share her bed at night, having her husband, her lover, lying right next to her. But, even with such a peaceful feeling running through her mind as she drifted off to sleep, Jennifer was gripped in her first real nightmare she had since childhood. And while the feelings of the scene seemed so real, the images were hazy and cloudy. In fact, the dream sequence opened with her lost in a fog:

She was trying to get somewhere, but all she did was run around in circles, desperately trying to find a way out of the fog. Then a shadowy figure approached. At first, she feared the apparition because it beckoned to her like the ghost of Christmas Future, but then she realized it was showing her which way to go. She followed behind at a distance. She was led to an old, colonial-type mansion that appeared suddenly out of the haze. Jennifer paused at the doorway, afraid to enter. But, in the shadows of the gaping mouth doorway, an arm waved, beckoning her to follow. She walked cautiously across the threshold, and the doors magically closed behind her.

At first, Jennifer thought that she wasn't inside a building at all, but rather back outside as the fog swirled around her. But, in the dim light, she could sense that she was walking down a long hall. She thought the hall would never cease, until it stopped abruptly at a large, wooden door with a brass gargoyle adorning the front of it. Jennifer sensed there was evil behind that door, and she resisted opening it. Then she looked up and saw the shadowy figure standing beside her—a faceless man in a heavy winter overcoat and a fur hat with earflaps. She tried to run, but a hand fell onto her shoulder—

And she awoke with a start. There was a hand on her shoulder, but it was Paul's. He had turned over in his sleep and absently lay his hand on her. When she jumped, Paul did not waken, but just rolled over again back to the other side of the bed.

The nightmare recurred several times in the next few months, and Jennifer always awoke at the same point in the dream. The spookiness of the scene frightened her, but the vividness of the details that she could recall after waking also troubled her. Most of her dreams were forgotten as soon as she employed her mind to remember them. But, for some odd reason, she clearly pictured the exact same sequence of events, as if watching a movie over and over again, or as if it wasn't even a product of her own mind, but someone else's. Jennifer did not tell Paul about the dreams because he might think it was silly. But why would she still be haunted by the mystery man from Washington? She still didn't know who he was, or what he might have been trying to do. And any possible threat he may have been to her was now over, wasn't it?

The nightmare only recurred sporadically and without reason. One time, two weeks went by and she almost forgot about it, thinking it had ceased, only to pop up again to remind her. Of what she did not know. But

Jennifer did her best to not dwell on it during her waking hours.

In the next few months, Jennifer and Paul tried to live a normal life in their new home. Paul found a job quickly, and now worked for the University of Ottawa as a research assistant, helping set up a computer system to organize and analyze data from the research team's experiments, and also tutoring science and engineering students on computer applications. He enjoyed the academic life again, and was thinking about going back to class himself to get his master's degree.

Jennifer remained unemployed, however. First, there was the fallout after her letter to the editor was published, which caused a lot of commotion in her life again. She granted a few interviews to set the record straight about her arrival, in hopes of getting the message back across the border. She reiterated that she had defected and had not been abducted. Jennifer became a celebrity all over again, as everyone looked to her as another symbol because she had chosen their system over the American system.

And the residents of Ottawa especially took to her when they found out that she was in their midst. At the market, at the laundry, at the doctor's office, Jennifer was inundated with supportive greetings, comments and opinions. They had first learned about her from news reports of that summer of an event they considered more a pathetic debacle than anything else. Of course, at first, she was only part of the generic U.S. troops involved in a border skirmish. But when Jennifer was awarded the Medal of Honor, she was considered a mere dupe of her own government because the Canadian press published interviews with the Canadian soldiers involved in the incident, and they, of course, told what actually happened. The folks north of the border didn't take the incident seriously at all, but saw it more as a sham and an embarrassment for the other side. And now Canadians were not holding Jennifer's part in the fiasco against her. And Ottawans, in particular, pictured themselves in direct competition with their Washington, D.C. counterparts, and they saw Jennifer's presence as an affirmation that their government's version of what happened at the Maine/Quebec border was indeed the cor-rect one. They knew that Jennifer was an unwitting character in that morality play, but was no less heroic for trying to save a fallen comrade. And now this main character, an American hero and symbol (and federal government em-ployee, no less), openly rebelled against what she thought she had stood for and chose the right. She chose and openly embraced their system.

When the receptionist in the doctor's office waiting room had said Jennifer's name, a pregnant fan seated nearby asked, "Are you *the* Jennifer Kennedy?" Then she answered her own question. "Yes, you are. Now I rec-ognize you. I've been reading the stories about you, and I saw you on televi-sion."

Jennifer smiled, acknowledging her, but didn't know what to say. However, the woman continued despite her silence.

"We're very proud of you, Mrs. Kennedy. It took a lot of courage to do what you did, yes indeed. I mean, there you were being a model, liberated girl, working for the government, serving your country as you were asked, just as any self-respecting person would. And you probably had a pretty good life over there, if I'm not mistaken?" Jennifer didn't have time to comment as the woman just continued on. "But you gave it all up because you had the natural urge to become a mother. You had a choice to make then, and, by God, you chose motherhood. And you chose us. Well, we're glad to have you. I tell you, if they had more people like you over there, maybe we could avoid going to war."

Jennifer thought about that for a moment, and she hoped that there were millions more like her. Not that she thought she was especially coura-geous or special, but she hated to think that everybody who was left was happy with the way things had turned out back home.

The woman continued to talk to Jennifer until she was called in to see the doctor. She sounded as if she were gossiping about someone, only she was gossiping about Jennifer, to Jennifer.

Similar scenes played themselves out almost any time Jennifer went out in public. She tried to put it all behind her and let her celebrity status die down once again, but she was confronted with it whenever she was interviewed for a job. It seemed everyone knew her story, especially the job interviewers, who had her summarized life history on paper before them.

The interviews had become so repetitious to Jennifer that she had begun to think she was simply a character in someone's play, performing the same scene over and over, each time opposite another leading man. She could have scripted it:

(Scene: Harsh, morning light streams through Venetian blinds of a small, stark business office. A middle-aged man sits in a leather, rocking-swiveling, office chair that creaks discernibly at each movement, behind a gray metal desk with matching cabinets around. On the opposite side of the desk sits a young woman in an unpadded, straight-backed chair. The man is a job interviewer preparing to interview the woman for a job opening. He shuffles and glances over papers in front of him.)

'INTERVIEWER: Let's see, graduated Georgetown University, cum laude, 2008. Poly-sci major. Member of Kappa Delta Epsilon honor society and Delta Pi Rho sorority. Member of junior varsity women's crew as a sophomore. Member of debate team, junior and senior years. Very impressive.

'JENNIFER: It's not on there, but I was alternate on the national semifinalist debate team in 2007.

'INTERVIEWER: Excellent. Member of District of Columbia Chapter National Organization of Women, 2005-12, secretary, 2010-11. District Chapter League of Women Voters, 2005-12, treasurer, 2009. Campaign volunteer, summer 2008, campaign worker, fall 2008, for Representative Marilyn Connors of Virginia. Nice. What kind of duties and responsibilities did you have during that campaign?

'JENNIFER: Well, I gained a lot of useful experience from my work on that campaign. At first as a volunteer, I helped pass out buttons, bumper stickers and campaign pamphlets at the candidate's appearances. I went door-to-door a few times to talk to people about the candidate to help with name recognition. Then later, as a member of the campaign staff, I did a lot of phone work, answering questions or soliciting campaign contributions. I was even recognized for taking in the most money during one week in October. After that I was promoted to assistant to the campaign manager, and I was involved in the consultations on campaign strategy and eventually put in charge of coordinating the schedule of events in the final week before election day and handling travel arrangements for the candidate's appearances. So I had the chance to do it all.

'INTERVIEWER: outstanding. But you realize that we don't have anything relating to politics here.

'JENNIFER: But the experience I've gained in my political job can relate to so many other business fields. The sheer variety of tasks that I've undertaken, I think, shows my versatility. From my previous employer, I've gained a working knowledge of law, obviously, and finance from the budget process. I'm confidant my skills could be useful in your legal or finance departments. And even my brief military service further demonstrates my ability to adapt to different situations.

'INTERVIEWER: Ah, yes. You did have some military service, didn't you? I've read news stories about you recently. Don't worry, though. Despite the current state of crisis between our two countries, we won't hold that against you.

'JENNIFER: Thank you. I appreciate that.

'INTERVIEWER: Yes, we're not all that worried about spy stuff around here. Basically because we have nothing to hide, I guess. Anyway, I also understand that you're pregnant. Congratulations.

'JENNIFER: Um, thank you.

'INTERVIEWER: I am kind of curious, though, why you seem so eager for employment right now when you'll be taking time off in a few months, anyway.

'JENNIFER: Basically, I need the job. I want to get started on my new life.

'INTERVIEWER: Is your husband out of work?

'JENNIFER: Well, no. He's working. But I don't see why that's important.

'INTERVIEWER: It's not really important. It's just that it's going to be hard to recommend you to the department heads if you're going to be taking time off, basically, just when you're getting acclimated to your new job. We'd have to replace you temporarily, and, by the time you came back, your replacement would be as trained as you were. So, you see where that would leave us. It would just be prudent for both of us to wait until after you've had your baby. Otherwise, I'm very impressed with your credentials.'

Jennifer wanted to belabor the point. After hearing the same story, she wanted to tell the interviewers that maybe she wouldn't take any time off. But then she thought about what it might be like—she had never been pregnant before—she wasn't sure how long it would take to recover. Her own mother didn't work while pregnant, or for five years after.

Then she thought maybe it would be different with a female interviewer, someone who could understand her desire to work. But then again, she thought she was just succumbing to the women's lib rhetoric from back in the U.S. They were just looking at things from a business standpoint, she guessed. They were just being fiscally practical, right? Maybe it would be best to wait until after. But it was kind of odd, she thought, that she didn't come across one single female interviewer.

By the end of the year, Jennifer had given up going out each morning to search for work. She thought it would get tougher and harder to justify with her ever-expanding abdomen. She still got out of bed each day when Paul got up to go to work. She would start his breakfast while he showered, and then they would have chats during the meal until he had to leave. Mostly,

Jennifer wanted someone to talk to before having to face the next eight to nine hours with no one to talk to.

The mornings were routine, but they were sweet routines for Jennifer. The otherwise mundane times she now considered special because she was sharing them with someone. In their brief relationship so far, they had fun and exciting times, and that was easy. And they certainly shared times of crisis, which Jennifer thought were just as easy to remain strong, if not grow stronger, because they had a rallying point and common goals to guide them through. But the real test would come every ordinary day, when nothing earth-shattering or piquant happens. Jennifer felt that if Paul stuck around after days like that, it would prove that he really loved her. And he was proving it each day, so far.

An ordinary day like that, one morning in January, Paul looked at his watch and said, "Ooops! I'd better get moving." He got up from the table and kissed Jennifer. "Bye, hon."

"Bye, dear. You have a wonderful day," Jennifer said.

Paul scampered out of the kitchen and went to the hall closet by the front door to bundle up in his overcoat and snow boots, while Jennifer turned to the morning paper and sipped the rest of her herbal tea. Then Paul searched for his gloves and car keys.

"Okay, all set," he said to himself. Then he called out to Jennifer, "I'm leaving now."

Jennifer was about to call out goodbye, when she remembered something suddenly and jumped up to see him out.

"Oh, honey, I forgot to ask you. What would you like for dinner tonight?" Jennifer asked.

"Oh, I don't know. But you don't have to cook for me again," Paul said. "Isn't it my turn?"

"No. Anyway, I want to. It gives me something to do around here. Besides, you work all day."

"Why don't we go out to dinner tonight? We used to go out a lot when I first got my job."

"Well, you know, dear, we should save money now," Jennifer said, patting her stomach to remind him of an upcoming event. "There'll be a lot of things we'll need. And I'd just as well not even go out in public for a while. I don't want people to recognize me and interrupt our dinner."

"Okay, if you insist. How about spaghetti and meatballs, then, with your famous garlic bread?"

"You got a deal. Be home by six?"

"Absolutely." Paul kissed her again. "Bye, Jennifer."

"Bye, Paul. Be careful. Keep warm," she yelled after him as he headed down the icy walkway. Jennifer shivered as a gust of wind blew in the open door. She quickly shut it, thinking she must be crazy standing there in only a nightgown and robe.

For the rest of the morning, Jennifer did her kitchen chores, washing and drying the breakfast dishes, then sweeping and mopping the floor. In her Washington apartment, she cleaned the entire place once a week on Saturday mornings. The Ottawa apartment was only slightly larger, but since she had the time, she thoroughly cleaned one room each day, thereby paying closer attention to details. Her career might have been on hold for the time being, but at least she could have the cleanest house around.

After the kitchen got the once-over that morning, Jennifer gave herself an inspection. Almost subconsciously, she played the role of a chief petty officer on a galley inspection. When she caught herself and realized what she was doing, she said aloud, "See what the military does to you. I wasn't in very long, but I'm still thinking military."

When she broke for lunch, she just fixed herself a sandwich and read the rest of the newspaper.

After lunch, she had to decide what to do next. 'I could dust,' she thought. But she had dusted the past two days. And yesterday's dusting wasn't actually necessary, so she was fairly sure that another round wouldn't be nec-essary today. Dust only falls so quickly.

So Jennifer stretched out on the sofa while she pondered how to fill her afternoon, and absently thumbed through a housekeeping magazine to possibly pick up some ideas. 'Redecorate, perhaps, she thought. Maybe—new wallpaper—mmm—

She dozed off for a bit, effectively solving her dilemma. But, during her afternoon nap, the nightmare returned:

It had started off in the fog, just as in every previous dream. But she subconsciously told herself that she was in charge of her own thoughts. The only person frightening her was herself. She didn't even have to go into the mansion, if she didn't want to. She could turn and run. But she didn't. She entered, as she had every other time. She didn't have to walk if she didn't want to. But she did. When she reached the final door, she stared at the grue-some gargoyle, eye to eye. 'What am I afraid of?' she thought. Was it not the mystery man but what was behind that door? 'Open that door. OPEN THE DOOR!' The dream Jennifer placed her hand on the knob and slowly turned it. The hinges creaked as the door opened. 'Walk in.' The dream Jennifer did. More fog swirled around her head in the dim light. 'No, that isn't fog,' the dream Jennifer thought, because she could smell it. 'It's smoke. Cigar smoke, most likely.' The shadowy figure of the mystery man beckoned her to step further into the room, and as she did, he stepped underneath one of the nu-merous shaded lights hanging low overhead throughout the large room. She actually could see his face!

He smiled at her with his round, pudgy, florid face. He was a middle-aged man with sparse, graying hair, drooping jowls and a pug nose. The dream Jennifer almost chuckled. This was what she had been frightened of all that time? He certainly didn't look threatening at all. And he seemed to be inviting her to join a party. She looked around the entire room, and she could see people gathered around a number of tables, playing card games—mostly poker, she thought. The tables were littered with gambling chips, drink glasses and ashtrays. It seemed as if everyone had a cigar going. There was a bar at the far wall with more people gathered around it, perched on stools. Then it struck Jennifer that all the people at the tables and at the bar were men. And just then, a busty young woman, dressed in a skimpy costume—a short, tight skirt and sheer, low-cut, off-the-shoulder, above-the-midriff blouse—carrying a tray full of drinks, excused herself and cut in front of the dream Jennifer. Jennifer's glance followed this waiter as she arrived at a table to deliver the drinks. The woman bent over from the waist, exposing part of her derriere to one customer and her cleavage to another. The customer behind her felt obliged to pinch her exposed lower cheek, and the woman jumped with a start, playfully brushed his hand away and wagged her finger at him as if he were a naughty boy. Jennifer also noticed other buxom young women scurrying from table to table, openly flirting with their customers. Then suddenly, as raucous rock music filled the room, a cheer arose from the crowd of men. They paused in their games to pay even closer attention to the drink-serving women, who had begun to dance provocatively, one at each table. Upon the urging of one table of patrons, one woman shed her scanty top while gyrating to the beat. Then the other men joined in the chant: 'Take it off! Take it off!' and the dancers obliged by tossing their tops and shimmying out of their skirts. The dream Jennifer watched the dream scene in shock and horror. But, just as she got the urge to flee, she felt someone pinch her buttock and she heard a rough, gravelly voice say, "Hey, honey. Are you going to dance for me or what?"

CHAPTER NINE

"I'm leaving now, hon!" Paul called out across the apartment from the foyer.

"Do you have to announce your departures and arrivals like some goddamn train station or something?" Jennifer called back from the kitchen. And noting the jagged-edged sarcasm in her voice, Paul poked his head back into the kitchen, where Jennifer was finishing her Saturday morning breakfast, to see if she was all right.

When Jennifer saw Paul's head in the doorway, she said like a station announcer, "Now arriving, Track Six, the Maple Leaf Express from Thunder Bay, Winnipeg, Saskatoon and all points west."

Paul smiled at her spoofing humor. Jennifer did not smile.

"I just wanted to let you know that I was leaving in case you wanted something before I left," Paul said.

"No. Nothing," she said. "I want you to stay home today. Why do you have to work today? It's Saturday. It's supposed to be our time." Jennifer pouted.

"I told you, " Paul said, walking over to her. He put his arm around her shoulder and kissed her on the forehead. "The kids have a computer project due Monday, and this is the last chance they'll have to get help. I just have to be there, you know, to be handy and answer questions. I should be home early. Probably two or three o'clock."

"The kids. You know you have a kid of your own to take care of. You should be playing catch with him today or taking him for a walk in the park."

"There'll be plenty of time for that. We can go for a walk after I get back. What do you say, slugger?" Paul leaned over and put his hand on Jennifer's swelled abdomen. "Whoa! He kicked. I guess that means yes. Did you feel that, honey?"

"Of course, I did," Jennifer said flatly. She had been just as excited when she first felt her baby kick a couple of months earlier, but now, late in her eighth month, the event was kind of losing its charm. "Quit squirming already, will you?" she said to her own stomach. "I wish I could deliver this baby right here and now to get this whole mess over with. I mean, when do I go back to being the old me? I may not ever be the same again. What if I'm never thin again? Look at you. How come you haven't changed into a different person? It's not fair. Oh, Paul, I don't think I'm ready for this. I don't know how to be a mother. What are we going to do?"

Paul tried to dry her weeping eyes. "I know what this is. I read it in the pregnancy book. It said you'd have sudden mood swings and anxiety attacks. Any minute, you could swing back and be happy-go-lucky and see things totally differently. It's all hormones, darling. Nothing has really changed, you know. Everything's fine," he said, kissing her on the forehead again. "I just hope you change back soon because this is supposed to be a happy time."

"Thank you for your insight, goddamn Doctor/Mister Spock," Jennifer chided.

"The book also said that you'd say things that you don't mean, and that I shouldn't pay it any attention."

"Well, don't pay any attention to this either." Jennifer punched Paul in the shoulder, not violently, but with conviction.

"Oww! What did you do that for?" Paul asked.

"It was nothing. Just a mood swing, dear," Jennifer said in her sweetest, most pleasant voice and then smiled at him. "Oooh!"

"What? What? Are you having labor pains?"

"No, I got to pee. Get out of the way."

Paul helped her up out of the chair. "Wow. I'd better go. I'll call you around lunchtime. And I'll try to be home early. Bye, hon." He kissed her goodbye. "I love you."

"Yeah, yeah. So, get out already, before I leak all over the floor." Jennifer blew a quick kiss to Paul as she rushed to the bathroom.

Almost in one fluid motion, Jennifer pulled up her frilly nightgown, pulled down her flower-print briefs and sat down on the cold plastic seat. When she let go after holding it back and only a few drops trickled out, she cursed out loud. "Damn." Then she thought, 'I feel like I have to go almost all day long. My bladder feels like it's bursting now, but there's nothing there. How am I supposed to know when I really have to go?'

Jennifer dropped her chin into her hand as she sat there despondently, almost in the pose of the classic sculpture *The Thinker*. And while she was sitting there, she did some thinking about what was happening to her. 'I'm getting exactly what I wanted, aren't I? I eschewed the liberated lifestyle and embraced the old-fashioned gender-based values. And this is my reward? Of course, it is,' she told herself. She wanted to be a mother. But why did it seem that she was still haunted by her exodus, after everything was supposed to be settled? She thought back on her recurring dream—the one she had the past couple of months, the one where she opened the door. She just had another one the night before. She tried desperately to analyze its meaning.

'That room must represent the decadent sexploitative society that I have chosen. I guess it shows that I'm still horrified by that kind of world. It shows that I, as a woman, will only be thought of as a man's servant or as an object of his lust. And the mystery man is my escort. He only wanted to see that I got there safely—the ferryman showing me the way to—hell? Oh, that can't be it. I didn't believe all the propaganda, and that's why I left. I must've been brainwashed by that equality rhetoric that I've heard all those years, and it is just my subconscious mind showing that it is still influenced by it. I didn't choose evil over purity. I chose happiness over unhappiness. Maybe the dream doesn't mean a damn thing. God, I'd like to believe that. But why does it re-play over and over? Is someone trying to tell me something? What is it? I don't like mysteries. I want to know now. I just want to get this nonsense out of my head so that I can get on with my life. I've made my choice, damn it, so just forget about trying to make me feel guilty. Just let me be!'

Tears trickled down Jennifer's cheeks. But she quickly dried them with toilet paper and stood up defiantly. 'I'm still in control here,' she told herself. 'The dream world has no connection to the real world.'

Jennifer took off the rest of her clothes to take a shower. It was time to get a start on the day, she thought. Even though there was no one else in the house, Jennifer closed the bathroom door. There was a full-length mirror on the inside of the door, and in the quick motion of shutting the door, she was somewhat startled to catch a glimpse of her full figure. It was as if she didn't recognize the person in the reflection. But, after looking more intently, her initial surprise was replaced with glowing pride. She turned this way and that in front of the mirror like a model, trying to capture her own image from different angles. At other times when she had seen her profile, Jennifer thought that she looked as if she had a beer belly. But now, she didn't see fat at all. She saw a baby snuggling up against her body. She had never felt more feminine than she did at the moment. Not when she got her first period, or went on her first date. Not when she had lost her virginity, or even when she felt Paul's intense, intimate love. Maternity itself was only another part of being a woman. She knew it wasn't what defined her, but it was her strongest feeling yet. She felt a special connection to her mother when she thought about what it all meant, the connection of carrying on the matriarchal line. They each had a different last name, but it didn't matter because she had a spiritual and biological connection to the beginning of humankind. She had a mother. Her mother had a mother, who had a mother, who had a mother, who had a mother and so on and so forth. Jennifer recalled references to the pre-Ratification era that described life as being all about sex. You were defined by your sex back then. You were judged on how well you attracted the opposite sex. You were told what you could accomplish based on your sex, regardless of your ability or desire. You even wore the uniform or your sex. But, despite all that, Jennifer realized that life was not all about sex. She wasn't sure what life was all about. People over the centuries have been trying to figure it out, but one thing it was *not* was all about sex. But she finally figured out what sex was all about. Sex was all about life. And the more people realized that, she thought, the less frustration there would be between the sexes. Sex was not all about feeling good, feeling dominant or feeling submissive. It's all about giving life, nurturing life and celebrating life. Life, of course, didn't necessarily mean just having babies, she thought. It was just the most obvious. The joining of two souls also creates life. So childless people are far from absent in the equation, she surmised. Jennifer was so excited by her revelation that she shared her discovery with Paul when he came home that afternoon. She greeted him at the door naked as a pregnant jaybird. And they gently made love to celebrate their life.

When Jennifer's contractions began in her 36th week, she knew it was time. She'd had false labor contractions a few times in the previous week, but now she also had some of the other signs that the doctor had told her to look for. She felt that the baby must have engaged because she could breathe much easier than at any time during the past two months. She also saw the bloody show. And when her water broke, Jennifer felt flushed and relieved. She knew it was only the beginning of labor, but she also thought of it as the beginning of the end to her pregnancy.

Jennifer had not been alarmed at the false labor pains. She just waited to see what happened. And it was with that same calmness that she told Paul, "This is it."

Paul tried to hide his anxiety, but Jennifer could sense his nervousness. He tried to talk slower to show his calmness, but he did a few things out of order from his prepared plan. He also talked more than he usually did. As he walked her to the car, he rambled on, but in his slow, methodical tone, while Jennifer nodded and smiled.

"Are you all right, honey?" Paul asked.

"Mmmm." Jennifer nodded.

"I knew I should have gassed up the car yesterday. But don't worry. We can still make it to the hospital. I hope. Okay, easy does it. In the car you go. And then off we go. Okay, close the door nice and tight, and ready to roll." Paul jogged around to the driver's side and got in. "All set now. Should take only ten minutes—fifteen, tops. Are you all right?"

"Mmmm."

"Are you timing contractions?"

"Mmmm."

"How far apart?"

"Ten minutes."

"Okay, no problem. Plenty of time. No hurry. We just put this into gear and off we go." Paul slowly put the car into first and eased off the clutch, lest he stall the engine in anxious haste. He followed his own mental map and called out the course changes. "Okay, turn right on Foxhaven—left on Morrow—pass two signals—One—Two—"

Paul looked over and saw the pained look on Jennifer's face. "Another contraction?"

"M—mm—mm. Hoo—hoo—hee—hee!" Jennifer noticed the car accelerating. She knew it was tough for Paul to deal with the fact that something was happening to his wife that could cause her great pain. Jennifer found it hard to deal with it herself. She tried to tell herself that she was going to the hospital to meet her new baby. And she tried to concentrate on the positive points.

"Okay, here we are, Carpenter Hospital." Paul pulled into the driveway leading to the front doors. When he stopped the car and put on the parking brake, he raced around to the other side to assist Jennifer. He flung open the passenger door and took her hands. "Okay, one, two, three, up we go," he said as Jennifer eased out of the seat.

"Can you walk?"

"Mmmm."

They walked, arm-in-arm, to the reception desk, and the nurse immediately brought a wheelchair for Jennifer. The nurse took some preliminary information and then said, "We'll take you up to a labor room now, Mrs. Kennedy, so that you can get prepped. Then the doctor will be in shortly to examine you."

Jennifer didn't say anything. Paul said, "I guess I should find a spot for my car. You know, you people should really think about having valet parking out there. That would be great. Wouldn't it?" He laughed at his own attempted humor and darted off to the car.

He was only trying to lighten the moment, but Jennifer didn't pay any attention to him. Even though he was her coach, he was just along for the ride now, as far as Jennifer was concerned. So was everyone else, and she also paid them no heed. She was beginning to sense an impending doom now. It was as if everyone in the hall was watching her being wheeled to the gallows, or better yet, to a torture chamber. She knew what was coming, and so did everyone else. She saw it in their eyes—the orderlies, the nurses, the doctors, the other patients. It wasn't a happy event yet. The contractions were intense enough now to make her sweat.

In her Lamaze class, when she showed some anxiety after the graphic video depictions of childbirth, Paul said to her, "Don't worry, hon. I'll be with you every step of the way." It seemed like a nice gesture of support at the time, but it echoed back to Jennifer as something completely ludicrous. It did make about as much sense as her husband taking her to that torture chamber and saying, "They're going to torture you, honey, but don't worry. I'll be with you the whole time." She conjured up a mental picture of Paul holding her hand to comfort her as bamboo shoots were being shoved under her toenails.

After her preliminary examination and an enema (which she requested due to the same graphic birthing film), the nurses set Jennifer up on an IV and then let Paul in to see her. When Paul tried to comfort her, she recalled her mental picture and said, "Just leave me alone, will you?"

"I'm supposed to be your coach, remember?"

"Well then, coach, damn it!" After she said that, she wished she hadn't because Paul became a veritable Lamaze textbook.

When she gritted her teeth and clamped her hands around the cool, aluminum bed rails during one particularly intense contraction, Paul said, "Okay, concentrate on your happy thought."

Jennifer pictured her mother's face. It looked as it did when Jennifer was seven years old. Then she saw her mother in the old kitchen, baking cookies on a cold winter afternoon. She let little Jenny lick the raw cookie dough off the spoon. Jennifer remembered how her cocker spaniel puppy did a funny dance and rolled over when she held up a ball of cookie dough to him. She had giggled hysterically because she was so surprised at how she could control the dog's movements. Move her hand to the left, the pup rolled to the left. Move it down closer, closer, then yank it up high, and the pup stood up on his hind legs and eventually toppled over backward. Then she gave a little piece to the pup. She remembered the warm, wet, gentle, tickling kisses he gave her to get every crumb off her fingertips. "Not too much," her mother had said, "or else he'll get a tummy ache." Mmmm, the smell coming from the oven. Little Jenny ran to the oven door window and flicked on the little light switch. She watched the dough magically transform into finished cookies. They turned from yellow to brown, got bigger and flattened out. The sight fascinated her. It *was* a happy time, a time when there was no such thing as sex to her. After she ate her fill of cookies, her mother would bundle up little Jenny in her little snowsuit and take her outside to play in the snow. Oh, Daddy was out there, too, building snow people. He already had finished snow 'man' and snow 'woman.' He was busy working on snow 'baby.' Little Jenny walked up to it. It was the same height as herself. She didn't know why, but she quickly made a snowball and threw it at Daddy. He just laughed when it hit him in the back of the neck and trickled down inside his overcoat. Daddy playfully chased Little Jenny around the yard, saying, "I'm going to get you, you little sneak." He threw a snowball at her. THUD! That didn't feel like a snowball, but more like a chunk of ice. Little Jenny was dazed. She looked down at the snow around her feet. But it couldn't be snow because it was pink. She felt her throbbing head and saw the blood on her white mittens. She cried and looked around for Mommy and Daddy, but only saw the snow people surrounding her. THUD! Another iceball to the head, and then she was pelted with them—'WAIT!' That's not what happened.'

"Oh, God. This isn't working. I'm still in pain!"

"That's because you're forgetting to breathe," Paul said. "Come on now. Do more rapid chest breathing. In—out—in—out. Now try to relax your body. Let the contractions come to you. Don't meet them head on. Don't tense the rest of your body. Come on now, loosen that jaw muscle. Okay. That's good. Now let your arm go. That's it. It's not even there. Just let go of it. Now let the left arm go."

Paul massaged the back of her neck. "I know you're in pain, baby, but I'm here for you," he said.

'Why did he have to say that?' she thought. After that contraction eased, Jennifer shot back at him. "What do you know, huh? You know I'm in pain and what to do about it all. Do you know what kind of pain, too? Of course you do. You're *there* for me. I guess that means you can just take my place, and I can go down to the waiting room and have a cup of coffee. Then you can tell me when it's over. And don't touch me."

"I—I just thought I could help you through this."

"Well, you're not! Why don't you just get out, and I'll call *you* when it's all over?"

"Maybe I should get some fresh air, and then get something to eat in the cafeteria. This could take a while. I'll be back." Paul turned to leave, possibly hoping Jennifer would call him back, not really wanting to be left alone. But Jennifer said nothing.

After Paul left the room, however, Jennifer felt even more anger. "Just great, leave when the going gets tough. Just call time-out and relax, get some fresh air, get something to eat. Well, I can't call time-out!" she yelled into the empty room. 'This is just wonderful,' she thought. 'I'm about to have my baby, and everyone leaves me alone. No doctor, no nurse, and no husband. I guess it's just you and I, kid.' Through all the physical pain, she did not cry. But now, after she thought she was abandoned, a few tears trickled down her cheeks.

Contraction after contraction, Jennifer tried to remember her breathing and not to tense up or push. For some reason, while searching her brain for happy thoughts, her mind drifted back to boot camp. She immediately thought of those cranking sessions when she thought she would surely die on the spot. There were exercises that made her think her abdomen would explode, about the same feeling she had now. She had to lie down on the ground and hold her feet six inches off the ground, or do as many situps as her body would allow. When her feet hit the ground and her legs felt like lead weights, or she just couldn't pull herself up for one more situp, the company commanders understood that the body only could go so far, it seemed. But they would get in her face if she quit trying. So they ordered her to continue to struggle and strain, even though she didn't accomplish another lift or another situp. Even though the body quit, the mind shouldn't be allowed to quit, because, as Jennifer came to understand after graduation, it was the only way she would ever know that she did everything that she could do. If she stopped at the first obstacle, she'd never know if she could've gotten around it. But if she tried everything in her power and still couldn't get around it, at least she would've known it couldn't be done. Then, of course, there were those instances when she makes it through and goes even further than she ever expected from herself. Jennifer came to understand that almost everyone could accomplish more than he or she expected, and that's why people needed to be pushed. It was all a form of conditioning that forced Jennifer to improve her own capabilities. But, after a few minutes of straining during those exercises (that only seemed like hours), the company commanders let them up and let them recover. Her current pain felt like that, but instead of being able to recover, the cranking session was repeated over and over, sadistically, hour after hour (that now seemed like days). Jennifer pictured Kaminski's uptight face barking out commands and obscenities as each contraction began. "You'd better not give up now, you lazy-ass piece of dog shit! Get 'em up there. You going to quit on me, you crybaby?"

"No, chief."

"I can't hear you!"

"I won't quit, chief!" Jennifer said aloud to the empty hospital room. 'Oh, God. I must be going nuts,' she thought. After what seemed like an hour, and no one came to check on her, Jennifer called the nurse.

"How're you doing, Mrs. Kennedy? Is everything okay?"

"I'm fine, I guess. Is my husband out there anywhere? I need him here."

"Yes, I just saw him. I think he's in a consultation with your doctor. But I'll send him in as soon as possible. Is there anything else I can get for you?"

"Yes, more ice, please."

"Certainly, right away."

Jennifer collapsed on the bed trying to enjoy the respite as much as possible before the next contraction came. Paul came in carrying the ice.

"Oh, Paul, come here. Why did you leave me?"

"You said that I should get out."

"I'm sorry. Why do you even listen to me? I'm a raving madwoman. Please promise that you won't listen to me anymore. Whatever I say or do, just promise to stay with me until it's all over."

"Okay, I promise." Paul gave her some ice to suck on.

"What did you and the doctor talk about?" Jennifer mumbled through the ice.

"Oh, he just wanted to let me know what to expect in case something comes up and they have to perform a Caesarean."

'Oh please, God, no. Not a Caesarean. If they're just going to take it from me, why did I have to go through all this? I'm ready to go all the way.' "What did he say?"

"He asked me if I would want to stay in the operating room with you."

"And what did you say?"

"I said yes."

"Thank you." Jennifer reached out her hand to him, and another contraction began. She gripped his forearm like a vice. "Anything else?" she said through clenched teeth.

"Not really. He said not to be offended if I was told to back away from the table to make room for a medical team. Breathe, breathe, quick shallow breathing, just like we practiced."

"Huh-huh-huh-huh-huh-huh—"

"There you go."

The doctor entered with a nurse. "How are we doing?" the doctor asked as he went to turn up the volume of the fetal monitor.

"I was hoping *you'd* tell *me*, doc—" Jennifer said between pants.

"Well, everything looks normal," he said while checking the monitor. "We'll do a quick examination to check your dilation." The doctor lifted off the sheet and felt around her abdomen, checking the baby's position. After he had Jennifer spread her legs, he asked the nurse for the speculum. "It looks like you're almost fully dilated. You're at nine centimeters now." He looked at the other monitor that graphed her contractions. "About two and a half minutes apart now, I see." Jennifer nodded. "Well, your progression is just fine. You should be ready for the pushing stage shortly. I'll be back in to check on you in a few minutes." The doctor and the nurse left them alone again.

"Hang in there. You're almost there," Paul said.

"No. *We're* almost there," Jennifer whispered. While the pains became even more intense, she now felt happier. She was one third of the way through her ordeal. One part was already past tense. And the pushing stage could be just as painful, but she could at least do something. It wasn't just happening to her. She felt she could be more in control. It seemed to fly by because there was so much excitement around her and in everyone's faces. Paul and the nurses were yelling out encouragement. "Come on, push, push! That's it. That's it. Okay, relax. Breathe in and out, in and out. Okay, ready, deep breath, hold it and push, push!" and when she felt some movement, her own excitement skyrocketed. "I'm doing it! It's happening!"

When it was time to go to the delivery room, it felt like being put on hold. They told her to stop pushing, but, at that point, Jennifer didn't feel much in control about when the baby would come, and the rest of the delivery was a blur. She was almost exhausted and her eyes didn't focus well. So she concentrated on the voices around her. She didn't feel as if she were in it alone anymore, and she didn't know what she could've done without their help. The doctor, the nurses and Paul were very much an integral part in the birth. Paul looked as if he'd actually been pushing, as well, sweating profusely and looking exhausted.

When Jennifer felt at the breaking point, the point where she couldn't give anymore, the doctor said, "We have the head. Push, push—Okay we have a shoulder—" After the widest part of the baby's body passed, there was a gush of relief, like the ecstasy of a thousand orgasms at once. In a whoosh, she felt as though not only the baby had left her, but also every organ and every life-giving fluid drained from her until she was a mere shell casing, completely empty. There was nothing left to give. She could now die in peace. But—

"It's a girl!" Paul shouted, repeating the doctor's pronouncement.

"A girl?" Jennifer responded weakly. The doctor held up the tiny human form for her to see—a glistening, pink, doll-like figurine, seemingly too fragile to touch. The doctor placed the baby on Jennifer's abdomen, and Jennifer reached her arms up to gently embrace the child, who looked almost asleep already, and Jennifer instinctively rubbed her back to coax her breathing. It was a bit tentative, but it was the start of a lifetime of breaths, as she cried for the first time. Jennifer cried at the same time, and then looked up and saw tears slowly rolling down Paul's cheeks. Jennifer had never felt so happy. But in only a few moments, she had to turn around her emotions quickly and also let go for the first time. The doctor cut the umbilical cord, and the nurses took care of the routine details of cleaning her up. Jennifer was not quite finished either. The pains started again as she delivered the placenta. But after such recent memory of even greater pain, it didn't faze her much, and it was over in no time. Jennifer had insisted on no drugs being used unless absolutely necessary, but her exhaustion felt like a drug-induced daze. Paul kissed her on the forehead and said something to her as she was being wheeled down to recovery. And only the orderly, whose face loomed over hers, could hear her mumble, "Mommy? I want to talk to my mommy."

Nothingness. Darkness. Black hole. Sleep. Void. Vacuum. Blank. Empty. Siren. Shadows. Ambulance? Police car? Fire engine? Piercing. Shrill. Trouble. Danger. Where? Emergency. Life or Death. Siren. Baby's crying.

"Baby's crying."

"Wha—?"

"Dawn is crying," Paul said as he crawled back into bed. "I checked her diaper, and it's dry. I think she's hungry. Your department."

"Right." Jennifer groggily sat up, rubbed her eyes and tried to focus on the alarm clock on the night stand. 1:32. "You're right. Feeding time." She swung her legs over the side of the bed and blindly felt for her slippers. "I'm coming, baby Dawn," she said softly, as Paul snuggled his head underneath the pillow.

Jennifer shuffled her feet as she walked into the adjacent room to the baby's crib. She switched on a soft light and a radio with soft music on low volume. She picked up the wailing Dawn and said, "Shush, little pumpkin. Don't cry. Mommy's here."

She unbuttoned her nightgown and unhooked the flap of her nursing bra covering her right breast, which was engorged with milk. It was round and plump, and noticeably larger to Jennifer. Now that she wore a bra again, she had to go from an A-cup to a B-cup. Nothing earthshattering, but actually a pleasant difference to Jennifer. She had felt she wasn't exactly normal before, even though she realized there was no such thing as a normal breast size. Wasn't everyone either too big or too small, she thought?

Jennifer cuddled up Dawn to her breast and the baby latched onto the nipple like a pasty. "There, that's what you wanted. Yes. My little angel. Drink up and grow big and strong. Just think, you could be doing this for your own daughter some day."

She wondered if this was what her own mother had thought 29 years ago. Jennifer didn't know if she'd have more children, but she was so glad to have a girl. A cycle was completed. A generation added to a line of women who had given birth to at least one daughter. Dawn might not end up having a daughter, but that was too far away to worry about. But it would seem like a shame for such a long line to come to an end. 'Maybe a son for Paul? He must feel the same way about his own line.' Jennifer didn't know if it really held any cosmic significance to carry on a line like that. There had to be millions and billions of lines ended throughout the centuries with childless couples, childless people, mothers with no daughters, and fathers with no sons. 'We are all related anyway, right? But, when it does happen, it still feels quite special, regardless.'

Baby Dawn drew away from her nipple signaling that she had her fill. Jennifer hiked her up on her shoulder and gently patted her back to coax a burp.

"Ahh, that's a good little girl. You're Mom's little girl, aren't you? Yes, that's right." Jennifer put her back in the crib without any protest and tucked her in her blanket. "If you ever get hungry again, call me. You know my number. Remember, day or night. I'd much rather have you interrupt my nights than those silly old dreams."

Jennifer had to think back. She didn't know why she thought of them now. The dreams stopped a few weeks before the baby was born. She seemed so exhausted at the end of the day now that she felt knocked out when she went to sleep. Maybe she had been too tired to dream. Maybe they were finally over. Dawn was proof positive that she had made the right decision. Her mind wasn't wrestling with it anymore.

She straightened up a few things around the baby's room, then turned off the radio and the light. As she slipped back under the covers of her bed, she wondered why she thought about the dream again. 'When something you come to expect disappears, you eventually wonder about its absence, that's all. Yes—(yawn)—That's it. But now it's time to forget.'

The next day she would wish she hadn't thought about it at all because during her sleep, the nightmare returned.

It began the same way as always, night fog swirling. She couldn't be sure why, but the fear associated with being lost in a fog wasn't there. Maybe, because of the sheer routine of the situation at this point, she knew she would find her way out of the fog, and she knew where she was going. And she knew what the mystery man looked like. Instead of cautiously following his beckoning, she dutifully walked behind him to the room. Yes, the room, some perverse kind of men's club, she guessed. The same horseplay was going on, the naked women dancing in front of the rabid men. And, as she watched the scene again, the dream Jennifer felt a pinch. The same gravelly voice said, "Hey, honey, are you going to dance for me, or what?" She turned around to slap the face of the old man who had accosted her, but her arm was caught. She turned around quickly again to see the piggish face of the mystery man.

"I'm deeply sorry. I apologize for his boorish behavior," the man said. "It's just that we've never let any women in here before who weren't dancers and waitresses. Please, come on over to my table. We can talk."

The dream Jennifer followed, hoping to finally get some answers. The man pulled out a chair at an empty table away from all the action and offered it to her. Very old-fashioned and gallant, but it made Jennifer even more upset because it subconsciously suggested that she was somehow incapable of the action herself, and that she depended on him to do it for her. Where did that come from, she thought? Anyway, she sat, and he pushed her in, then sat down opposite her.

"You look extremely familiar," the dream Jennifer said finally. "Weren't you President Jordan's—?"

"Chief of Staff, yes," he responded and held out his hand. "Arnold P. Quisenberry. You have a good memory. It's been almost three years since I left the public spotlight."

"So, what is this revolting place, Mr. Quisenberry?"

"Call me Arnie, please."

"Okay, Arnie," she said with contempt.

"This is just a little place we like to call the 'Animal Farm.' You know, where some animals are more equal than others." Quisenberry burst out laughing.

"I don't get it," Jennifer said.

"Oh, pardon my manners. Would you like anything to drink, deary?"

"No, thank you, *Arnie.*" Jennifer looked up at the naked waitress who had stopped at their table, and their eyes met for a moment, but the woman cast them down as if embarrassed. Jennifer had just seen this woman gyrating around in front of frothing groups of men, and she thought that she couldn't possibly have any modesty, but she seemed to be ashamed to be in the presence of another woman who was not like herself.

"Then I'll have a Scotch and Soda, sweet cheeks," Quisenberry said to the waitress and gave her a pat on her bare rump as she turned to go.

"Where am I, Arnie? And why did you bring me here?"

"I just wanted to thank you in person."

"Me. For what?"

"For what you've done for all of us—for me and everyone in this room tonight." He waved his hand to indicate the other men in the room. Jennifer looked at them again, and their faces looked familiar, too. "You see, everyone here has been rejected by his woman, and you, dear Jennifer, have helped them forget and begin anew."

"I don't understand," Jennifer said.

"You probably don't recognize all the faces out there, but I'm sure some you do. These people were senators, congressmen, Supreme Court justices, cabinet members, and the very powerful captains of industry. Most were turned out of office with the Ratification of the ERA. I shouldn't say that because most wanted to leave. They saw the ERA coming. Smart men."

Quisenberry was interrupted by the waitress bringing him his drink. Jennifer was starting to think that she looked familiar, also. Sort of like her old college roommate, Sheila. But she had no room for a name tag.

"Thank you, honey. Oh, as I was saying, these were smart and powerful men. And powerful men don't like to give up their power. They thrive on control. And with the help of other smart men, like myself—" Quisenberry looked absolutely smug. "We devised a way for us to keep control and give you women exactly what you wanted, and what you deserved."

"And what was that?"

"Why, equality, my dear. Equality. We stripped down every law, every scrap, every idea, every last bastion of the male-dominated society, except, of course, this one you see before you. And then we handed it all to women on a silver platter, and they ate it up like a Thanksgiving Day feast. It was quite ingenious, if I do say so myself." Quisenberry seemed almost giddy.

"And why did you go through all that trouble?"

"Control. I told you, we're used to controlling things. We couldn't let the women do it. God knows what they would do with this country."

"But we have a woman president."

"Absolutely necessary for the plan. Our first objective was to find a female candidate we could control. Someone for the masses to rally around when we introduced our newfangled ideas. But people don't respect presidents the way they used to. Not a lot of charisma these days, you know. And anybody who can be controlled doesn't have much charisma to begin with. So you could see our problem. What we needed was a truly heroic figure, someone we didn't really need to control. A war hero perhaps."

"Me?" Jennifer asked, astounded.

"Someone who could clearly symbolize all the right ideals, make the issues black and white. She came to us quite by accident. But when we found her, we knew she would make a great martyr."

"I—I still don't understand. Even if it is about control, why couldn't you remain in control and use your power to create a better society? Why outlaw sex, for instance?"

"I'm glad you brought that up." Quisenberry looked incredibly animated. His eyes almost lit up. "That was the ultimate challenge of our control, to see if we could rule people's lives, right down to their sex lives. You can imagine how difficult that could be. Sex is such a personal thing. And you know how some people can't seem to resist those biological urges." He winked and smiled at her.

Jennifer felt guilty. 'He does know,' she thought.

"We're not a hundred percent yet, but, by God, we're doing it. We're getting there."

"You—you were following me. Why did you let me get away?" she asked.

"Another fortunate coincidence. In part, we owed you some debt of gratitude for all you've done for us. I understand you've started a new life. Congratulations on the baby, by the way."

"Um. Thank you."

"It just seemed to suit everyone's purposes just fine that you left the scene. No reluctant messiah hanging around to gum things up. You got what you wanted, and we got what we wanted. So, thank you again."

"But—are we in Washington now? Is this the White House? What am I doing here? How am I going to get home?" The words just echoed in Jennifer's head as the dream scene dissipated, and she awoke in a cold sweat.

CHAPTER TEN

The taxi pulled up in front of the Ottawa Royal Grand Hotel, and Marilyn Connors paid the fare with the strange-looking Canadian dollars. It almost felt as if she weren't paying anything, as if it were play money. But she needed only to remember that she had traded her 'real' dollars for these 'fake' dollars at the customs office in the airport.

When her luggage was placed on the sidewalk, a bellman approached her and said, "Carry your bags, ma'am?"

Marilyn resisted her natural aversion for such a repulsive greeting—she hadn't been a ma'am, lady or miss in years—and reluctantly relented. 'He's just doing his job,' she thought, 'and my bags are a bit heavy and awkward.' But of course, she kept her diplomatic satchel firmly clutched in her hand.

When she walked into the lobby ahead of the bellman, she was visibly impressed with her accommodations. 'They certainly gave it the right name,' she thought, 'because it is grand.' The room was ornate and antique, and there was a dazzling chandelier hanging overhead. It was actually her first trip abroad, and she was excited by all the new sights she had seen already. Washington had its own unique architectural style, borrowing a lot from Athens and Rome to create a new Americanized version call 'colonial.' But Ottawa looked like a combination of Paris and London, or what she thought they might look like. It was elegant and Old World. Marilyn couldn't help thinking about all the heads of state and other world dignitaries who had passed through those same doors over the years. It was the same feeling she sometimes got while sitting in the House chambers.

When she got to the desk, she proudly announced, "Marilyn Connors, of the United States of America."

"Yes, Miss Connors," the concierge said. Again, Marilyn cringed, but said nothing. "Your suite is ready. If you'll just sign in here, please."

She did so.

"I also have a message for you already," the woman said and handed Marilyn a fancy envelope with her name written on the front and a gold sticker seal on the back flap. She broke the seal and took out the note inside. It read:

'Welcome to Canada. I hope everything about your stay in our country will be satisfactory. And just as a reminder, my driver will pick you up at the hotel at 6:30 p.m. Enjoy your visit, and I look forward to meeting with you later.—H.S.'

Harold Samuelson, she thought. Marilyn would be attending a state dinner at the Prime Minister's residence at 7 o'clock that evening. But she wondered why the big reception for her. Relations were very strained. The diplomatic corps had been recalled over the very incident that brought her there. So, she would not have the ambassador to present her. Marilyn had begged for such a meeting for months to negotiate the release of Jennifer Martin, but the response was always the same, plain and simple: There is nothing to negotiate. She had to fight with her own State Department to keep lines of diplomatic communication open. The Secretary of State only would issue his own simple message: We demand the immediate and unconditional release of Jennifer Martin. Then finally, seven months after her disappearance, a response came back agreeing to a direct meeting with the Prime Minister, if the diplomatic team consisted of one and only one person—Marilyn Connors. Then, for another month, the State Department rejected the proposal, saying that Marilyn would then be in danger of kidnap herself. But Marilyn insisted. And the State Department finally relented. So now she was alone in her attempt to free her former employee. But it was also more than that. It was also her personal attempt to save her friend.

Marilyn went up to her suite to relax, but, with the thoughts running circles in her head, she began jotting down notes to organize what she wanted to say. She never had been involved with diplomatic negotiations before, although she was an experienced wheeler-dealer on the House floor. But while Marilyn was good at drumming up support for her positions, this was quite different. On the floor, she dealt with numerous differences of opinions, but, in essence, they all were on the same side; they all were interested in passing good legislation. But, in this case, the other side was all but officially called the enemy.

As seven o'clock approached, she changed into the official 'new-traditional' formal suit. It was similar to the new-traditional business suit that she wore while traveling, except for the color. The business suits ranged in colors from brown to gray to blue, while formal was always black. At any rate, Marilyn thought they looked like a combination of the Western-style suit and the Mao suit. The lines were predominantly vertical and effectively hid the bosom of female wearers.

At 6:30, Marilyn received the call from the desk informing her that the car had arrived and would be waiting for her right outside the front door of the lobby whenever she was ready. She knew it was only a five minute drive to the Prime Minister's residence, and that she could've walked, just as well. But she waited fifteen minutes to collect her notes and bundle her nerves before she went down. She was nervous about the dinner where she would have to be nice and observe protocol, when the first thing she actually felt the urge to do when she met the Prime Minister was discuss the whereabouts of Jennifer. Marilyn didn't know how the subject could not eventually come up anyway, and thus turn the dinner into a defacto negotiating session. But she had to remember where she was. She had to play by their rules. 'When in Ottawa—' she thought.

When she did go down to the car and the driver took her through the inner section of the noble city, she felt the power in the elegant old buildings, much as she had in Washington. There seemed to be something distinctive in a seat of government, she thought.

She arrived at the residence at 6:57, and she was politely greeted by the Prime Minister's aide and escorted in. He offered to take her jacket, but she declined.

"Please, this way to the dining room," he said, and Marilyn followed him down a narrow, dimly-lit hall. Oil portraits periodically broke the expanse of wood panel, along with sconces holding flickering candles. The scene was somewhat Victorian, she thought. The aide led her into a large room with more subdued lighting. There were tapestries hung from the walls, and a suit of armor stood in one corner holding a battle ax, and a large escutcheon was displayed on one wall, with the Canadian Maple Leaf and the American Stars and Stripes dangling below it. The room looked as if it might be in the Royal Governor's residence instead of the Prime Minister's, Marilyn thought. But then she recalled her visits to the White House, and there was some odd stuff there, too. There seemed to be only one thing missing in the room, however—other people. There was a very large table in the center of the room that looked as if it could seat 25 people, but it was bare. There was another smaller table on the other side of it by the draped picture window, and it was fully dressed and furnished, but with only two place settings.

"What's going on here?" Marilyn asked.

"The Prime Minister will be in shortly to answer your questions," the aide said and then left Marilyn alone in the dining room.

Marilyn paced back and forth across the room. Already things were not going as she had imagined. 'Something odd is going on,' she thought. Just as she was trying to reorganize her thoughts, however, Harold Samuelson strode into the room.

"Ah, Representative Connors. How nice it is to finally meet you," he said, offering his hand to her. Marilyn refused it.

"Will you explain what the hell is going on here?" Marilyn asked as two waiters rolled in a food cart behind the Prime Minister.

"Well, we like to receive important dignitaries such as yourself with a state dinner," Samuelson said. "But then I thought, you have something important on your mind, and I figure you are a person who likes to get to the point. So then I decided we should skip all the frivolity and the formality and have a little one-on-one session right now. But I also figured we could still do that over dinner. I hope you don't mind."

Marilyn looked at him, somewhat bewildered. "No, I don't mind. As a matter of fact, I was thinking the same things."

"Good. Then let's have a seat." She did so, and the waiters served sherried veal pot roast with golden crumb broccoli and baked potatoes with sour cream. She was offered her choice of wines and chose the Chianti. After the waiters finished pouring, they left the room. Marilyn and the Prime Minister were alone in the warm light of the dinner candles. 'Time to get down to business,' she thought.

"As you know," Marilyn began, "my primary objective is to obtain the release of Jennifer Martin—"

"Whoa, whoa, whoa," Samuelson said. "This is a difficult situation, and it's the reason why I asked you here personally. I understand that you were Miss Martin's employer, and that you care very much about her well-being. But we did not kidnap her, and we are not holding her against her will. She defected. She came to us, and we granted her political asylum."

"I've heard all that before. I just can't believe it," Marilyn said. She had to find a way past this point of tossing the same accusations back and forth. She wasn't an experienced negotiator, but it seemed she had to lay everything on the table now. "Just tell us what you want for her release. I can't offer you anything because I'm not in the position to do that. But I can take your demands back to Washington for approval. We're willing to negotiate anything."

"There is nothing to negotiate. I told you, Jennifer Martin defected. I know you represent your government, but your government is lying to you. I thought that by bringing you here I could get you to understand that."

"I just can't believe what you're saying. Not Jennifer. I've known her for years."

"But it's absolutely true," Samuelson said.

"Then tell me where she is. Let me see for myself that what you're saying is true."

"I can't do that. Despite how I respect you personally, you are a representative of your government. If I tell you where Miss Martin is, it would put her in jeopardy of being kidnaped by your government. She came here to escape. She deserves to be left alone and to live in peace."

Marilyn felt very frustrated, and she began picking at her food. How could what this man was saying be true? Yet he looked so sincere. He looked genuinely troubled that he couldn't do anything for her. He was a tall, but stout man, rugged-looking even in his tailored suit. But was it just her old notions of what an honest face looked like?

"I'll tell you what I can do, though," Samuelson said to finally break the impasse. "I can have my people contact Miss Martin. If she is then willing to meet you, we can set something up. It just won't be at her residence. She could meet you at your hotel, or here. It's basically all up to her. Is that fair enough?"

"Yes, I think that is fair enough as a start," Marilyn answered. She thought if Jennifer refused to see her, she would know that Samuelson was lying. Jennifer would never refuse to see her, she thought. And if they did meet, Marilyn finally would get the answers to what really happened.

"Now that *that* has been taken care of, I hope you can still enjoy your meal," Samuelson said.

"Oh, yes. It is delicious, I must say. Thank you for inviting me," Marilyn said.

"It's my pleasure." Samuelson poured more wine after Marilyn emptied her glass. A very polite person, she thought. In the old days, he would have been referred to as a gentleman. "I hope you don't mind, " he continued, "but it's sort of a personal thing with me to really get to know the people I deal with. And I happen to believe that you can tell a lot about a person by finding out about their childhood. Once they reach adulthood, most people forget the first twenty years of their lives. But almost everything that happens during that time helps determine the way you are as an adult. So I was hoping you wouldn't mind talking about your childhood. And I'll tell you anything you want to know about mine. Anything you may have heard already probably isn't true."

Marilyn thought it somewhat strange at first, but she said, "Okay, sure." So they started talking about their younger years. Samuelson thought it would be better to go back to a time which they both could relate to, instead of discussing the current state of affairs between their two countries. He was certainly intrigued with Marilyn and wanted to get to know her better. At first, Marilyn was a little reluctant, but when she started reliving her memories, she realized that she had almost packed them away forever. But now she remembered events she hadn't thought about in years. And she remembered the people whom she hadn't thought about in years. There were Mom and Dad; her brothers, Joey and Stevie, and her sister, Sue. There was Fourth of July's with Uncle Bob and Aunt Fran in North Carolina; Christmases with Grandpa and Grandma Connors in Richmond, or Grandpa and Grandma Harrison in Connecticut; birthdays and other celebrations with other aunts and uncles and all the cousins.

Marilyn began to feel funny. She felt warm and tingly. She didn't know if she were blushing after revealing her hidden personal life to this virtual stranger, but she did know she was having fun, for the first time in a long time. Then she listened with fascination at Harold Samuelson's life story. She heard about how his father was a hard-working wheat farmer in Alberta, until oil was discovered on his land. And when his father shifted his focus to developing oil resources, he reaped the financial reward. And little Harold might not ever have had to work a day in his life. But he wanted to work. Starting at age 12, little Harold worked for his father, and worked hard, learning everything he could about every aspect of his father's business. And he was eventually able to take over when his father died. He did go to college before that happened. So he was extremely prepared, and he thrived. He first got interested in politics when he thought the government was trying to regulate his industry to death. Harold was drafted by his father's friends to run for a seat in the Canadian parliament to directly represent their views. But once he arrived in Ottawa, he soon realized that there was more to government than just trying to fulfill his own needs. He realized that there was a whole country out there, and a whole world. Each person he met had his own views. But he still had the knack to get his own way. So he quickly rose up the political ladder. Yet he was determined to use his new power to best serve everyone.

Marilyn was amazed. She knew that they had a strong-willed independent nature in common, but she felt almost embarrassed about her comparatively pampered childhood. Her father was an executive for a large tobacco company in Petersburg. Marilyn and all her siblings prepared for college by concentrating on school work. They would take summer jobs if they felt like it, to have a little spending money, but once school started in the fall, the jobs were forbidden.

The conversation lasted much longer than the food, but eventually the tongues grew tired. It wasn't at all what she expected in this meeting, but she enjoyed it. And there was something about him that told Marilyn she could trust him. So, when he reiterated that he would contact Jennifer for her, she believed him intuitively.

"I will call you personally when we get a response from Miss Martin," Samuelson said, offering his hand once again. This time Marilyn accepted.

"Thank you." It was a firm but gentle handshake. Marilyn felt that, with his huge hands, he easily could've broken bones in her hand if he weren't careful. But his hand was soft, while not being limp like a dishrag.

When he walked her out down the hall, he said to an attendant, "Tell the driver to take Miss Conners back to her hotel."

"Yes, sir." The attendant picked up the telephone to call the driver to the front door.

Samuelson turned to Marilyn. "I know you came here with one express purpose, but I hope you enjoy your stay in our country. Good night."

He shook her hand again and bowed his head slightly, as if he were starting to kiss her hand, but stopped.

"Good night, Prime Minister."

"Please, call me Harold."

"Okay, Harold. And I hope this trip eventually leads to better relations," Marilyn said, "between our countries."

"Yes, of course." He smiled and left to return to his private residence.

Marilyn climbed into the cavernous back seat of the stretch limousine. She had to fight the urge to lie across the seat and go to sleep. Wine made her sleepy. But she made it back to the hotel.

As she walked past the front desk on her way to the elevator, the clerk flagged her down.

"Oh, Miss Connors, I have a message for you," he said. "It was a phone message from a Mrs. Jessica Lodermeier. I have the number here."

He handed her a slip of paper, which she looked at with puzzlement. She didn't think she knew anyone in Canada. Then, she thought it must be a reporter. She had held a brief news conference when she arrived at the airport, and it was fairly routine, as everything was at a preliminary stage. But, she figured that a reporter might have called with some follow up questions.

Then, she thought more about the name. Actually, it was somehow familiar to her. She had met many people in her political career. It was even impossible to remember all the names of the other representatives. But Marilyn thought back. She didn't know any Lodermeiers. Except one. Darrell Lodermeier from high school. 'Jessie! Jessica, of course. It has to be. But how? They must have gotten married and had to move to Canada,' Marilyn thought. 'But how did she know that I'm here?'

Marilyn went up to her room as quickly as possible and immediately picked up the phone to call. After a few rings and a female voice said hello, Marilyn said, "Hello—may I speak to Jessica Fernandez—I mean, Lodermeier, please?"

"Marilyn?"

"Jessie, it is you!"

Jessica Fernandez Lodermeier stepped off the bus from Toronto the next day looking for a familiar, but slightly more aged face—the face of her best friend in high school. It had been 23 years since she had seen her last.

Marilyn Connors, who was waiting at the station, recognized her almost immediately, and waved frantically to catch Jessie's attention. "Over here, Jessie! I'm over here!" she yelled from amongst the crowd waiting to board.

"Oh, my God!" Jessie said when she finally saw Marilyn face to face again. "I can't believe it's really you!"

The pair embraced clumsily, as Jessie clutched her overnight bag in one hand. When Marilyn had said that she may only be in Canada a few more days, Jessie insisted on seeing her before she left, and she caught the first bus to Ottawa the next day. She had recognized Marilyn's name in the news stories about Jennifer Martin, and did some of her own detective work after she learned that a meeting was set and that she would arrive in Canada for a negotiating session. Jessie now lived in Toronto with her husband Darrell, and they had three children.

"It's so wonderful to see you again," Marilyn said. "We've got so much to catch up on. Come on, let's take a walk." After Jessie put her bag in a locker at the bus station, the two old friends took a short walk along the riverside in downtown Ottawa to get reacquainted.

"So, you've got to tell me everything," Marilyn started. "How did you end up in Canada? And how did you end up with Darrell? I thought you broke up with him after high school."

"Yeah, I guess I did," Jessie said.

"I mean, the last time I saw you, you were on your way to Florida. And I expected the next time I would see you would be in the Olympics or something. So fill me in—how did you get from Florida to Toronto?"

"It is a long story," Jessie said. "I did go to the University of Florida for my freshman year. And Darrell and I did break up because we got into this big fight about where to go to school."

"I remember," Marilyn said.

"Then you remember that, with his parent's money, Darrell could have gone anywhere to school. But he didn't want to go to Florida. Either that or he didn't want to be with me, I thought at the time. So we went our separate ways. I went to Gainesville, and he went to Charlottesville. I had a great first year, by the way. I even went to a couple of national meets."

"But, obviously, you must have seen him again. When did that happen?" Marilyn asked.

"It was the summer after my freshman year," she answered, as they started walking across a bridge over the river. "I was home for a few weeks. He also was home for a few weeks, and I guess we did sort of run into each other. I still missed him, but I tried to be cool. We just talked like old friends. You know, 'Hey, what've you been up to?' He told me what he was doing. I told him what I was doing, making sure to let each know that we were doing fine without the other."

Marilyn and Jessie stopped in the middle of the bridge and stood solemnly at the rail, looking down at the brown water rushing past. "And because we could talk like that, I thought it was really over right then," Jessie continued. "I mean, we both seemed comfortable with the idea that we weren't a part of each other's life anymore. But then he asked to see me again. Asked me to a movie. I said sure. I thought it could be nice just for old times' sake. And then we could go back to our separated lives with no regrets. We went out, you know, and I don't know if it was just comfortable to be with him, or if I really still loved him, but I ended up sleeping with him."

"Oh, my," Marilyn said. "And afterward you realized that you were really still in love with him?"

"No. We both left to go back to our separate lives. But then, a few weeks later, I found out I was pregnant. I called Darrell and told him. I really didn't know what kind of response I would get. But when he dropped everything and drove down to Gainesville to see me and then proposed to me, that's when I knew I still loved him. And I finally knew he really loved me, so I said yes. We both dropped out of school and got married. And, of course, had a baby. A boy. Dennis. He's my oldest. He's twenty-one now. He's just about to graduate from the University of Toronto. Anyway, Darrell's parents helped us out a lot those first few years. And Darrell ended up going into his father's line of work, selling insurance. And he found that he was really good at it."

"But how about your swimming career? Didn't you go back to school?" Marilyn asked.

"Oh, I thought I could come back after I had the baby, no problem—but I got pregnant again," Jessie said with a smile. "Danny. He's twenty. Takes after his athletic parents. He plays college hockey in Montreal. Then I got pregnant again. Jill. She's my baby. Seventeen. Poor girl is torn over whether to become an actress or a doctor. Sharp as a tack, and gorgeous, too. All the boys are really after her. She doesn't have a steady because she says she doesn't want to be 'tied down.' She's so cute. I just think she likes all the attention she gets from different guys. Anyway, after trying to raise that bunch, the swimming career got put on the back burner."

"It's such a shame. You were so good. Don't you regret giving up your shot at the Olympics?"

"No, not really," Jessie replied. "I'm very happy with the life I chose, and I couldn't imagine it without Darrell or any of the kids. I mean, if I chose to focus on the Olympics, winning the gold would have been a very satisfying experience, but how long could that have lasted? You go to one Olympic Games, two if you're lucky. Swimming was fun, but it wasn't my life. Even if I would've won, then what?"

"Then you concentrate on your next career, whatever you went to school for," Marilyn replied.

"Just like you did?" Jessie said.

"Yes, sure. Sort of. I guess."

"I'm not going to argue with you over who made the right choice or the correct choice because it's not even about that. I realize that I could have made different life choices and still have found happiness. I could have done it exactly the way you said, and I could have been just as happy because I never would've known what I was missing. I can say now that I'd never trade the joys of having children for anything, but that's because I know how satisfying it is. If I chose the career path like you, I would've never known and never missed it. But since I did choose the other path, I know it was what I wanted. You see, I admit that I made a choice, but you seem to be saying that you didn't have a choice. You seem to be saying that you couldn't be happy being married and raising kids."

"Maybe you're right," Marilyn said. "I don't think I could be happy just being someone's wife or mother."

"I don't believe that. I mean, it isn't magical. Just because you choose to marry, doesn't mean you'll be happy. It depends on meeting the right man."

"My life shouldn't have to depend on any man. My life should depend entirely on me!" Marilyn drew back from the rail and faced her directly. She felt a little uptight about having to defend herself, and, basically, her entire country.

Jessie was not looking for a confrontation either. She only wanted to understand her old friend. She was only looking for an explanation now about why she had felt compelled to leave her own country. Jessie searched for the words in her mind to better help Marilyn understand her point of view. And then she said, "If you remember me in high school, you know I was never liberation-minded. But, you see, I never needed to be liberated from anything. I chose my own life. I'm not a slave to my husband. I was sort of a slave to my kids. But that's not the right word. I was bound to the responsibility of raising them after I chose to have them. And that's not being trapped into doing something you don't want to do. You want the responsibility when it happens. You can even thrive on it. And it doesn't mean giving up who you are. You can be just as independent being married as you are now, as long as you choose to be. That's where the right man comes along. You have to find one who doesn't try to restrict your independence or impede your growth as a person, like I did. And it doesn't just depend on the right guy coming along. It also depends on you being the right woman and meeting him half way."

Marilyn looked back at Jessie in silence, trying to take it all in. She felt like a pupil struggling to understand the mystical lesson from the teacher/sage. Jessie started again, "You were wondering why I came to Canada, right?"

Marilyn nodded her head. Initially, she was excited to hear from her former best friend again, but, in the back of her mind, she also was a bit disappointed to find out that Jessie was one of 'them.'

"Well, it all started after the Ratification," she began. "You remember how rapidly things were changing back then, things a lot of people didn't even seem to notice. All the elementary kids started boarding at their schools to 'enhance and maximize the educational experience.' My kids were older than that, but I heard from other parents that they felt they were losing touch with their children. And when they finally did have some contact with them, the kids had changed completely, as if they were brainwashed, spouting equality slogans and rhetoric. And when the parents went to the school boards, the commissioners said that they were just following federal guidelines passed by the Congress."

"Are you blaming me?" Marilyn asked, looking shocked and defensive. "Because I didn't know of anything going on like that. I never heard of anything like that. Brainwashing?"

"Yes, absolutely! I've seen some of the results. I'm not saying you're personally responsible because some of this started before you were elected. But how could you have not known anything about it afterward? You were a member of Congress, and you didn't do anything to stop it."

"I swear I never knew about it."

"It was happening all over the country," Jessie said. "It's true that the parents only talked about it reluctantly, and the media didn't talk about it at all. So maybe you didn't know. But just what did those federal guidelines say?" Jessie demanded.

"Something to the effect of providing the proper environment to ensure a quality education absolutely free from sexism."

"Was there something about isolating children from negative images in there?"

"Yes, but we only thought it was necessary to undo centuries of discrimination and distortions of the truth in a short period of time. I don't see how anyone would describe that as a call for brainwashing."

"But some did," Jessie said calmly, trying to contain her own emotions. She stared straight down at the water while she spoke. "When you present only one view, at the very least it's propagandizing or indoctrinating. Well, anyway, then they were talking about doing the same thing for middle school students and then the high schools students. The dormitories were being built when we left. I didn't know what to do, but I was scared that they were trying to take my children away."

Marilyn watched a tear drop off Jessie's cheek and fall down toward the river. She was tempted to repeat the party line about how the family was just an archaic, outdated institution that was no longer necessary, or that the family structure itself was created by men to keep women dominated and under control. But it didn't quite seem to fit here.

Jessie wiped her eyes and looked back up at Marilyn. "But then I knew exactly what was going on when Barbara Thompson was elected and she outlawed sex and marriage. She was trying to take my children away, and I couldn't allow that to happen. So we left. And it wasn't because I couldn't give up sex like you've probably been told. I couldn't give up my family. I still love my husband and my kids. You've got to believe that's why I left."

"I do, Jessie. I really do." But Marilyn didn't tell her that she did believe it was because of sex at first. Theoretically, she had thought it was possible, with the advances in technology, to keep families together while getting rid of sex. Sex had nothing to do with the kind of love given to a child, and Marilyn thought that kind of familial love could be transferred between husband and wife. That's what Marilyn had wanted for the country: loving families. But the situation was out of her control, especially due to the fervor of the president's proposals.

"The only thing I can't understand," Jessie said, "is how such a loving person like you could support such a decision that, in effect, made love illegal."

"I don't think I supported that," Marilyn said, staring blankly upstream, not looking at Jessie. "I did think the country would be a better place without sex, and that by giving up sex, we weren't giving up anything truly important."

"Forgive me for asking such a personal question, but have you ever been truly in love with a man before?"

"Yes," Marilyn answered nervously. "Or, at least, at the time I thought I was. There was someone I met while in college. We had talked about getting married. But he wanted kids right away, which meant he didn't want me to go on to law school. I told him that was absolutely out of the question. There was no way I was going to give up my career just because he wanted me to. And I guess he couldn't wait. So we went our separate ways."

"So it was just a question of one wanting a family and the other not? It was just a question of when, right?"

"Yes, I guess so."

"So you must have been extremely close to this man to consider raising a family with him?" Jessie said.

"Yes, I was. I thought he was a very special person."

"But that was obviously pre-Ratification."

"Right."

"What if you had married this guy, and then sex and marriage were outlawed? What would you have done?"

"I don't know. There's no way to answer that because it's a moot point really."

"Then what about this?" Jessie asked. "What about after the Ratification? Have you been in love with any other man since?"

"Not that way, of course not," Marilyn replied. She was a bit confused as to where this line of questioning was leading.

"So don't you see that, while you gave up sex willingly, love went with it?"

"No. Wait a minute. There's not an absence of love in my life. I love the people who work for me very much. That's why I'm here in the first place. And one of those people happens to be a man. And I think they would say that they love me. It's just a different kind of love, like I've been trying to say. It's just not sexual. But I care for them very much."

"But even if they are friends, they're co-workers. You're not as close to them as you were with that guy in college, are you?"

"No," Marilyn answered apprehensively.

"And, even with your newfangled, new-age ways of having babies, there isn't anyone in that group, male or female, that you feel close enough to raise a family with, right?"

"Right. But I think I could be capable of raising a child without a partner. It's been done many times before."

"But, don't you see that there is a difference?" Jessie asked. "You've experienced both feelings. Don't you miss that kind of closeness you felt with the guy in college?"

"I guess I do, in a way." Once she admitted it, Marilyn expected her to say, 'I rest my case.' That's the point she was trying to make, right? She really wasn't any different. She was giving up more than sex. But, when Jessie didn't say anything, Marilyn made one more point to defend her position. "I do miss it, but I still don't think it's absolutely necessary to live a happy and fulfilling life."

"For some people it's not, I agree. For you, it's not. But, for some people, it is essential to living, period," Jessie said. "It just should be a person's choice, not the government's."

With the argument deadlocked, the two participants fell awkwardly silent. Marilyn now had her back to the rail and watched the cars roll by on the bridge, while Jessie watched the boat traffic on the river. Then Jessie broke the silence.

"Listen, I didn't come here to win any arguments, or to convert you to my side. I've chosen my life, and I'm going to stay on my side of the line. You clearly care a great deal for this woman you work with, or you wouldn't be here trying to rescue her. I wish you the best of everything when you go back to your side. There is only one thing that I ask of you."

"What's that, Jessie?"

"That you do everything in your power to stop a war between our countries. It wouldn't be beneficial to anyone. We just want to live in peace."

"I agree with you there. I certainly will."

Jessie started by offering her hand, but Marilyn surprised her by hugging her. As the two old friends walked back off the bridge, they continued to talk, but not about political affairs. They reminisced about the old days in high school, and had an enjoyable rest of the afternoon challenging each other about who remembered what. Marilyn couldn't recall when she had as much fun. Despite their differing opinions, Marilyn was glad they still were friends after all those years. She helped Jessie get a room at the same hotel for that night, and they planned to stick to more reminiscing for the remainder of Jessie's visit. After an enjoyable dinner together, they made plans for breakfast the next morning and then retired to their rooms.

When Marilyn entered her room, she was surprised to see a package sitting on the bed. She walked around the bed, eyeing the package suspiciously, suddenly recalling the warnings the State Department gave her before she left, not only about being a target for kidnap herself, but also possible assassination by Canadian radicals who were itching to start a war. Was it a bomb, she wondered? The package had markings of a fancy Ottawa boutique, but she didn't order anything, and the thought never crossed her mind to do so. As she made another pass and drew closer, she saw a note was attached. The note read:

'Dear Marilyn,

'I was just thinking that, while touring our fair city, you might be more comfortable in the customary attire of our country, to possibly avoid drawing attention to yourself during your very sensitive mission. I sincerely hope that you don't find it insulting that I took it upon myself to do this for you, but I just thought that, by blending in more with the local residents, you could maintain a certain degree of anonymity.

I hope you find everything satisfactory.—Harold.'

Marilyn opened up the box to find a red silk dress, old-fashioned women's undergarments and a selection of four pairs of shoes. She instantly felt nostalgic at the sight of the items and thought it would be better to be just another face in the crowd while she was there. It surely would be frowned-upon behavior back home, if they ever found out. At least, she could try them on. What would that hurt?

She peeled off her new-age clothes and tried on the antiquated garments. Marilyn wriggled into a pair of pantyhose for the first time in ages, and she had to think a moment before she remembered her old bra size. Samuelson had provided an assortment, and she picked the one that was closest in size. Marilyn mostly remembered how her brassieres had felt so confining and cumbersome. Sometimes it was akin to strapping herself into a straight-jacket every morning, she thought. But now, after a few years of bouncy freedom, and the effects of age and gravity, it felt somewhat comforting.

The smooth, silk dress slipped easily over her head and hugged her curvilinear frame. Marilyn tugged here and there to straighten it out, and then walked to the full-length mirror to check the look.

Marilyn was taken aback for a moment at the sight of her figure, mostly because she had forgotten she'd had one. After years of being hidden in frumpy, dowdy clothes, Marilyn, like most women of the day, didn't have to care as much about her appearance. No longer needing to attract the opposite sex, she could've gained 10 to 15 pounds without much of a real difference in her appearance, as long as she was comfortable about her own weight, for her health's sake. That's why she supported many of those fashion measures when they came to vote, so that women might find it easier to be at more normal weights instead of some ideal 'fighting' weight, or 'bikini' weight.

Now, as she gazed at her reflection, Marilyn felt as if she were transported back ten years. Her hips were a little wider, and her short-cropped hair was more salt and pepper now, but her figure was still there. She whirled around to see the entire view, her hemline ruffling just above her knees. She pivoted back and forth to see her legs. Still shapely, she thought, even though with a little help from the hose. She felt almost giddy, like a young child dressing up in Mommy's clothes for the first time.

Marilyn thought that Jessie was right. She was missing something. Not the love of a man in her life necessarily, but feeling special about being a woman. They had gained equality with men now, and so no one was special. But she had just realized that she did miss that feeling.

As she admired herself in the looking glass, she wondered how Samuelson could have guessed her dress size so perfectly. Maybe, if all those stories about him were true, he had a special talent for it.

Marilyn also kept thinking about Jessie. She didn't enjoy having to defend herself and her country's chosen path to equality. But did she just defend herself because she was coming under attack? No one would want to admit to being wrong for all those years. Was Jessie right? Would she be happier with the love of a man in her life? And what kind of man? Would she need to find the perfect man to be happy, or could she still be happy settling for a decent man who was less than perfect? But it was all a moot point anyway, wasn't it? She had to return home in a couple days. And to ever find out, she would have to—stay here. 'Stay here?' she wondered. 'What could possibly be in store for me here? Hmmm. Who knows, maybe I could become the first lady of Canada,' she mused. 'Harold Samuelson did seem to be flirting with me. He seemed very much the gentleman. And quite dashing. A bit of a rogue, perhaps, but just on the adventurous side. But he's certainly responsible enough to run an entire country. But he is a chauvinist, remember? What about all those rude comments he's made about our president? Although, I never cared for Barbara Thompson much myself. In a lot of ways, she seems too artificial. He was just speaking his mind, as is his nature. He would certainly respect a good woman. Like me? Oh, this is nonsense. I don't even know what he's thinking or how he feels. But I should call and thank him for this lovely dress.'

Just then as she eyed the telephone, it rang, and it spooked her. Was that he, wanting to find out her response to his gesture of goodwill?

She picked up the receiver tentatively. "Hello?" she asked nervously.

"Hello, Marilyn. This is Jennifer."

Like a ghostly voice out of the past, Jennifer's voice brought Marilyn back to the reason she was there to begin with.

"Jennifer! My God, I'm so happy to hear your voice. I didn't know what happened to you."

"I know why you're here, Marilyn, and we need to have a serious talk."

CHAPTER ELEVEN

The ceremony was glorious. It seemed the whole city turned out just to honor them, the dashing groom, Prime Minister Harold Samuelson, and the blushing bride, Mrs. Marilyn Samuelson, nee Connors. Fancy tuxedos, opulent gowns, a Gothic cathedral, an angelic-voiced choir, bows and vows. In his toast at the reception, the best man made it sound like a 'brave new world' in which they were entering. The band played, and the people danced and swayed.

Jennifer was almost overcome by emotion. It had only been a month since she had been reunited with her former boss, and now, she was the maid of honor at Marilyn's wedding. Jennifer could have been knocked over by a feather when Marilyn told her of the engagement.

Marilyn had been in her own state of shock when Jennifer told her the truth of her departure from the United States. She felt very confused and quite betrayed. For Marilyn, something was running roughshod over democracy in her country if she, a member of the government, did not know the truth about what was happening. Then, it all became so very clear to her. Marilyn went directly to Harold to plea for asylum. All the while, Harold had been in love with Marilyn from afar. It was love at first sight when Harold first saw Marilyn's face on the television news during the Jennifer Martin defection. Harold had arranged the diplomatic meeting with Marilyn alone, and when he was able to profess his feelings for her, she reciprocated.

While Jennifer was performing her maid-of-honor duty of socializing at the reception, Paul took Dawn home after she had become cranky. Meanwhile, Jennifer flitted about the ballroom, greeting and shaking hands with the guests, mostly Canadian government dignitaries she didn't know.

After one of the countless introductions, forcing a smile, pretending she was having a good time, Jennifer heard from behind her a vaguely familiar voice calling her name. "Jennifer Kennedy! I've waited a long time to finally meet you."

Jennifer turned to see the all-too recognizable face of Arnold P. Quisenberry. "You? You? What are *you* doing *here?*" Jennifer asked while recoiling from the sight of the man who had haunted her dreams the past few months. She almost had to wonder if she were dreaming now, but unfortunately, she wasn't and couldn't simply awaken to escape.

"Ah, you recognize me," Quisenberry responded. "Since you know who I am, I won't have to introduce myself."

"Of course, I know who you are. You're Arnold Quisenberry, former President Jordan's chief of staff and the man who was following me before I left the United States." Jennifer's tone was almost hostile and accusatory, even though she still wasn't sure about the accuracy of her statement.

"Oh, my," he remarked, "you recognized me from *that?* And I thought I had done a good job of disguising myself. I had better be a bit more careful in my surveillance. Although, I should have realized that I am more well known to people from Washington, like you."

"Why were you following me, and what do you want with me now? I just want to be left alone," Jennifer said angrily. Because of the dreams, she was thinking that this man was the one responsible for all the problems back in America.

"I think, perhaps, I need to explain," he began. "Although you recognized me from my former position, I don't think you are aware of my current endeavor. I am one of the leaders of the resistance movement back in the States."

"The 'resistance'?" Jennifer asked with confusion. She had wondered about the existence of such a movement, but she thought it would be composed of people who thought like she did. Her dreams perplexed her, and she had to try to separate the dream world from the real world. Maybe Quisenberry wasn't the behind-the-scenes leader of the 'revolution,' as she had dreamed, but instead was the leader of a group trying to restore the old system.

"Yes," Quisenberry continued. "Not many people know about our organization, but it is out of necessity, as we are attempting to topple the current government. And I was following you because I was trying to contact you, to recruit you to our little rebel band."

"Me?" Jennifer queried. "You wanted to recruit me? Why in the world would you want me?"

"Since you were involved in that little border skirmish in Maine, you, no doubt, understood the truth of the situation. And very few people actually know the truth these days. We thought you might feel the same urge to do something about the incredible injustices being perpetrated by the current U.S. regime. I mean, that is why you left, isn't it?"

"And why would you think that?" Jennifer asked. "Do you think that just because I disagreed with the new system, I'm going to help you try to re-install the old system, where you could have your lost power back?"

"I think you misunderstand our goals, Mrs. Kennedy, because I'm fairly sure we both want the same things. I happen to believe there is a happy medium between the two extremes of the old and new systems, and that is what our organization is fighting for. We don't want to replace the current female power structure with the old male power structure."

"You don't?" Jennifer looked at him with skepticism.

"Why, no," Quisenberry continued. "We are attempting to have power shared equally between the groups, as I think the ERA originally was designed to accomplish. Even though you were part of the new women's movement in the beginning, you probably didn't realize that it wasn't simply a movement to obtain equal rights and opportunities for women."

"It wasn't?"

"No, it wasn't. It actuality, it was a power struggle, pure and simple. It was very similar to the Communists in the first Russian Revolution. Lots of people thought they truly had some good ideas, you know, about equality and not profiting on the labors of others. Well, once they had the power, they had to maintain the power. And to maintain the power, they needed to have control. To create their Utopian system, with all their lofty ideals, they needed to have an incredible amount of control. Sound familiar?"

"Yes," Jennifer responded submissively. She was almost mesmerized by the way he spoke, seemingly taking all her loose, scattered doubts and fears, and tying them up into one logical, tightly rolled ball of yarn.

"It was simply a case of replacing one dictatorship with another. And as it turned out, the Soviet Communists were among the most brutal, ruthless dictatorships in the history of the world. All in the name of equality."

Quisenberry's manner had the same smugness that Jennifer recalled in her dream, but instead of finding it terrifying, she found it oddly assuring. "That does sound a bit like the way I feel about things," Jennifer said. "So, what do you call this organization of yours, anyway?"

"It's called, 'Consanguinity,'" he replied.

"What does that mean?"

"It means a group that is related by blood, a kinship. In our case, it's more like a brotherhood or sisterhood, a group with common aims, except that it doesn't denote gender."

"I like that." Jennifer had finally found someone who expressed the same troubled feelings she had about the current state of affairs, and it was the most unlikely person. Her dreams just may have been her attempts to fill the holes in her understanding, to explain something that scared her, which was being followed by a mysterious man. There wasn't enough of a glimpse for conscious recognition, but there was enough for a subconscious one, for she previously had known of this man. "But why all the intrigue?" she asked. "If you wanted me to join your group, why not just come right out and ask me?"

"As you can imagine, we have to be extremely careful about whom we contact, as we are an underground organization. Our main objective has been to infiltrate the power structure to find out what *they* are doing. We can't afford to be infiltrated by them and expect to survive long. I followed you to gain information on whether you were 'right' for us. As I've said before, you were brought to our attention for possible contact, but before we could come up with a definitive answer, you already were on your way out of the country."

"So, what you've concluded now is that you think I would be right for your organization?" Jennifer questioned.

"Yes, indeed I do. You already have demonstrated many admirable qualities, and I have a few ideas how we could use a person of your stature. It would mean some traveling, and, obviously, some risk. What do you say?"

"Whoa, I'm sorry, Mr. Quisenberry, but I don't think so. I have a husband and a baby at home. I can't simply take off and traipse around playing spy or soldier, or whatever you have in mind for me, to fight a battle I don't even care about anymore. I am no longer a citizen of the United States. Why should I care about what goes on there?"

"Ah, but I sense that you still do care very deeply. And you may become an American citizen again whether you wish to or not. Sooner or later, you'll end up fighting the same battle, if things come to pass as I suspect. America has had its eye on Canada for quite some time, and I feel that an attack is imminent. While the blessed nuptial of your good friend to the Prime Minister is a cause for celebration here and now, it is a cause for war back in the States. Of course, Americans aren't aware of the wedding, but instead are led to believe that Marilyn Connors also was kidnaped. The U.S. administration is thinking that it's enough to justify their actions to the American people."

Jennifer tried to digest everything Quisenberry was saying, but her stomach was beginning to churn. "I don't see how my participation will have much of an impact on any of this," she said.

"Actually, I think you could have a major impact," Quisenberry responded. "Don't sell yourself short. I have a plan in mind that could use your notoriety to diffuse the powder keg for now, possible giving us enough of a delay to affect changes from within. It is crucial that we avoid war at all costs. It's a big responsibility, I agree, but for people who feel as we do, we can't shrink from that responsibility just because it doesn't happen to be convenient at the time."

Jennifer was surprised at the patriotic feelings that Quisenberry was stirring inside her with his speech. Maybe it had been all that talk about being a hero. She wanted desperately to do something to actually earn the adulation she had been shown already. And he was right; she did care deeply about what had happened to the United States. Simply spending the rest of her life with her loved ones could make her quite happy, if she did not have to worry about anything outside her private, family triangle, but that was selfish, when all her compatriots could not enjoy that same freedom of choice, including her parents. Being separated from her mother at this moment in her life was especially hard on her.

Instead of fighting a war, maybe she could stop one, and in the process, if it was meant to be, she could play a part in freeing a lot of people from a restrictive, almost thought-controlled society.

"I can't make any decisions without talking to my husband first," she told him.

"Fair enough. Talk to him, and then, we'll talk some more. I'll answer any questions you still might have concerning our organization."

"How do I contact you?"

"Don't worry," he said with a smile, "I'll be contacting you. You just think about it for now." Quisenberry turned and melted away into the crowd, leaving her to wrestle with her muddled thoughts.

Jennifer could hardly stand any more of the gaiety and frivolity of the party. However, she waited to see Marilyn and her new husband off before returning home.

After she arrived, though, she didn't want to confront Paul just yet, not until she had a handle on the situation herself.

There were certain things she wished to be accomplished, but could she expect that they would be done despite her? No, and she couldn't simply allow others to do all the dirty work while she was safe at home and then reap the benefits afterward. Then again, how could she leave a husband and child to fend for themselves while she was hunting for glory? When she realized that men basically had done the very same thing for centuries, she decided she could do it, too.

But if she did get involved, there was one thing that worried her. Jennifer hoped that equal rights weren't turned into dirty words while they tried to trash the system. She realized that, sometimes, revolutions can't be controlled, even by the people who lead them. And that may have simply been the case with the ERA in the first place. She still thought it best that instead of protecting any group's rights, the Constitution worked best by protecting any individual's rights, and that's what she had always loved about her country, and what had made it so strong to begin with. She knew the ERA wasn't intended to protect women's rights, but the individual's right if she happened to be a woman, and also if he happened to be a man.

Even though only a few words were exchanged between them that evening, Jennifer and Paul turned to each other and engaged in their most intense lovemaking session since the birth of their child. Perhaps Paul also sensed something major was about to happen, Jennifer thought. In any event, she felt snug and secure for the moment as she lay in his arms.

Exhausted and satisfied, Jennifer lapsed into a dream world once again. It was a dream of a new society, revised edition. Big Sister was not watching them. Jennifer was involved in another female candidate's campaign for the presidency. She could picture the signs that had a twist on Barbara Thompson's twisted Orwellian slogans. One read: "Equality is Slavery." And another: "Inequality is Freedom."

She knew exactly what they meant. They were her slogans. Equality *was* slavery if it meant that people were forced to be the same. And if people had the freedom to be whom they wanted to be, they obviously would be unequal. That was one of the campaign's goals, because, while some people might be more equal than others, no one is more unequal than anyone else.

Jennifer thought back to the days when the ERA was first proposed. Women *were* seeking equal rights, but they didn't want to be the same as men; although, that's what some men believed. The name of the movement, after all, was in fact the women's liberation movement. And that's the only thing she ever really wanted. Jennifer just wanted to be free: free to be any kind of person she wanted to be.